Shudder

Colossians 3:13

"Bear with each other and forgive one another. If any of you has a grievance against someone, forgive as the Lord forgave you."

Dedicated to my family

Chapter 1

May 6th, 2000

Darkness surrounded 8-year-old Katie. The hairs on her arms stood up, both from fear and the cool temperature of the garage. She could feel the hot breath from her brother, Jay, puff on her face. His maniacal laughs sent shivers down her spine. Katie's body trembled as she tried to get out from the ropes that restrained her.

She flinched at the sound of her father's blowtorch. She imagined the powerful blue flames rushing out of it, burning to a crisp whatever it touched.

The thick tape over her lips masked her screams, unleashing a high-pitched humming noise instead.

She'd frantically wrestled with the rope that bound her hands and feet, but her trembling sweaty fingers hindered her effort.

Her tears reached the gorilla tape over her mouth, as her 12-year-old brother laughed coldheartedly.

She couldn't imagine the pain she was about to feel, and with her vision obscured, she hadn't even known where to expect it.

"Katie? Jay?" she heard the glorious but faint sound of her mother's voice from upstairs.

Katie wanted to scream the thoughts in her mind. *Yes! Please, I'm in the garage, Mom! I'm in the garage with Jay alone. Come get me!*

As she heard her mother's footsteps drawing closer, she felt her heart dancing inside her chest. Now her mother was finally going to understand. She was finally going to see what Jay did to her when they were alone.

Her saving day had finally come. The blindfold over her eyes prevented her from seeing anything in the room, but she could imagine the panic in her brother's eyes at her mother's voice, especially since their mother wasn't due back for another hour.

After the torch shut off, Katie could hear him scramble to put it back in their dad's tool case. She could hear her mother's footsteps approaching the garage.

Swiftly, he untied her hands and feet.

"I'll kill you if you tell her," Jay whispered before tearing off her mask. His words were terrifying because she knew he meant it.

Knowing a quick rip would cause her to scream, he attempted to take the tape off her mouth slowly. When the knob turned, he'd swore under his breath, and took his hand off the tape.

Just as her mother opened the door, Jay faked laughter. "My turn next, okay? You've had your fun!"

Her mother's steps down the creaking garage stairs came to an abrupt halt. Her eyes darted from Katie's to Jay's. "What's going on in here?"

"We're playing torture dungeon," he answered playfully, "and Katie's been playing victim too long."

Her mother watched Katie's helpless, desperate face, and the gray Gorilla tape that hid her lips. Alarm filled her mother's face as she watched Katie's bulging eyes and muffled pleas. She stared at Jay, who maintained his fictitious smile. Her eyes lingered on him, then flickered to Katie and back again.

"...Jay?" she swallowed, discomfort clear in her voice.

"Yes, Mother?" he responded with his hands behind his back.

"Don't... be too rough with your sister." She cleared her throat, casting one final look at Katie.

"This game is over. Both of you come help with the groceries."

January 7th, 2024

"So, this is it," the tall, handsome man in front of Katie stated. His fingers buried deep in his coat.

"I guess it is," she replied.

It seemed they both sensed something was off in the relationship, and Katie was just the first to address the issue. He didn't appear fazed by the breakup; the slow nod he gave suggested he had seen it coming. Katie hadn't felt deeply for anyone since her high school boyfriend, Lincoln Riles, whom she had followed to college in Virginia. They broke up just two weeks later. Katie vowed that would be the last time she would ever move to a place where she hadn't known anyone, and the last time she'd move anywhere for a man.

He turned away without another word; his shoes crunched into the snow. Katie walked opposite him, traveling under the succession of lamp posts aligning the street. Along the narrow road were the conjoined buildings still adorned with holiday wreaths and Christmas lights; It was the typical scene in Sperry, Virginia, in early January. She dug her numb fingers deeper into the pockets of her red trench coat as she approached her apartment complex.

Katie had become used to the same result happening over and over again with past relationships. She was surprised this one lasted as long as it did. Nobody seemed to have what she was looking for. Was it too much to ask for some ambition, stability, maturity, or direction? The man walking opposite her had lacked them all.

Katie couldn't help but blame herself. She had focused on her career throughout her 20s, studying hard while pulling all-nighters and becoming one with caffeine. She had put off serious dating so long she feared that the men who possessed all the qualities she wanted were gone. This struggle was the reality of dating in her 30s.

The lobby of her apartment complex was nearly empty. Most residents were probably huddled in their units, keeping warm on a cold night like this.

Mr. Jones, who'd lived alone on the 6th floor, approached her. He was a brown-skinned, middle-aged man with a shiny bald head. Divorced twice, he was a friendly neighbor who occasionally had his kids come visit him—kids from which former wife, Katie didn't know. He took out a napkin from the pocket of his black overcoat and sneezed into it. "Hi, Katie," he said, sniffling in passing.

"Hello," she replied, discreetly shifting to the side.

The elevator opened on the third floor. She walked the dark and narrow corridor to her unit; the faint noise of kids bustling had grown louder as she approached. They'd come from unit 305, where a couple with young kids lived.

Katie dug inside her purse just before she arrived at 311. She set her purse down on the counter and checked her missed calls. All of them were from her younger sister, Max.

With the phone secure between her cheek and shoulder, she unbuttoned her red coat, placing it on the bar chair.

When the call had gone to voicemail, Katie put the phone in her back pocket and opened the kitchen cabinet door. Her hand slowly moved past the red wine bottle, grabbing spices instead. The recipe she was about to prepare would indeed go well with wine. However, since she'd used alcohol as a crutch in the past, she'd quit drinking altogether. She hadn't even had a beer since college. The wine bottle sat in her cabinet now for guests mostly, and as a mere reminder of her success and self-control. There were so many memories of her drinking to numb the pain of the past. She'd rue the day she ever went back to it.

The phone vibrated from her pocket. *Max*, Katie thought as she pulled it out. When she looked at the ID on the screen, her suspicion was confirmed.

"Hello?"

"Hi, Katie!" Max's tone was high-pitched and extra sweet, like she'd wanted something.

"Hi," Katie muttered, her tone flat.

"So, as you know, I got a job in Stockholm…."

Katie was silent on the other end, waiting for Max to make her request.

"I wanna get some of the family together. Like both a reunion and a going away-party."

Max knew Katie didn't do reunions or any family events. Besides Max, Katie hadn't kept in contact with anyone in her family for years. Having lost 100 pounds since then nobody would recognize her anyway. They'd likely ask questions about her weight that she'd be forced to answer. Questions like *What did you do to lose it, and how long did it take?* Initially, the inquiries from high school friends and acquaintances had given her a sense of pride for her accomplishment, but after a while the comments had grown tiresome. Katie didn't like talking about herself. She'd learned to be a solid listener of other people, and that's what she was good at.

"Maxine," Katie said. If only Max could see her expression through the phone. "No."

Max, Katie's naive 24-year-old sister never gave up easy. Max was used to getting what she wanted. The parents of the Mackenna children spoiled their youngest daughter almost rotten. It was like once they'd realized their parenting style had failed on Katie and Jay, they gave up and supplied Max with anything she wanted, and now she didn't comprehend the concept of no.

"Okay, I know this is a lot to ask Katie, but please please please be there for me. Mom's not doing well, and this may be the last time you see her alive. Maybe it could be a chance to reconcile, ya know?"

Katie didn't know which was worse, Max using Ruth's illness as a way of manipulation or the fact that it was working. Ruth's leukemia had become untreatable. If Katie saw her at Max's going away party in Huntley, it might very well be the last time.

Though her relationship with her mother wasn't spectacular, the thought of seeing one specific family member was notably alarming.

Her body tensed. She bit down on her lip so hard she expected it to bleed. It had been so long since she'd mentioned the name of her brother. Suddenly an image popped into her mind. 12-year-old Jay Mackenna was being escorted out of their childhood home by her father. Jay froze at the doorframe to look back at her. His chilling smirk had caused her to flinch. Katie knew the message he wanted to give her was in that expression alone. She'd worked so hard to learn to put away those memories that'd haunted her all her life. She knew she would never be rid of them completely, but after years of struggling and counseling, she'd learned to put them in their proper place. Katie wondered what Jay would be like now that it had been so long.

It'd been over 20 years since she'd last seen him. Of course he'd look different physically, but Katie wondered about his psyche. Was he normal? Patient? Kind or charming? Was he any of the things people assumed he was just by looking at his captivating eyes and warm smile? She wouldn't know nor believe it unless she went.

"Will Jay be there?" she asked.

Neither Katie nor Max spoke, creating a painful silence.

"Yes," Max finally answered, sighing under her breath. "Yes, Jay will be there."

Again, there was silence.

"Look, you don't have to come, but I'd love it if you did. I gotta go."

With that, Max hung up. Katie tossed her phone on the black couch, where it bounced and landed on the carpet.

She sat on the couch next to Casper, an American Curl cat with fur white as snow. Sitting still, he watched her as his tail lightly swayed. As the tall mug of tea spun in the microwave, her mind had leaped from scene to scene in her head, revisiting old memories of terror at the hands of her brother. She took her reading glasses off and rested them on top of her dark bangs, sighing to herself. Her brown eyes had once again met Casper's baby blues. "What?" she asked.

He jumped down as if he'd just been insulted, trotting toward the kitchen.

As she sank further on the couch, her thoughts had returned to her home life back in Huntley. For years, Jay had gone undetected. Her concerns about him had been dismissed by Ruth and Allen until they were both unexpectedly faced with the truth. The incident in the garage as children was one of the last memories Katie had of Jay. In the following weeks after that, Katie's parents caught him in an inexplicable position. Left with no choice, Ruth and Allen had finally sent their oldest child away. His first destination was to his grandparent's house, and when that didn't work, a reform school, and then finally a bible college.

Katie hadn't seen her brother since she was eight years old. She'd received many texts from him over the years though, and only a few had she actually read. They were meant only to stir up fear and paranoia in her, promising to get her back for causing him to be sent away. As much as she tried to put the threats deep within the back of her mind, they would still pop up every now and then, causing many sleepless nights and provoking her to take every pill known to man to calm herself from fear and stress. She never knew when it would be her time, when her brother would finally come back to finish what he'd said he would. She didn't hate her brother. She didn't despise him either. She was scared to death of him.

Chapter 2

A blanket of snow still covered Sperry—whitening roofs, cars, and the sidewalk. With no sun present, Katie wondered how long it would stay or if more would fall later. Against the forceful wind, Katie tightly held her arms while trudging through the snow. Across the street, the chubby, middle-aged woman rose from her mail truck, carrying a stack of envelopes. They both shook their head as they locked eyes—a mutual disapproval of the weather. Thankfully, it wouldn't be long until Katie reached her destination. Since Heart-to-Heart Family Therapy was only a block away from her apartment, Katie often walked it, despite the conditions outside.

The room's warmth was a sweet relief as she walked in. The waiting room was nearly empty as it often was at opening time. The patrons inside looked up as the door opened, and then they'd gone back to their phones and waiting room magazines.

Katie stared at the list on the white door to the hallway; the list of names of mental health clinicians employed. Her name was toward the middle, Katie Mackenna, LPC. For some reason, it'd perturbed her that she wasn't first. A petty, yet very real feeling.

Gianna, the young twenty-something receptionist greeted her behind the door.

"Heeeeere you arrrre, Kaaattttieeee," she sang while handing her a cup of coffee.

Gianna had a new wig or a new nail color almost every time Katie saw her. Being a college student on a part-time receptionist's salary, Katie wondered how that was feasible, though she'd never asked.

"Thank you, Gianna. You're wonderful you know?"

"Anything for my favorite therapist. You'll have to remember me when you get your own practice. I'll definitely join," she whispered.

Katie had been wanting her own private practice since college. It was another way of proving herself. She'd poured a lot into this goal, saving up where she could as she followed the financial advice from Max, who'd been saving like a financial wizard since she got her first piggybank at five. Despite Katie's high rent and adverse student loans, she'd never given up hope. She believed with all her heart that she would start her private practice someday.

The phones rang on and off the hook as Katie walked down the narrow hall, repeating the typical generic greetings to everyone she passed.

Harold Dyson, the owner of Heart to Heart had given her one large smile and nod in passing. Katie knew she'd become a favorite of his ever since her presence here had drawn in a number of clients and referrals. It was just another reason to appreciate her job.

In her office, Katie walked along the large rug of multi-colored squares, hanging her coat on the rack by the window. Her desk was decorated with notepads both large and small, a tiny holder of pens and markers were beside them. Two pictures were placed in the middle; one was of Max and Katie for Max's 22nd birthday. A lanky Max smiled widely as she stood close to Katie. Her arm rested on Katie's shoulder. Max's hair was thick with tight curls, stopping short of her chest since she'd just cut it. A birthday girl banner hung from Max's shoulder to her hip. Katie's smile was less prominent, but still visible. Her hair was thin as usual. The atmosphere was dark, with surrounding lights inside. It was a karaoke bar, one of Max's favorite things to do. Even though Katie couldn't sing well, she'd gone to support the only family member she'd kept in contact with.

A picture of Jay's young children was the other picture on the desk—children she'd never met. Max had given her the picture as a Christmas gift years ago.

She unlocked the faded pink filing cabinet beside the desk, rummaging through the files. While blowing the steam from her coffee, she scanned the notes of her newest client, Colin.

Name: *Colin Kellam*

Age: *6*

Subject: *Mute client*

Symptoms:

—*Not speaking*

—*fidgety*

—*avoidance*

—*lack of eye contact*

—*isolation*

Session number: *1*

Even though she'd been a child therapist for years, there was still the occasional nervousness with a new client, not for herself, but for them. She'd always wanted to be a good fit for anyone who sought her help. It was her desire always to make the hour worth their money. Most of the time it was exactly that. First timers would often come looking confused or anxious, but by the end of the visit many of them softened up quite a bit. Her reputation was excellent for a reason, and it was her goal to keep it that way.

She opened the door to the waiting area, capturing the attention of nearly everyone inside.

"Colin Kellam?" Katie called from her chart.

A pale faced boy with auburn hair shot his head up. Sitting beside the boy was a woman named Angela, who Katie met last week. She'd come in requesting therapy for Colin. Having filled out her child's intake form already, this would be his first official session—and the first time Katie had ever worked with a mute child.

Angela rose from her seat. The bottoms of her loose gray sweatpants were tucked inside tan uggs. Her green sweater looked about three sizes too large. She took Colin's hand and escorted him over. He was walking very close to her, clinging to her tightly as if she might disappear. He was careful not to meet Katie's eyes.

She greeted them both with a friendly smile. Angela looked dangerously slim, with slightly curled flyaway hairs, and a loose bun likely to crumble at any moment. Her eyes were baggy, with dark circles surrounding them. Women who looked like this in public often fell into two categories:

One. A drug addict.

Two. A battered woman.

Katie quickly discarded the thought as the woman approached.

"Hello again," she said, extending her hand out to Angela.

Angela returned the smile, as she shook Katie's hand. "Nice to see you again, Ms. Mckenna."

She lightly brushed back the hair of the boy beside her, "This is my son, Colin."

Katie bent to the boy's level, offering her hand even though she was sure it would be rejected. And it was.

Angela closed her eyes, an apologetic expression appeared on her face. "Sorry about that."

"No need to apologize," Katie said, rising up to Angela's level. "Please follow me."

Katie guided them down the long narrow hall, making small talk with them as they walked. Katie tried to fit in jokes as much as

She could, hoping to ease Colin's discomfort.

"I've heard great things about you, Ms. Mackenna."

"Please, call me Katie, and thank you."

Every case that she had she'd given her absolute all to it. She'd spent several nights going without food or sleep, glued to her case files. She'd read and re-read all the information of her clients, going over the faces, the expressions, the gestures all in her head. Replaying them all in her mind like a movie.

She wasn't sure why, but children were often drawn to her, and ready to open up, sometimes without much effort. Perhaps it was her soft tone and youthful face to credit. Progress would often come quicker than not. No one had ever stopped coming until the end of treatment with positive results.

When they reached the door of Katie's office, Angela stopped. "Go ahead inside, Colin."

He glanced at the door and then back at his mother. Angela nodded. "It's alright. Go."

When Colin closed the door behind him, Angela turned to Katie.

"We recently moved here from Boston. My husband and I thought he was just looking for attention, you know, trying to tell us something by not speaking. But it's been a month."

Her puffed eyes were becoming glossy. "What do you think is wrong with my child?"

There was no way for Katie to know for sure without speaking to Colin first. She had her theories based on the information already provided; anxiety, fear, depression, selective mutism, or autism. The list was quite long.

"I'm not sure yet, Angela. But I'll do my best to find out. You have my word."

****

Colin sat on the red beanbag chair opposite Katie. His body language closed—crossed arms and eyes that wandered everywhere but in her direction. He watched the rug that was nearly large enough to pass as carpet, studying its colored squares. His gaze then shifted to the little clock embellished inside the red cat on the wall, as if to count the minutes he'd had left in this session. Katie pondered how this was going to go. A mute child was rare. She'd had many shy clients, but none that she could say were partial or total mutes—until today.

"Colin?" Katie called.

His eyes met Katie's, but he didn't speak.

She expected this reaction, but she wanted to test his gestures, and his facial expressions.

He went back to exploring the room once again, playing with his fingers. Katie watched his every move—from his fingers, his breathing, to everywhere his eyes had landed. He watched the toys in the light green bin used for play therapy, and then the small dry-erase board in the corner.

"Would you like to draw, rather than talk?" she asked.

When he hadn't responded, Katie gently tried again, and again, she was met with silence. Katie surreptitiously glanced at the tiny clock strategically placed in the room. Time was moving very slowly. She caught him watching the candy dish on the desk.

Her eyes followed his. "You want some candy?" she asked, her voice an octave higher.

She grabbed it off the desk behind her and held it out. "When you're ready, you can come get whatever you want."

He hesitated at first, and then he'd left the bean bag chair. Slowly he approached, keenly watching Katie as if he feared she'd make a sudden startling attack.

He looked down at the candy bowl, scanning all of the left-over taffy, fun sized skittles, and chocolate inside. He grabbed straight for the red colored blow-pop and headed back toward the bean bag chair.

"So, Colin," Katie said, after he'd sat back down. "I hear you like to build things."

Colin didn't respond, nor did he budge—not even at the mention of his name. It was as if Katie had said nothing. It was as if she weren't there at all.

He began peeling the wrapper until it'd separated—placing the pop inside his mouth.

"What kind of things do you like to build?"

Predictably, there was no answer.

"Colin?" she called.

He watched her, but no words made it out of his mouth. He leaned further back in the chair. His eyes dropped to his lap; his free hand lightly rubbed at his thigh. Katie could tell his mind was busy. Hungry for more, she leaned forward, calling his name again. This time he didn't look up.

"You can speak when you're ready," she said. "This is a safe space."

He looked up again, but not at Katie. He'd gone back to exploring the room—and once again, ignoring her.

The hour with Colin went by excruciatingly slow, mostly because he'd only opened his mouth to suck on the blow pop. The only time he'd looked up again was to watch the red cat on the wall. Colin would be a challenge for Katie. Still, she was excited for this new case. She loved challenging herself, testing her abilities to see how far she could go. She'd been this way ever since she was a child. Most of the time, she didn't know when to stop. She also loved helping other people with their healing. It was fulfilling to be there for people the way she wished someone had been there for her as a child. It brought her peace, and it'd made her feel useful in a way that nothing else ever had. It was her purpose in life.

Colin's father came to pick him up at the end. His name was Reed, tall and thin with glasses that flattered his face. His reddish-brown hair matched Colin's, and his skin was every bit as pale. Katie reported to him every behavior Colin displayed and the plan they'd take moving forward.

To Katie's surprise though, Colin's father hadn't asked the questions she thought a concerned parent would; questions like *how did my son do?* Or *was the session good?* Instead, he'd just nodded while checking his watch and phone as Katie gave her assessment. When she'd finished, he'd thanked her, took Colin by the hand, and rushed out of the doors.

****

Katie's apartment was quiet, a modest two bedroom with basic colors, and it was decorated with various types of snow globes. Katie started collecting as a child, and it'd followed her into adulthood. She had gotten a new snow globe for nearly every birthday and Christmas, sent to her by close friends, clients and colleagues. Katie was quiet in nature, but when she'd grown close to someone, they'd know about her collection.

She'd glanced at her phone on her dresser, and the time read 3:15a.m. Her apartment was empty, but sometimes she felt like she was being watched. At night she slept with the covers over herself. Like a child, she felt protected from what was outside of them.

Katie scratched her elbow, nursing the itch over a bruise she'd gotten from Jay when they were children. She figured it was strategically placed on her elbow, making it easier to explain away. In the woods that day, after biting her, Jay pushed her down. Kiko, a stray cat Katie had found and fed became a victim of her brother's wrath. Katie helplessly watched Jay strike Kiko with a very long stick he'd found. One hit after the other, more and more blood would soar up, smearing Jay's face, but he didn't stop. He swatted harder after every strike.

Katie screamed the loudest she could, causing the birds perched above them to scatter, but nobody was around in the woods with surrounding trees that all looked the same. It wasn't until Kiko stopped screeching and moving that Jay dropped the stick.

Deep within those same woods, Jay would watch her run, allowing her a head start as if to enjoy the sport of the hunt.

She would run for her life, never knowing if today would be the day that he ended her suffering. Eventually she'd stopped fearing for it and began hoping for it. To live in fear was to have no life at all, so why not die?

Chapter 3

February 2nd, 2024

Katie reluctantly agreed to go to Max's going away party. The loud screeching cheers of Max's excitement had played on repeat in Katie's mind. Rather than fly or opt for a bus, she decided to drive herself to her hometown in Huntley, North Carolina, taking a long circuitous route. She kept herself entertained with music, and on occasion, an audiobook.

She hadn't been back in her childhood home since she was 18. When she started college in Virginia she hadn't looked back. She wondered what it would feel like to see her relatives again after all these years. It would of course be a little awkward—something like; *Hey, I know I've ignored and or blocked your attempts to bond all these years but…What's up?"*

Every family member knew the truth about Jay and Katie's history, although her parents worked hard to conceal the more appalling details. It was one of those very uncomfortable situations everyone pretended had never happened.

While holding the wheel, Katie looked out of the window. Unlike back in Sperry, the roads of North Carolina were clear of any snow or ice, and the temperature, Katie was sure hadn't dropped to what winter nights in Sperry had been.

Not much had changed in town. The old bank, and grocery stores remained where she'd last saw them, with little changes to the exterior. New buildings had gone up at the intersection before the long road, a Piggly wiggly, and a Tropical Smoothie. She traveled six miles down the narrow country road, passing homes with several acres of land behind them. Old memories of being driven around the area by her parents inevitably entered her mind. She'd lightly raised her foot from the gas, remembering how dangerous this road was. With its sharp sudden turns and lack of streetlights, the road had a reputation all its own. It wasn't uncommon to see flowers, ribbons, and crosses with the names of people who'd become victims to this road.

Finally, she pulled up to the old house that she grew up in—a big white box in the middle of nowhere.

Dozens of cars were lined up along the lengthy driveway. Parking behind the last car in line, she was just inches away from the narrow country road. Even though it was 10:30 at night, the house was still lit up. Every window had light shining through the Christmas wreaths.

Unlike in Sperry, there was no blast of bitter cold smacking her face when she'd opened the door. Instead, the temperature felt like a comfortable mid-60s.

Katie reached the top of the steps with both her purse and a duffel bag. The familiar long porch bench by the windows was still in place, now decorated in holiday garland. She stepped on the face of Santa Claus and cleared her shoes. Closing her eyes, she whispered, "What am I doing here?"

The temptation to turn around had followed her since she left the Sterling Pointe apartment complex. There was still a chance. If she turned back now, no one would know. Suddenly, the door opened to Uncle Rudy; now gray haired and chubbier than Katie remembered. His puffed cheeks were filled with whatever he was eating.

Too late.

His eyes lingered on her, as if to wonder who she was. They hadn't seen each other in person in over a decade, but Katie remembered his thick eyebrows and prominent nose. When Katie moved to Virginia for college, she cut contact with every family member except for Max. Since she was a mental health professional, she opted out of social media altogether, so any trace of her in the digital world was non-existent. She might as well have been dead.

She shrugged. "It's me, Uncle Rudy…Katie."

His eyes widened. "Katie," He chomped. "Of course I remember. You're so grown up! You look great—almost like a different person."

Katie expected this reaction, not only was she 100 pounds lighter than before, but she was also much older. A lot had changed after

Katie left for college, her self-esteem, her motivation, and more notably, her appearance.

He forced a hug, holding her so tightly she struggled to breathe. He smelled like he'd been smoking. Katie assumed he probably opened the door, blocking her only escape, to indulge in more. Behind him, she could see the familiar light wooden floors and neutral-colored walls of her childhood home. She recognized the family pictures that hung close to one another on both walls of the narrow hall. All pictures of a seemingly happy family of five. Pictures of Allen and Ruth, Katie and Max's graduation photos and pictures of Jay as a toddler up until age twelve—just before he was sent away. He asked if he could take her luggage, and she wasted no time thanking him. When she was younger, road trips were fun and something to look forward to. As she got older though, they'd become more draining.

When Katie stepped foot inside the house, she could smell the lingering scent of cooked meat and something sugary. Uncle Rudy led Katie into the living room. Her Aunt Cheryl and Max were close together on the couch. Max's already slim frame looked even smaller next to Aunt Cheryl's plump figure. A big book, most likely of family pictures covered Max's lap.

"Katie has returned!" he announced. They both looked up. Max swiftly handed the book to Aunt Cheryl and sprang up.

Her perfume was strong and smelled sweet like starburst. Her curls seemed tighter since the last time Katie had seen her, and her parting pink lips revealed the same bright white teeth that she remembered.

"How was the trip?"

"Long."

"Thanks for coming," she said, before they pulled apart.

Aunt Cheryl struggled to get up. She held up her hand, stopping Uncle Rudy from approaching her. "I'm fine, Rudy…I'm fine."

She gave Katie a heavy embrace once she'd gotten up, twirling her around after they parted. "You're so thin now. You look like a different—"

"Person," Katie finished, with a smile.

Katie knew this type of reaction was going to get old quickly. The only person who was used to seeing her with this body was Max. They lived in different states, but Max would visit and video chat with Katie periodically.

"We've got to get you fed, Katie. We can barely see you now." She turned to Max. "Go ahead and get her some cookies in the kitchen."

The idea sounded great, and the smell was greater. Katie knew she'd smelled something sweet when she'd walked in. She just wasn't sure of what it was.

"Okay," Max said readily. She disappeared into the hall, following Aunt Cheryl's orders.

Katie watched Aunt Cheryl waddle back to the couch, easing herself down slowly. Katie sat next to her. When their eyes met again, she returned the smile Aunt Cheryl gave.

She looked older and plumper than Katie remembered. She had tired brown eyes and a pale face on the verge of wrinkling. Her hair long, and white, flowing down her back from her ponytail.

"It's so good to see you, Katie," she said.

"You too, Aunt Cheryl."

"Will you be staying a while?"

Never.

"Just until tomorrow," she replied.

It wasn't long at all. Katie was dead set on leaving right after Max's party. Her heart had longed to turn back the moment she'd left her apartment complex, which she'd almost done if Uncle Rudy hadn't caught her at the door.

"Where's she staying, Cheryl?" Uncle Rudy asked.

"Up the stairs to the left."

Translation: Jay's old room.

She recognized the man who'd just appeared from the hallway, wobbling toward the front door. His limp was likely from the car accident he'd had in the past. Max told her the night that it happened. The man walking toward the door, also known as her father, Allen, had a head-on collision with a guardrail years ago. Katie asked if he was alive, Max answered yes, and then Katie changed the subject. She heard the sound of a knob turning amid the surrounding conversations. Soon after, he was visible again.

Uncle Rudy looked from Katie to Allen and then back at Katie. It was as if to wonder if she'd alert him that she'd come home, but she sat quiet as a church mouse, watching her father until he disappeared behind the mint green wall.

Uncle Rudy cleared his throat and then bent to reclaim her duffel bag. "I'll take this up for you."

"Thank you," Katie said.

Max came back with a tray full of sugar cookies. Katie grabbed two and passed the tray to Aunt Cheryl upon her request.

"Let's see here," Aunt Cheryl said, while chewing. She held the thick picture book in her lap; one hand turned the pages, the other held the bitten cookie.

Aunt Cheryl turned the page to an enlarged photo of Max as a baby, crawling on her hands and knees while gleaming up at the camera. She had nothing but a diaper on. Her cute and cheery grin resembled a model for baby products. Aunt Cheryl looked up at her.

"I still can't believe you're going away, Maxine. We'll miss you dearly."

"Oh, I'll definitely be back. I promise to come back every year for the major holidays."

Katie figured Max made those promises without knowing for sure if it was feasible. That was typical of her. She was always getting ahead of herself. However, even though constant trips back to the US would be expensive, Max had always been responsible with her money. She had big plans to travel, and she was now doing what she'd always wanted to.

Katie yawned as Aunt Cheryl continued turning pages. The truth was, she was ready for bed as soon as she entered the room. When Cheryl stated it was getting late, Katie took that as her cue to leave.

Jay's childhood room was clearly different from when he was a kid. Rather than white walls, scattered science books, and an overflowing hamper, the room was now well groomed and beach themed: Baby blue walls, a giant seashell rug, coastal accent tables, and netted lamps on top of them. Katie knew this design had to be Ruth's doing. Ruth loved the ocean so much it'd been her idea to book multiple family trips to Allen's Hawaiian childhood home, rather than Allen himself.

Katie set her things beside the bed and then scanned the walls; she folded her arms tightly, as if a chill had just entered the room. It was a weird feeling being home again. She didn't exactly hate it, but she didn't like it either. She was just here until she didn't have to be anymore.

The next morning, all the women gathered in the kitchen, preparing one big meal for breakfast. Most of the men were packed in the Livingroom with the TV on, watching a football game.

Katie was rejected at the kitchen entrance by Aunt Cheryl, who hadn't allowed any more help in the crowded kitchen. As she lingered in the hall, she heard her mother's name in their conversation. Katie hadn't seen Ruth in person since the day she'd left for college. Ruth was healthy then, strong, and young looking. Initially, Ruth acted in denial of it. She was dying, but she lived like she was a healthy 25-year-old. From what Katie heard from Max, Ruth was gardening, eating a diet of whatever she wanted, and was making plans for 10, and even 20 years from now. Though, according to Max, lately her condition has worsened. She was sleeping longer, eating less, and was in constant pain.

Aunt Cheryl allowed her to help with the setting of the long table in the dining room. The room was different than she remembered. The once beige walls had been painted teal. The glass light fixture above the table, and the dark maple chairs had remained the same.

"Could someone get Ruth?" Aunt Cheryl asked.

"I will," Max cheerily volunteered. She'd been standing at the doorframe for God knows how long.

"Katie," Max called. "Wanna help?"

Clearly, Max was serious about her and her mother making up, though there was nothing to really make up. Katie didn't feel angry at her mother, not anymore, rather she was just done trying to pursue a relationship that was already dead. She'd tried many times as a child, hoping one day Ruth or Allen would apologize or make it up in some way. However, both were preoccupied with creating stories to tell friends and neighbors, explaining Jay's absence rather than making things right with Katie.

Her acceptance into a Virginia school was Katie's ticket out of Huntley. Stepping outside of the front door of her childhood home that humid August morning, bound for college, was a dream come true. The only thing she'd miss was the face of a then ten-year-old Max, who'd stood on the long driveway, waving her off. Originally, Katie's destination was Santa Barbara, intending to get as far away from Huntley as the American map allowed, though she ended up settling on Virginia with her then boyfriend.

Katie followed Max to the door. Max knocked three times. "Mom?"

There was silence behind the door. "Mom?" she called again.

Max looked back at Katie; fear filled her eyes.

"Come in," Katie heard from the other end.

She sounded older, and sick, her raspy voice broke in between coughs. Katie braced herself for what she may find behind the door. It opened to her mother lying on her back, coughing hysterically with only a few strands of hair left on her head.

A trail of crumbs started parallel to her chin and ended at the tied belt of her purple robe. She held a crumpled napkin to her mouth that she used to catch what came out. Age and illness had clearly caught up to her. The wrinkles on her cheeks were just as blatant as the hairs left on her head. Her baggy red eyes revealed several hours, possibly days of missed sleep.

The room had stayed the same, just as Katie remembered; A teal bedspread and two overhang paddle boards above the bedframe. Ruth's fervent love for the ocean made it seem like she'd grown up in Hawaii. However, it was Allen's family who'd owned a home right on the shore, and it made Katie assume that same shared interest of the ocean was one of the reasons they'd come together as a couple.

Ruth held her arms out to her. Katie hesitated for a moment, and then proceeded to lean into her. Ruth's body was so dangerously slim and frail that Katie felt she could almost break her.

"Hand me my wig," She whispered, as they came apart.

Katie's eyes followed Ruth's finger as she pointed across the room.

A black wig styled in a short bob hung from the accent cabinet. The large nautical fishnet with starfish and clams hung above it.

Katie gently placed it on her mother's head, shifting the synthetic hairs out of her face.

"I haven't seen you in so long," she said, in between coughs. Her eyes scanned Katie's body up and down. "You've lost so much weight!"

"Yes," was all Katie could say at the moment.

"How did you—"

Ruth was cut off by a series of her own congested coughs. Max handed her more Kleenex from off the nightstand. "Are you ready, Mom?"

"Yes," Ruth replied, wiping her mouth.

Max held her right shoulder, signaling to Katie to take her left.

Ruth groaned as Katie tried lifting her shoulder. "I'm sorry," she said, freezing in place.

Ruth shook her head. "It's not you. It's my bones. Everything hurts."

Katie glanced up at Max, who'd already been staring at her. "Let's try again," Max said. "One. Two. Three. Go."

Katie and Max helped their mother to the dining room with the rest of the family.

After Aunt Cheryl blessed the food, they began to eat. Max went on and on about how excited she was about her new life. Katie was happy for her, and everything she's accomplished at such a young age. She would undoubtedly miss her.

Ruth asked Katie basic questions like how her trip was, how long it took, and how work was going.

Katie answered casually to all of them.

"When are you getting married, Katie?" Aunt Cheryl asks. "You're 32 and still—"

Katie tuned her out. She was well aware of her age. She'd been keeping tabs since she first learned what numbers were. She didn't need others keeping track as well.

"Katie?" Aunt Cheryl called. Clearly noticing she hadn't answered her.

"Well. . ."

"Maxine tells me she's seeing someone," Ruth said, winking at Katie.

She was referring to Tim, the man Katie had been dating for the past six months. Her hesitation on their future wasn't working for Tim. When he'd asked her about marriage and where she saw herself in five years, he wasn't in any of those fantasies, and that's when she knew his pace was faster than hers.

"Not anymore," Katie said. "But there's always other fish in the sea though am I right?"

There were a few head nods at the table. Katie's eyes had landed on her father, Allen. He didn't speak, but his lingering eye made Katie wonder what he was thinking. Had he already suspected Katie would never get married and he was now settling with the thought? Or does he think there's more to the story than what she'd led on? It was hard to tell with her father. He was a reserved man who spoke only when necessary, and who loved spending time alone. When he wasn't working, he would spend several hours fishing at the local lake. He brought Katie and Jay with him once. Jay had overkilled the fish, and Katie simply stood in the background, swatting irksome flies.

Katie hadn't seen much of her father growing up. After joining the AirForce at eighteen, leaving Hawaii behind, he worked as an airline pilot until he retired. With such a busy pilot's schedule, his presence at home wasn't frequent. Allen hadn't seen anything that Jay had done in the past, and he didn't believe something about his oldest child that he couldn't see. When the truth had come out about Jay, he didn't know how to face Katie, and Katie didn't know how to face him. And that was the nature of their relationship.

In the afternoon, Katie joined the other family members outside.

Max got a moment alone with Katie on the porch. Despite it being early February, the weather outside was warm, somewhere in the high 60s or low 70s it felt like. Max certainly took advantage, dressed in a tight yellow crop top and jeans that met her ankles.

"Happy for me?" she asked, excitedly.

Katie nodded. "I'm proud of you."

"You too," she said as her foot tapped the floor of the porch. Katie watched the old bench they were sitting on, studying it as if to search for hidden markings. "I wish this thing could swing," she said.

Max chuckled. "I'm surprised it still holds." As kids, they'd stood on it, crawled on it, laid on it, slept on it, and Katie remembered Jay even bouncing on it. Somehow, though, it had survived it all.

"I see great reviews on your yelp," Max said.

Katie smiled. She'd worked so hard to maintain a high approval rating. Her whole life she'd spent wanting to make a difference and be useful in some way. She was grateful to have fulfilled her calling.

"Thanks for coming by the way. I know this is hard."

Katie shrugged her shoulders, "Well this will be the last time we see each other for a while since you're moving."

"True," Max replied. Her expression was now sorrowful. "What do you think of mom?"

"Sad. Very sad. . .How long does she have?"

Max shook her head. "Doctors say a month—2 at best."

Katie muttered a curse before turning her eyes to the long and narrow driveway.

"I'm sorry," she said.

"Sorry for me or for us both? She's your mom too."

"I didn't say she wasn't."

Silence took the moment until Max broke it. "Did you speak to her?"

"I said hello, and you heard us talk at breakfast."

"You know that's not what I meant."

Her eyes darted to the silver Elantra that approached from the country road. "There's dad and—"

Max neglected her sentence, but Katie didn't need her to finish it. She held her breath as her body tensed. What would it be like to see Jay again in over 20 years? What would he look like now? Had he gotten taller? Fatter? Most importantly, what would his behavior be like? Max told Katie he got married and was the father of two children. But she wondered what kind of father he was, and if his family was safe.

Allen was the first one out, wobbling toward the porch. Jay rose out of the car and assisted Allen with the groceries. Katie couldn't take her eyes off of him. He was clearly older, but he still maintained his good looks over the years. His build was bigger, and he'd of course gotten taller.

When the storm door closed behind Allen, Jay and Katie shared a quick exchange of eye-contact. He gave her a brief smile before shyly looking down. This was the first time she'd laid eyes on her brother face to face in 24 years.

Rather than a skinny twelve-year-old, he'd filled into a grown man's body. He had minimal facial hair and those same cold dark eyes that she never forgot. She nearly shuddered looking at him. Almost like instinct, her heart had plummeted to her stomach, and then she ached.

Jay followed Allen into the kitchen. They set the groceries down, and then they began preparing for the cookout outside.

Katie headed back into Jay's room to catch a breath. She sat on the twin sized bed huffing and puffing as if she were having an asthma attack.

Why had she come here? She could have said goodbye to Max over skype or something.

She could've—

There was a knock at the door. She took a deep breath before opening it. Jay's cold dead eyes stared at her. Katie thought back to when they were kids, when she used to search his face for any ounce of truth, remorse, or humanity, but there was nothing in those hollow eyes.

"Hi, Katie," he said. He looked her up and down. "Wow, you really lost a lot of weight."

"Yeah," she replied.

After a moment of silence, his expression shifted to apologetic. "How are you?"

"Fine," she said.

"I got you something." He swiftly reached into the brown satchel slung across his body, pulling out a medium-sized snow globe. It was Christmas themed with three snowmen standing inside. Katie didn't bother to shake it. She had about 12 just like it already. Did he even try to make it unique?

"Thanks," she said, dryly.

Jay nodded at her apathy.

"Look, Katie—"

Katie slammed the door in his face, her impulsiveness overrode any clear thought.

She remembered her years of training as a therapist. *You control your emotions. Don't ever let them control you.*

When she cracked it open again, he was still standing there with hope in his eyes. He was taller than her, but he was slouched with his hands leaning on her door frame. As he looked up at her, a single strand of hair swayed at his eye. "Can I come in?"

"No," Katie blurted.

He chuckled. "I can't come into my own room?"

His smile faded when it was clear to him that Katie wasn't amused. The room hadn't been his since he was twelve.

He nodded. "Okay, then I'll say it here. Please listen to me. I know you don't owe me anything, but if you could find it in your heart to at least hear me out it would mean a lot."

After a moment, Katie slowly pushed the door wider.

"I put you through so much when we were kids. I was the worst person—the worst older brother a person could have, and for that I am sorry, Katie. I'm so sorry. I want you to know that I've changed. Please forgive me."

Katie sighed.

"I do forgive you, Jay. I wouldn't be as good at my job if I didn't, but right now you've bought memories back that I don't want to think about. I need to be alone for a while, okay?"

Jay nodded. "Okay."

When the door closed, she felt like crying. Ninety percent of her memories of Jay had been negative. Throughout her childhood, Jay had been mysterious and unpredictable. He'd spent so much time in isolation when he wasn't at school. The only close friend Jay had that Katie remembered was a boy named Craig, who always reprised his role of detective whenever he and Jay would play cops and criminals. As far as she knew, he was the first boy to have a crush on her, which she had found out from a classmate. Nothing had happened though. Both were too shy and awkward. He, just like many other faces from her childhood, had disappeared over the years.

Katie never knew the things Jay had done inside his room for hours on end. She suspected that Allen and Ruth hadn't known either. Jay had two sides to him when they were young: on the surface, he was an outgoing, normal kid; but in secret, he was a torturous and dangerous boy who craved power and control.

Katie would have to deal with this now and be done with it. She had a reputation to maintain as a professional, and family waiting for her out there. She could not, and would not, stay hidden here.

Most of the family had moved indoors, bought on by the unexpected weather change. Rain fell from the gray clouds, despite the earlier forecast.

Only Ruth and one of Katie's cousins were left outside on the bench. Katie stood by the window and watched the rain drench the front lawn. From the inside, she could hear their mumbles, but she couldn't make out any words.

Ruth sat with a gray throw blanket over her body, nodding along to the conversation. Part of Katie felt obligated to join them, but she couldn't get her legs to move.

Allen's reflection appeared in the window. "How does it feel to be back?"

When Katie turned around, she saw a piece of green stuck between his teeth.

"It's. . . Different," She replied, tapping her tooth.

Allen quickly responded, digging out what was between his. Katie turned back to the window, wondering if Allen would stay or leave, unsure which one she wanted.

"She's really glad you came back, Katie."

Katie turned to him, her brow furrowed. "Yeah?"

She wondered if he was going to add more, and clarify that he was included in that, but Allen was never that forward.

His eyes met Katie's, but nobody spoke. Allen cleared his throat.

Katie returned to staring out the window. She wondered if Allen would take this as a sign or an opportunity to leave.

"She won't be here much longer," he continued. "She mentioned you, and how she wanted to leave you this house after we pass."

Katie sucked her teeth, her focus still on the porch. *All this time and he still doesn't get it.*

"I don't want this house," she grumbled.

"I know you don't, so it'll be your choice what you want to do with it."

"Why not give it to Max? She's the youngest."

"Because we're giving it to you."

Katie looked back at him. The two stared at one another, but nobody spoke a word. Allen turned to leave, and Katie returned to the window.

Why would they think she'd want anything to do with this monstrosity of a house? There was no way they would think she'd want to raise a family in it, did they? She'd left Huntley behind for a reason, and she'd left it for good…so she'd thought.

Allen had said after we pass, implying that both he and Ruth's time on earth would soon end—Ruth with her debilitating cancer, and Allen with his heart disease, both conditions she'd found out about through Max. Sometimes Katie wondered if her parents' health problems were karma for how they'd handled Jay's abusive behavior, but the thought was never satisfying.

The kitchen was packed just like it was this morning. The cake was large enough to feed the entire family and more. Its base was white, with yellow along the sides; the latter was Max's favorite color. The center read, "Goodbye Max. We'll miss you!"

The family stood in a circle listening to Max talk about missing them and loving them dearly. Katie smiled as she watched her. Sometimes she was just a little dramatic, speaking like she was going off to war and would likely never see family again. Still, she was so spirited and passionate in the way that she said things. She was confident and happy, void of any damage by Jay. That was what Katie wanted for her baby sister.

When Max finished her speech, the room erupted in conversation, and the line for cake began to form. Jay walked up to Max with something he held behind his back. Katie winced.

He took a quick peak at her before revealing it to Max. He'd been eyeing Katie ever since he got here, which did nothing but make her nervous.

When he revealed the gift to Max, she cheerily took it. It looked like an oversized book straight out of Harry Potter; a thick brown book with an old buckle around it. Max always loved Harry Potter, and every other popular fantasy story. Katie figured the gift would fit right in with all her other items.

"So, you can document your new world," She heard Jay say.

Max hugged him and then whispered something Katie didn't catch. She couldn't blame Max for being comfortable with Jay. She was just a baby when he started abusing things weaker than him. A human baby hadn't interested Jay when they were young. With the ability to cry when her parents were home had made it harder for him. The fact that the baby's body was well looked after had also deterred him. Jay was young, but he was very smart and skilled in the art of manipulation and deceit. There was good reason he'd gone undetected for so many years.

Jason Mackenna's ability to woo people had not only come from his charm, but his looks. With warm eyes and a symmetrical face clear of adolescent acne, his appearance had made people of both genders treat him like royalty; dismissing any otherwise obvious imperfections. With his intellect, he excelled academically. All the nights Katie had stayed awake studying for her exams, Jay was the type to take a glance at his textbook and still pass with a near perfect score.

However, Katie's middle and high school days consisted of not only long studying but also struggling to control her weight. By age 17, she had reached 257 pounds. She was happy nobody at her high school had known Jay, since he was sent away before he could attend. She feared that if anyone knew they were related, they'd take one long look at the both of them, and then they'd laugh.

Katie took a seat beside Ruth in the living room. Her coughing fit started again. Katie stared at her, taking in her woeful condition. Then the coughing became so bad she had no choice but to run and get a bowl.

Her mother threw up inside of it when the bowl met her mouth.

Katie grabbed the napkin box on the coffee table. It was empty inside, so she ran and got paper towels from the kitchen.

"Thank you, Katie," Ruth said, taking them from her.

This was her mother's condition now. All this time it hadn't kicked in as a reality yet. But seeing was believing. Ruth was dying. The two of them had barely spoken in years, and she was dying.

Katie reclaimed the seat beside her mother.

"I'm sorry," she said. "Katie—" another cough, and another one, and one after that.

"Your brother being here…"

"Where's his family?" Katie interrupted. "He's married right?"

Ruth glanced at her amid her coughing.

Katie wondered how long that union had lasted. Perhaps his wife had experienced enough of the lies, cruelty and manipulation, and left with their children, as she should've.

"Beth, their daughter, has been having some behavioral issues. His wife, Jenna, stayed behind to deal with it."

Ruth's coughing had settled, and then she leaned over for a hug. Katie hesitated a moment, then slowly drew closer.

Hugging her mother's frail body felt like she was hugging just skin and bones. She was warm at least.

Ruth reached for the vase on the stand beside her, taking out the drooping flowers that'd looked as though they'd been dead for weeks. She placed them in her lap and handed Katie the vase. It was quite beautiful, a glass vase shaped like rose petals in the colors of blue, purple, and a hint of pink.

"I want you to have it, Katie—my favorite vase. It's beautiful, right?"

Katie smirked. "It is."

"Go ahead, put your favorite flowers inside."

Ruth commanded this as if Katie currently had any. She thought of her apartment, and which place the vase would go well in. Perhaps it would make quite the decorative mantel piece by the window, flowers inside or not.

Ruth opened her arms, awaiting Katie's embrace. Katie gulped, then slightly lifted the vase, indicating the barrier between them.

"We'll have the rest of our lives to make things right," Ruth said, pulling back.

Katie jerked her head back, unsure how to respond.

The five stages of grief for a cancer patient are:

One. Denial.

Two. Anger.

Three. Bargaining

Four. Sadness and depression

Five. Acceptance

Ruth was clearly still at the first stage, in denial of the true weight of her situation, but Katie wasn't going to be the one to unpack it for her.

"You'll come see me, won't you?" she asked.

Jay entered the room just as Ruth broke out into another raging coughing fit.

"Could we talk, Katie?" Jay asked.

Ruth nodded amid her coughing, letting Katie know it was okay to go.

Katie followed behind Jay into the kitchen, clear of anyone else.

"Jay, didn't I already say—"

"The money is yours," he said. "When mom and dad die, the money they leave behind for Max will be hers, and what they have for me will be yours."

"What?" Katie said. "What are you talking about? Jay, you can't buy forgiveness."

"I want you to give me a chance. I don't know any other way. Please."

Katie sighed. "What do you want me to say?"

"That you'll give me another chance."

Katie wasn't sure what to say. How did she know this wasn't Jay going back to his old antics of manipulation? And if so, why was it so important she forgive him? Katie wondered what he was up to.

When they were kids, Jay lied all the time, and almost every time Katie believed him. She wanted to believe so badly that he'd change, but he *never* did. Why would this be any different?

Even though Katie didn't respond, there was hope in Jay's eyes.

"There's a difference in me, Katie. You'll know it when you see it."

Katie raised her hand, stopping him from saying anything else. Without another word, she walked away.

****

On the way home, Katie finished the audiobook she was listening to. She decided to speed through the boring parts to get to the big reveal of who killed Sidney Wallace.

Jay's final words popped into her mind. She found them to be quite haunting.

You'll know it when you see it, was what he'd said. What was that supposed to mean? Surely, she wouldn't be seeing him again.

The car behind her beeped three times in a row, alerting her that the light was now green.

Immediately she floored it.

What did Jay mean? Katie smacked herself on the cheek for allowing the thought to travel with her. She wasn't going to do it. She wasn't going to let Jay and his lies rule over her.

After picking up Casper from the local kennel, Katie arrived home at her empty, dark, apartment. She'd taken her black flats off beside her doormat, while holding Casper's travel cage. He whimpered inside as she set it down. Her apartment was freezing. She raced to the thermostat and turned up the heat. It was nice to be back home, and even nicer to be done with the tedious drive.

Once settled, Katie lit a large lavender sage candle and took it into the bathroom. The sensation of the steaming water flowing down her face from the showerhead felt like a relief—like she was washing off all the stench and ugliness of the day's events. She'd left her childhood home as soon as she'd hugged her sister goodbye.

Again, Jay's words circled around in her head. "You'll know it when you see it."

The tears in her eyes flowed in sync with the water from the shower. She sank to the bottom and sobbed hysterically, gripping her shoulders as the water entered her open mouth.

Chapter 4

February 9th, 2024

The workday seemed to go by slower than normal. Katie found herself paying unusually close attention to the semi-hidden clock inside her office. Solutions to problems for her clients hadn't come as quickly. She hadn't even offered candy to her youngest clients, or cough drops to Niah, a sick 14-year-old who struggled with anxiety and bullying. She encouraged the girl as much as she could, but something was off.

Throughout the day, she had visions of Jay at their childhood home, and of the man he had become. The images were on repeat from the morning, growing more aggressive by the evening.

At home, Katie prepared a meal for herself. Ramen noodles in a white bowl. She had her chocolates from Godiva right next to her. Katie realized she was stress eating, something she hadn't done in years.

Her phone buzzed by the bubbling pot of Ramen. Katie had two new messages, one from Max, thanking her for attending her farewell party, the other was from Daphne, a friend she had made in college. Unlike Katie, Daphne had chosen to take the path of medicine. She was a standby nurse at a local clinic. Daphne would come over every once and a while for food, drinks, and to get out of the home she shared with her husband and 3 young children.

I'm here, the text read.

Katie opened her front door to a smiling Daphne. There was something extra in her eyes tonight Katie noticed.

Daphne followed Katie back into the kitchen, where she unloaded the snacks for tonight. Daphne was the mother of young twins and a relatively newborn baby. It wasn't often that Katie was able to spend time with her, but she was quite thankful when it did happen.

Daphne leaned on the counter as she scrolled through her phone. "I have a man for you."

Katie sighed. Daphne was persistent in her pursuit to make sure Katie didn't end up with Casper, and three or four more cats to spend her life with. "Good women should never be alone," she'd always said.

"His name's George. He's single, hardworking, sweet, *and* he's rich."

Katie folded her arms. "What's wrong with him?"

Daphne laughed. "Nothing."

Surely a man with that kind of profile wouldn't still be single at Katie's age, and if he were, she suspected there may be good reason for it.

"He's ugly, isn't he?"

She shook her head, "Not at all."

"Has he ever been married?"

"Yeah. He's divorced—just once though."

"Wow, just once?"

Daphne ignored her sarcasm. "And he has one child."

"Look," she said, placing the phone closer to Katie.

`George Harper,` his profile read. `Works in finance and is from Stamford Connecticut.`

The man had a lovely smile, with brown eyes, light brown hair, and no receding hairline. He was undoubtedly handsome, which immediately piqued Katie's curiosity.

"You should go out with him," she said. "He's a friend of Carson's. He's a good guy from what I hear."

Daphne's husband, Carson, was a good guy too. It wouldn't be out of the ordinary for him to keep company with others who were also good people. Perhaps she should give it a try. What did she have to lose?

"And if it doesn't work out," Daphne continued. "Come to my church. You'll hear a great message, *and* there are a lot of single men there."

Katie hadn't been to church in years. The last time she had gone was with her family. She didn't intend to associate it with the rest of her bad memories, but somehow that's what'd happened.

****

Daphne had left after they'd eaten dinner together. Katie rejected her offer to help with the dishes, suggesting she ought to head back home and help Carson with the little ones. Daphne, understandably, hadn't fought her on it.

Wanting dessert, Katie walked the sidewalk of Main Street, headed to a newly established business called *Molly's Tavern*. Since it was one of the places on the same street as her work, she was often tempted to go in. Instead, she ended up deviating from the path to the tavern.

Her fingers dug inside the pockets of her red overcoat as she walked. The temperature outside was cold, but thankfully not unbearable. She stopped in front of the familiar dark abandoned building. Her silhouette expanded as she approached the glass door. A white sign was taped to the glass, reading **"For Rent"** in bold red letters, with a phone number beneath it.

Katie had fantasized many times about this building. She'd thought about how many offices it could hold, how many clients, and how many clinicians she would hire. When she was in her sophomore year of college, she determined that she would dedicate her entire life to helping those who couldn't, or didn't yet know how to help themselves. It was her purpose, her life, something that'd made her feel useful, something that'd given her life meaning. She simply hadn't known anything else. To open up her own private practice would take a great deal of money she didn't yet have. The money that would come from her parent's death wouldn't come unless they died, and she wasn't exactly anticipating that. However, Katie was determined that someday, someway, she would make her dream a reality, with or without help from anyone else.

****

It was crowded inside *Molly's,* with groups of people both young and middle-aged crowding inside. Since Valentines Day was approaching, there were red paper hearts and pink paper lanterns hanging above the bar. Katie took a seat underneath one and scanned the above menu adorned in string lights. A dark-skinned girl with puffed curly hair and small nose ring approached her at the counter.

"Hi," she said, with a smile. "What'll you have?"

"Scone please, blueberry."

The bartender nodded. "Comin' right up."

Katie turned on the bar stool to people watch while she waited. A man was hitting on two women who were clearly uninterested, one repeatedly checking her phone, the other had her body turned away. Close beside them, a young girl, seemingly college age was chatting up a man who looked middle age.

A group of young guys and girls crowded a corner, laughing and enjoying each other's company. Katie reminisced her own college years, where she'd shared moments like these with her friends. After graduation though, Daphne had been the only friend she'd kept contact with.

A handful of people were by the pool table. A man was bent over the table, his arms stretched as he grasped the pool cue. After striking the ball, it'd soared straight into it's intended goal. He met Katie's eyes as he rose up, like he had several times since she'd entered in.

He was good-looking from what Katie could see: tall, with dark, silky hair, and a medium build. The sleeves of his green and black plaid shirt were rolled to his forearm. His keys dangled outside of his dark jeans, particularly when he'd bend to take a pool shot.

He was off to himself when it wasn't his turn, checking his phone whenever he could.

The bartender gave Katie her scone, striking up a short-lived conversation about new year's resolutions and how long the both of them typically stuck to them.

Katie turned back around to watch the pool game, but the man had shaken hands with his opponent, signaling the game was over.

Their eyes had met yet again. His lingering stare was empty, not accompanied by a smile or even a kind gesture. For a moment, Katie considered his gaze to be less flirty and more you've got huge fly-away hairs on top of your head, or you resemble my cat. The latter, a sad but true story.

His eyes dropped back to his phone again, his fingers raced across the screen.

Jeremy...

It was the name Katie assigned to the handsome stranger at the pool table. It was something she'd sometimes do just to see if she was right in guessing.

After slipping his phone into his back pocket, he approached Katie. She smiled as she watched him.

"Hi," he said. "How are you?"

"Better now," Katie replied.

He was even more handsome up close—full lips, a five o'clock shadow, and eyes a mix of blue and gray.

"Can I buy you a drink?" he asked.

She shook her head with a smile. "I don't."

He slowly nodded. "A non-drinker. At... a... bar."

"I can explain."

He chuckled. "No need. The food here's great." He reached his hand out. "I'm Ian by the way."

Rats.

"Katie," she said, shaking his hand.

"So, I take it you're by yourself tonight?" he asked, sitting on the stool beside her.

"At the moment. My fiancé doesn't get here till eleven."

Katie watched the embarrassment fill his face. "Sorry to have bothered you."

She reached her hand out before he could leave. "I'm kidding."

She felt a twinge of guilt for playing with him, but she wanted to check his character. If he entertained her after knowing she had a relationship, she knew he would be a waste of her time in the long run.

Voices grew louder from across the room. Katie glanced over, but she couldn't comprehend the words spoken. Judging from the tone and body language of the two men, Katie couldn't tell whether they were angry or joking.

"So, Katie," he said, retrieving his seat. "What do you do?"

"Therapy. I work with children."

His eyes widened. "Nice."

"And you?"

"Landscaping."

He dug inside his pocket, taking out a blue shaded card. "Been in business for 10 years," he said handing it to her.

Katie read it to herself.

`Ian Alexander. Freelance landscape designer.` His contact info was listed below.

Max had a theory about male designers: They were all gay, she had said openly. Even though the idea was farfetched and silly, the thought always crossed Katie's mind whenever she met one.

She could feel Ian's eyes on her as she read the card. When she looked up, her suspicion was confirmed.

"You've got beautiful eyes," he said.

He didn't seem gay from what Katie could tell so far, but she did wonder how many women he'd probably said the same thing to in a setting like this one, but she still answered with a simple, "Thank you."

His eyes had dropped from meeting Katie's, down to her chest.

Nope. Definitely not gay.

A loud crash of glass smacked against the wall. It was clearly aimed at the man who'd just ducked below it. Gasps and loud cussing quickly filled the room. A heavy-set biker club looking man tried punching a much slimmer man, who'd quickly ducked, causing him to punch the woman standing behind him. The enraged man beside her retaliated. Things quickly escalated into a full fledge bar fight, with Ian's pool opponent being one of the men involved.

"Time to go," Ian said, taking Katie's hand.

The two of them joined the growing throng of patrons rushing for the door. Once outside, Katie burst out laughing, barely able to sustain her balance.

Ian swiftly assisted her, keeping her from falling. "I thought you didn't drink?"

Katie laughed hysterically, unable to respond.

Ian pulled her upright, "Okay, okay," he said. "Easy." He leaned her against a building, where she closed her eyes.

"Not a very good impression I'm making is it?"

"I've seen worse. Can you walk?"

"I'm not drunk," she said, chuckling. "It's just—all the nights I've passed by this place, I always thought about stopping inside, and the one time I do, there's a fight."

"You're probably not in a hurry to go back then I assume."

She shook her head.

Ian stood smirking at her, "You want to take a walk with me?"

Katie stared at him. It was unlike her to go anywhere with a stranger. However, it was just a walk on a busy street.

"Sure," she said.

They walked side by side down the sidewalk, passing the many buildings joined together, shops, restaurants, and healthcare clinics.

From her peripheral vision, she caught him staring at her. "What?"

He cracked his knuckles. "Do you mind if I ask how old you are?"

Katie chuckled. Having such a youthful looking face, she'd gotten this question often.

"I'm 32."

"Wow," he said, his eyebrows raised. "You look very young."

Katie nodded. "That's what everyone tells me."

"Well, I'm 29," he said, before Katie could play her game of guessing.

He nodded. "So, what are your interests?" he asked, amid their shared silence.

"Knowing people. Understanding why they do the things they do. Learning more about them."

He nodded. "Spoken like a therapist."

"What about you?"

"Wait is that all you're interested in?" he asked.

"I don't enjoy talking about myself."

"Yeah, I picked up on that."

"I'd like to hear more about you," she continued.

Ian smirked. "What do you want to know?"

"Anything. Everything. Whatever you want to tell me."

They separated, allowing the oncoming group of loud teenagers to pass between them.

"Okay," he replied once they'd come back together. "But you've gotta give me something else first. Something about you I don't know. Can't be that hard since we just met."

Katie searched her brain once again. It was silly to make such an easy request complicated, so she knew she had to push herself.

"I like snow globes. I used to collect them when I was a kid—and even now. I have a bunch in my apartment."

He nodded. "Like Christmas snow globes?"

"Like any kind."

"Speaking of Christmas," he said, "Would you say that's your favorite holiday?"

"Actually no. I'd say Halloween is my favorite."

"Oh yeah? Why's that?"

"It's basically the start of the holiday season. It's in the fall, and fall is the best season. And it reminds me of *The Nightmare Before Christmas*, which is my favorite movie."

"Nice," he said.

"Your turn," Katie turned to him, quite pleased with herself.

"After high school wrapped up, I researched business owning, perfected my skills, and marketed the hell out of myself."

Katie nodded as she listened attentively.

"I was born and raised here. Been on my own for three years." Katie glanced at him. If he had been on his own for three years, where had he been living before? Was he now divorced? Widowed? Or had he been living with his parents? 20 years ago, a man still living with his parents would be outlandish, but it was becoming more and more common among men her age and particularly younger.

"I like hiking, food, and listening to podcasts in my spare time. I'm also in the process of learning a new language."

He pronounced the word process oddly, kind of like an old person who refused to conform to 'young people language'. A desperate need to seem different Katie considered.

"A new language," she repeated. "Why?"

He shrugged. "Why not?"

"Anything else?"

"Yeah. I also enjoy reading," he said, his hands sank deep in his pockets. "I go to a pretty nice bookstore around here a few times a week. *The Book Café*. Maybe you've heard of it?"

Katie nodded. "I know where that is."

It was a bookstore nearby the therapy center. She had been inside before on occasion, but she'd never gone back since she'd disliked the coffee. However, she hadn't disclosed to Ian the location of her work since she hadn't known him well enough. The last thing she needed in her life was a stalker who'd known where she was five days a week.

"I would go more often if I didn't throw myself into my work so much," he said.

"Looks like we have something in common."

"Do we?"

Katie nodded. "I'm a workaholic to—so much that I forgot the color of my kitchen."

He chuckled before turning to face her. "So how far do you want to go?"

"Ian," Katie gasped, "You haven't even bought me dinner yet." He laughed to the ground, smiling as he came back up. "I meant on this walk."

Katie's smile had matched his. It was nice when someone got her humor, and she didn't have to clarify her jokes, making her feel silly, and hideously unfunny.

"Actually, I should probably get going. It's getting a little late."

Normally, on a Friday night, Katie would be in bed with her reading glasses on and a mug of tea in her hand as the TV played.

As she stared into Ian's eyes, Katie wondered why a man this good looking was still single. Her mind went through a series of possibilities. Was he unstable with commitment issues? Was he indeed the man-child she'd feared?

Ian nodded. "Hold on to my card. Have a good night, Katie."

He passed her by, leaving her more than a little confused. He hadn't asked for her number. Instead, he'd given her his by way of a business card.

****

Katie had been texting George all week. It had begun just a day after Daphne had given him her number. George seemed to be an all-around nice man, and smart—qualities that had always been a plus for Katie.

After picking her up in a red Tesla, he took her to a very fancy restaurant downtown. Inside were dimly lit lights, soft classical music, servers dressed in black, and the patrons dressed in their Sunday best.

It seemed a bit much for a first date, but Katie wasn't going to complain.

"You can have anything you want," he told her, as she scanned the single page menu.

She looked up at him and smiled. Returning to the menu, she raised an eyebrow.

The cheapest entrées were nearly forty dollars. She remembered she never asked what he did for a living. She'd already told him her occupation, but he stopped her before she could ask his. He'd said they would have nothing to talk about on their date if they got too personal too quickly. That concerned Katie. It felt as if he was hiding something.

"You look beautiful," he said.

It was the fifth time he'd said it tonight. Katie was tempted to let him know that the first time was indeed enough, but there was no way to say it without sounding rude.

His eyes locked in on her unhappy expression.

"You don't like being called beautiful?"

Katie set the menu down. "On a first date if all a man can say about his date is how good she looks, the woman thinks that's all he's interested in."

"Noted. It won't happen again."

"It's not that you can't *ever* say it, I just don't need to hear it all the time."

"Okay," He smiled. "It won't happen again *tonight*."

Katie couldn't control her oncoming smile. When he returned it, she stared at how white his teeth were. She began playing her guessing game in her head. Perhaps he was a dentist. Or perhaps he just happened to be a secret agent with nice teeth. She found the mystery quite intriguing Afterall.

"So," he said. "Let's talk about your work. How are things at your job?"

"They're good," Katie replied.

"Good."

"And you? Am I allowed to know what you do now?" She asked, playfully.

He smiled. "I'm in finance—investment specifically."

Katie cocked her head. "Nice. How long have you been in that?"

"Since I was in my early 20s—started as an analyst and worked my way up."

He sounded hardworking, just like Daphne had said. Since he was in finance, Katie assumed he was good in math, which she figured must've meant he was smart. However, math was her worst subject, memories of struggling back in school with it had been well suppressed. Was she out of her element? Did he want his equal? Surely, he wouldn't choose her if he did.

He leaned toward the table. "I think it's great what you do."

"Excuse me?"

"Working with kids like you do," he said, cutting into his steak. "They need it."

He reassured her at the perfect moment—as if he could read her mind.

She smiled at him. "Thanks. It wasn't an easy journey, but I'm glad I made it. It's very fulfilling."

He took another bite. "So, Katie, what exactly are you looking for?"

She placed her glass back on the table. "Pardon?"

"With me—my work consumes me. I don't have time for a lot. I do want a future with someone in it, but I feel it's only fair to tell whoever I'm entertaining that my work isn't exactly part time."

Katie figured this kind of talk might turn many women off. However, she found his honesty refreshing. Katie was a recluse herself. She didn't exactly need the company of too many people, so his candor about it hadn't bothered her.

"Not a problem."

His smile had matched hers, which made her guess this date for him might've been going as well as it was for her.

George was straightforward, ambitious, and seemingly confident. Had she finally found what she'd been searching for?

Katie leaned back a little, taking another swig of her drink—well aware of how big of a thank you she was going to give Daphne.

After a long week of work at the therapy center and seeing George throughout it, Katie got home to a very cold apartment on a typical weekend night.

She ran to the thermostat in the hallway as if she were being chased.

Just as Katie was about to sit on her couch, there was a knock at her door. Swearing to herself, she wondered who it could be. Daphne hadn't mentioned coming over, and George didn't know where she lived.

She looked through the peephole and saw the face of a nervous looking girl. She had long brown hair with bangs just above her eyebrows. She held her arms as if she were standing in the bitter cold rather than a warm corridor. Her head was down like she'd spotted her loose shoelace.

Katie wasn't in the mood for any visitors, nor was she in the mood to give directions. Sighing, she opened the door anyway.

"Hi," the girl said, looking up, innocence written on her face. "I'm Beth... and I think you're my Aunt Katie."

Chapter 5

Katie sat her niece down on the couch and poured two glasses of lemonade, requested by the young guest. She handed hers to Beth and then took a seat on the opposite side of the room.

Initially, the idea of shutting the door on her had entered her mind, but those beautiful brown eyes and innocent face prevented her from doing it. The warmth in Beth's eyes was the opposite of her father's. Looking at her now, the only trace of Jay that Katie saw in her was her nose. She didn't know much about Jay's wife, only that her name was Jenna, which she'd learned from Max.

Beth lifted up the glass. "Thanks for this."

"It's freezing outside, and you wanted iced lemonade," Katie said. "You're welcome for it but I gotta assume you're a little nutty." "Weren't you drinking it too?" Beth fought a giggle. "Doesn't that make you kinda nutty also?"

Katie shrugged. "I never said I wasn't."

Beth laughed, but silence quickly followed. She tried not to look at Katie, but Katie had trouble doing the same. All she had of Beth was a picture from Max of her and her brother when they were four and six years old. She'd never had contact or seen any other pictures.

She didn't know Beth's likes or her dislikes, how old she was or even why she was here. Her presence struck a new curiosity in Katie.

"Does your dad know where you are?"

She stared down at the glass she held with both hands. "Not really. He's. . ."

"Good to you, right?" Katie finished with obvious alarm in her voice.

"He's so awful," Beth said, leaning back into the couch. "He and my mom never let me do *anything*!"

Katie relaxed at Beth's teenage whining. She was just about ready to call every emergency first responder that there was.

"Please don't make me go back," she whined.

"You have to go back. Call your mother and tell her where you are."

Beth scoffed. She started dialing and put the phone to her ear.

"Put it on speaker," Katie demanded.

If Beth was anything like her father, she was sneaky, and Katie wasn't about to let her pull anything straight over her head.

"Hello?" A woman's voice answered.

"Hi, Mom," Beth said, rolling her eyes.

"Beth, where are you?!" Her tone was a mixture of both concern and irritation.

"I'm fine. I'm at Aunt Katie's."

The phone went silent.

"Katie?" she repeated.

"Yes, Mom, it's a name, and it belongs to dad's sister. Remember?"

"She's there with you now?" she asked, as if to check if Katie could hear them.

"Yes."

"Okay," She finally said. "Your father will come get you. Apologize to Katie for intruding on her unannounced."

She hung up before Beth could reply.

Beth's eyes met Katie's. "Sorry. I would have gone to Aunt Max's place but she's in Sweden."

"It's alright," Katie replied. "But this is the first time we've ever met. How'd you know where I live?"

Katie's chest tightened. She could sense her blood pressure begin to rise.

"My dad brought me here once."

Katie dropped her glass. Beth's eyes locked on the now damp carpet. She then looked up at Katie, who hadn't glanced not once away from Beth.

"For what?" Katie studied Beth's every gesture and facial expression.

"He—he just wanted to show me where you lived when we were checking out the area."

Katie froze.

"Are you okay, Aunt Katie? I know you and my dad don't get along very well, but he wasn't here to argue."

Katie forced a smile. "Of course not. What did he want?"

"Just to say hi."

"Why check out the area?"

Katie's heart was on the verge of combustion. As if life and death depended solely on Beth's answer.

"We're moving here. It's why we came. We're gonna—"

"Stop talking," Katie commanded.

Beth pursed her lips.

Every kind of emotion Katie felt came in at her all at once.

Slowly, she rose from the couch. Beth's eyes followed her into the kitchen, where she'd bent to grab cleaning supplies from under the sink. She returned to the stain and started dabbing with paper towel. All Katie wanted was to go far away from here for the night. Anywhere but here.

Katie allowed Beth to continue watching Netflix while she excused herself to the bathroom. She ran the sink water to drown out her crying. It was happening again. The same routine of Jay promising something would change for the better, only to do something that frightened her beyond belief. But now was not the time for a melt-down. She had a young, estranged family member on her couch.

When Katie returned to the living room, she switched the conversation back to Beth. She was fourteen now, beautiful and boy crazy. In fact, the reason why she was here was because her parents wouldn't let her date a 17-year-old. Katie wished that was her reason for running away at a young age.

After the Netflix show, Katie darted through the dark corridor. "Why the hurry?" Beth said, rushing up beside Katie.

"I just… want to get you to your dad."

When Beth hadn't responded, Katie questioned the potency of her own lie.

After a moment of silence, Beth said, "Hey, Aunt Katie?"

"Yeah?"

"Go easy on my dad. He's annoying, but he's not gonna argue with you. He finally told Grandpa that he's the one who crashed the car."

Katie was thankful Beth wasn't facing her to see her eyes roll. The years of torment she'd suffered at the hands of her brother was apparently erased and replaced with a dispute over a crashed car. Her fingers formed a fist. Out of all the stories Jay could've told to Beth. The elevator doors opened to a young family of four. The woman smiled at them, and the man had kept his focus on controlling the children who rushed out.

When the doors closed, neither Katie nor Beth spoke. Beth was swiftly texting, and Katie watched the floor numbers decrease until the doors opened again.

Beth struggled to keep up with Katie as she zoomed through the lobby. Jay was there at the glass entrance, watching them. Katie had planned to meet him outside before he could even make it in, but he'd beaten her. After glancing at Katie, his eyes locked in on his daughter.

"Beth, go wait in the car," he said, with his thumb pointing in back. "Now. Your mom's pissed."

Beth rolled her eyes before she passed them. The smell of her sweet perfume lingered in the air after she left.

"Katie," he said. "Can I get a minute?"

"What are you doing, Jay? What is all this? Your daughter comes to my apartment?!"

He double checked that Beth was gone before speaking.

"You won't answer my calls. You left mom and dad's without really giving me an answer."

"An answer to what?"

"About what's going to happen between us. You never answered."

"So, you move to my city?!"

He slowly nodded. "She told you."

"Yeah, she said quite a bit," Katie said, tightly folding her arms. "She even mentioned a crashed car."

"I couldn't let her know what I used to be, Katie. That's my daughter."

"So, you lie to her?"

"If it helps protect her. I want her to feel at home, safe, and not think of me as the dangerous devious prick that I was."

Katie wanted to smack him. She wanted to smack him because he was saying all the right things. She wanted to believe him, just like so many years ago, but Jay had always been a liar and a manipulator. She'd never seen him any other way.

"How did you know where I live?"

"Huh?" he asked, as if he hadn't heard her.

"Beth said she came here with you. How did you know where I live?"

His eyes closed as he deeply exhaled. "Max."

Katie already knew the answer of course, but something within her wanted to hear it from Jay's own mouth.

"Don't be mad at her. She was just trying to help."

"Don't tell me what to do."

Jay said nothing. He just watched her until her breathing relaxed.

"Why are you moving here?" she asked.

"It's a good state."

She gave a disapproving look. Last Katie heard from Max, Jay was still living in North Carolina. Why had he done this? Something was up. It had to be.

Just then, Mr. Jones had come through the entrance, smiling at Katie as he always did. "Hi, Katie. Have you seen Xavior?"

Xavior was one of Mr. Jone's kids who'd sometimes visit. He was the tallest, and likely the oldest of the others.

Katie shook her head, "No, is everything okay?"

"Oh yeah yeah, he's with his mom, but apparently I'm late, and they've both been standing in front of the building for forever…And do you see anyone in front of the building?" he gestured.

Both Katie and Jay looked back.

"Nope," she said.

Mr. Jones nodded. He looked at Jay and then back at Katie, as if to request an introduction, which Katie denied.

Jay reached out to Mr. Jones. "I'm Jay"— his head cocked toward Katie. "Her brother."

Mr. Jones raised his eyebrows before shaking his hand. "Oh, nice to meet you, Jay. I'm Hubert. I didn't know Katie here had a—"

His eyes locked in on the entrance. "There they are," he said. "Have a good night, Katie, and it was nice to meet you, Jay."

Jay beamed. "Likewise."

He turned to Katie. "Nice guy."

"What were we talking about again?" Katie asked.

Jay inched closer. "Let me prove to you I've changed. Let's finally have a relationship. . . Please."

Her professionalism was coming back to her now. Her logical mind was back. She needed to hear Jay and not immediately condemn him.

"Beth's excited to meet you," Jay said. "And Griffin's never even seen you. Forget how you feel about me, just please be in their lives."

Katie felt a mix of emotions again. She didn't even know what to say or how to say it. She closed her eyes. Like she would tell her clients, think of a distraction. However, nothing could distract her from what was right here in front of her. Nearly every horror she ever faced was right here in human form in front of her.

"Excuse me," he said, digging his phone out. He swiftly texted and then returned it to his pocket. "I have to go. It's gonna be different though, Katie," he said, backing away. "You'll see."

****

The next day felt like she'd woken up from a horrific dream. She knew it was real because she found a pink charm from Beth's bracelet lying on her side of the couch.

She'd woke with a massive headache that proved too much for the four Advil she'd already taken. She had trouble keeping her eyes open ever since she'd left the house for work.

It was as if all the sleep she'd missed from last night suddenly crept up on her. There was no way she could sleep after last night anyway. Jay was here, at her complex. His daughter was here, and then he'd met her neighbor. *Good grief.*

The therapy center was full, just like it normally was on Monday mornings. William, her 8-year-old client, was her first session of the day. He sat still on the chair as he watched Katie. His weekly sessions would likely end sooner than Katie had planned since his improvement was rapid. His grandfather sat with his legs crossed while reading one of the table magazines. Katie smiled at the both of them, but for some reason the words *Good morning,* failed to come out.

"Morning, Katie," Gianna said.

Katie nodded without words.

"Are you okay?" She asked, handing Katie her schedule.

"Nope."

Katie hadn't planned on being so blunt, but it was almost as if she spoke before she thought.

Gianna stared at her, but when Katie hadn't expounded, Gianna moved on.

"You want your morning coffee? You seem like you need it."

The coffee she wanted, the day she could live without.

"Yes," Katie told her.

Gianna grabbed the mug beside her. "Here you are."

Katie smiled as she took the white mug of steaming coffee from Gianna. "Thanks."

Katie nearly tripped in her black flats on her way toward the hall. She passed her colleagues without a word. She pretended to be busy on her phone, so she didn't have to look up. When she got to her office, she tore off her coat and hung it on the rack beside the window. After putting her belongings down in her designated area, she unlocked the filing cabinet, sifting through her files until she reached the name, William. She pulled his file out and scanned the notes she'd written down, reading them to herself.

Name: *William Shepherd*

Age: *8*

Subject: *Divorce.*

—*Client expressed confusion, and fear of the future.*

Symptoms:

—*Academic decline.*

—*Changes in social pattern.*

—*withdrawal.*

Session number: *3*

She called William to the front. His grandfather gave her a smile that Katie failed to return. She grabbed William by one hand when he got close enough, and she closed the waiting room door with the other, cutting off his grandfather's gaze.

The session with William went by slower than she would've preferred. They'd still made progress though. This time she just hadn't felt what she usually did during her sessions. She was tired. Her eyes drooped, her attention was elsewhere, and for the first time in a long time she felt like she'd failed a client. She'd failed William even though he'd walked out smiling.

Back at the front desk, Gianna was writing something down with the phone pressed against her cheek and shoulder. She looked up at Katie and caught her rubbing her eyes. After hanging up the phone, she said, "Katie, seriously, are you okay?"

"Of course. Why?"

She answered before really thinking about it.

"Because, no disrespect but you look awful—I mean you look like you haven't slept for ten days."

"I'm good. I took some pain medication for—"

Katie froze before she could pull the bottle out of her purse.

The label read melatonin. Katie laughed while she stood there, probably looking like a fool to everyone who could see. She explained to them what she'd carelessly done, and they'd joined in laughing.

Katie shook her head before checking the time on the big black clock on the wall. One client down. Three more to go.

Chapter 6

February 24th, 2024

Katie realized she wanted to work in mental health while sitting in Dr. Kumar's office. He was a child psychologist with white hair, medium brown skin, and a broad nose. He had candy of nearly every type for her when she'd come in. However, it wasn't the candy that'd brought 16-year- old Katie itching to come back. Dr. Kumar was the only person she could be completely honest with.

What a difference he'd made in her life. Whatever she'd said to him, there was never any judgment, only helpful tips and wise words that'd lifted her spirits. Because of Jay's threats though, she was careful not to reveal too much. And Dr. Kumar was never forceful.

As a college freshman, Katie flirted with the idea of criminal justice and business before circling back to mental health her sophomore year. She realized that child therapy was the area best suited for herself. It was so hard trying to dive into the mind of her brother, Jay. After experiencing the helplessness, shame, and spine-tingling fear she'd experienced as a child, she decided to dedicate her life to helping others overcome the evils that exist. . . Evil that sometimes exists within the family.

George and Katie had been talking via text nearly every day for weeks.

Due to George's busy life, the messages they shared were typically very brief, like good morning, and goodnight, but it was those gestures of effort that let Katie know he cared, even if they were small.

They had a date planned for tonight. Katie had spent all afternoon getting ready. She'd gone from store to store picking out and trying on different outfits. She was torn between wearing a dark red dress, and a fancy yellow dress. She'd never been a fan of bright colors before, but something about the design of the yellow dress had stood out.

The news was playing loudly in the living room. A 30-something year old woman had gone missing after midnight in the nearby town of Del Ray. According to the news reporter, her ex boyfriend was the prime suspect.

Katie's phone vibrated on the glass coffee table.

A message from George was on the small screen. `Sorry. Can't make tonight. Raincheck?`

Katie sighed before texting a sad emoji back.

All the effort and excitement had gone to utter waste. She'd hung both dresses back on the hangers in her closet and put her perfume back on her vanity. *Won't be needing this anymore.*

There was a swift knock on the door. Even though George didn't have Katie's address or apartment unit number, she imagined it was him playing some kind of corny joke showing up at her apartment door with roses after he'd just canceled. Katie loved roses, particularly red. She loved the smell, the color, and the feeling she'd gotten when they were in her presence.

Katie looked through the peephole of her door, and to her surprise, she had in fact seen red roses, the face behind them though, was hidden.

As she opened the door, the flowers quickly swayed to the side, revealing Jay's smile and dark eyes.

"Hi, Katie," he said, handing her the roses—the type and color, she'd already known was probably Max's idea.

She reluctantly took them. "What are you doing here?"

"It's a nice day; thought I'd come see you."

"You could've call—" Katie caught herself. She realized she'd never given Jay her number, and even if they had exchanged numbers and he had called, she wouldn't have answered.

"So, you've moved already?" she asked.

"Not officially."

Katie stayed silent.

"Let me take you out," he suggested. "I'll get you anything you want."

What's he up to? What does he have planned?

Clearly, he was still in town. Katie wondered if he and Beth had been staying here in Sperry ever since he'd picked her up.

"I don't think so, Jay."

His shoulders slumped. "What do I have to do?"

"Nothing. I don't need you to do anything. In fact, I wish you wouldn't."

"Well then how are we supposed to have a relationship?"

She tightened her lips shut, letting her silence do the speaking for her.

"Come on Katie," he said in a hushed tone. "I'm trying here."

An image entered her mind. A time when one of her older clients, Jayla, who had anger issues, came in with a grudge against a fellow classmate. They'd been former best friends, but when drama rang out between them, she couldn't bring herself to forgive her. Even though the drama with her friend wasn't what brought Jayla in as a client, it was part of what they'd discussed that day. And Katie encouraged her, along with her many other clients she'd had, to forgive. Immediately she'd felt like a bit of a hypocrite. Even though she didn't hate Jay, she still hadn't wanted anything to do with him. It'd messed with her mind, as well as her performance at work. Still, if she were to give him another chance, another after so many others, it's not clear what he'd do next. Katie knew she'd have to keep a sharp, strong, very close eye on Jay.

"Okay," she said, finally. "Let me put these away and I'll be right out."

Katie shut the door slightly harder than normal. The idea of leaving the door closed until Jay figured out she wasn't coming back had crossed her mind. Instead though, she'd set the roses in the vase Ruth gave her, got her purse and keys, and returned to the door.

"What are we going to do?" she asked.

"I figured we'd take a walk."

Katie loved walks, just like she loved roses.

She thought back to her college years, where guys who'd wanted something from her did and pretended to be everything they knew she liked, so they could score what they'd wanted in the end. Even though Jay was her brother, similarly, she wondered if this was just a fake attempt to get close enough to hurt her. She was aghast by the thought of it. But Jay was older now, and probably had different interests.

As children, Katie was the closest human to him that he could manipulate, elicit fear, and torture. Since they were older though, would that still be his primary focus? Was he still out to get her since he'd blamed her for sending him away? He'd told her that many times in his texts. Many years had passed since then though, and Katie figured she probably had nothing to worry about. Still, she wasn't exactly thrilled to have Jay emerge back in her life.

They walked side by side in a nearby park. For once, Katie was thankful for the large crowd, a crowd of people who were also enjoying the late February weather.

"So, I really appreciate you taking the time to do this, Kay Kay."

"It's Katie, Jay. You know that."

He nodded. His eyes rested on the ground.

Katie hadn't been called that in years, used mostly by a then four-year-old, Max, who'd coined it.

An awkward silence emerged between them. Katie scanned her surroundings as she walked with her hands wrapped across her chest. Kids played with kites in the field. Couples walked hand in hand, and joggers dressed in athletic wear had quickly passed them by. The sun had beamed in the sky, with slight wind that'd brushed her face. She wished she could hold on to this type of weather a little longer, but the temperatures lately were unstable and unpredictable.

"How's Beth?" she asked.

"She's better," he quickly responded. "She's"—he trailed off. "She'll be alright."

The silence returned, but Jay didn't allow it to last long.

"I'm told you don't have kids yet," he said. "Are you wanting to settle down soon with someone?"

Jay would be the last person she would ever discuss her dating life with, but she wondered though—how had he actually gotten a woman to marry him? Jay was what many would consider attractive, but the terror he'd brought to her as a kid was all she could see of him for years. It was hard to see Jay as anything other than a manipulative, dangerous, lying, sack of—

"You don't have to answer," he said, interrupting her thought. He swiftly shrugged his shoulders. "Just making conversation."

"I haven't dated anyone seriously in a while," she blurted. "And if I don't date and get married, there won't be kids."

"Why don't you date seriously?"

Katie studied every gesture, every slight difference in tone, wondering what he could possibly be thinking or planning. She abruptly stopped and turned to face him. "What's the meaning of all this, Jay?"

"What do you mean?"

"I mean why now? Why are you wanting a relationship now?"

His blinks slowed to a steadier pace, and it gave Katie a slight chill. As a child, Katie desperately wanted to believe him every time he swore that he would stop. It was a false hope he'd enjoyed seeing her believe, over and over. She'd be damned if she fell for it again.

"I spent a lot of time thinking after dad sent me away."

"I'm sure," she interrupted.

Jay was quiet.

"Go ahead," she said, sighing.

"I want to right my wrongs—all of them; with you, with our family, and anyone else I've hurt."

"Why?"

"Because it's the right thing to do. I really messed up, Katie. I know, and I know I don't deserve your forgiveness or your respect...But if you'll allow me to, I want to make things right."

"Well—"

Jay put his hand up, cutting her off. "Before you say anything else, I'd like to help you."

He dug inside his back pocket, taking out an envelope. Slowly, he unfolded it.

"I heard about the business that you want to start," he said, handing it to her. "This should help."

Katie's arms slowly uncrossed. "Jay—"

"Just take it... Please."

Katie was speechless. She was stiff, baffled by his words. All her life she'd seen him as a liar, a master manipulator, and someone who couldn't be trusted. She thought she was free of ever seeing or dealing with him again... And now this.

She stared down at the envelope. His name was written on the middle of it. Below it was his ten-digit phone number.

He turned away from her. Katie stood with her hand still out in front of her, eyeing the weightless envelope.

Chapter 7

Katie watched Colin intently as he drew on the dry-erase board. He chose the blue marker—drawing faces on the board, some happy, others sad. He then went on to draw a tall building with surrounding blocks beside it. Katie watched how he filled the blocks inside. She then watched him open the green bin of toys, pulling out legos and then tearing them apart, putting them back together again the same way. He'd done it several times, as if he'd expected a different outcome—perfection perhaps.

Still, Colin hadn't said anything during their sessions. However, Katie noted that the fear, at least in her presence, was weakening. He seemed quite comfortable during play therapy. He wasn't looking around, watching the clock inside the red cat on the wall, nor did he sit with his face resting in his palm. This time, he appeared curious and imaginative.

She'd written down everything that she'd observed of him, preparing to let one or both of his parent's know his status. Angela had been the one she'd kept contact with the most. Her husband, Reed, from what Katie could tell so far, had seemed to take a less active role.

When Katie arrived inside her apartment, the smell from Casper's litter box had met her at the door. Without another moment to waste, she took him out and gave him a quick bath in the bathroom sink. It didn't take long since she'd rushed it, and as soon as she'd finished, she got ready for her date.

Katie waited outside of her apartment complex, watching the cars zoom by from both directions.

His shiny red tesla pulled up beside her. The windows were tinted, but she still managed to see his face. Katie opened the passenger door and slid inside.

George smiled at her. "Good to see you, Katie."

"You too."

George turned his attention to the large screen above the cup holders. His fingers tapped the screen several times, before he'd leaned back, relaxed, and allowed the car to do the driving itself. She wondered if this was how he normally rode, or if he was simply showing off in front of her.

"Where are we going again?" Katie asked.

"We're going to—" George neglected his sentence, swearing loudly.

Concern filled her face. "What?"

"My wallet. I left my wallet at home."

Katie's heart sank. A flashback of her college years had come to mind, where her classmate had taken her on a date and conveniently forgot his wallet. However, George was wealthy. Katie figured he could certainly afford to cover his meal as well as hers, so there didn't appear to be a reason why he'd pull something so tasteless.

"We'll have to make a quick stop at my place and get it," he announced.

Katie agreed to it, and the car proceeded to drive smoothly down the road.

George pulled up to the gated driveway of a luxury ranch style home. He rapidly typed numbers into the keypad, and then the black gates slowly parted. In this moment, Katie felt like a character in one of those popular romance novels—where the protagonist gets swept off her feet by the handsome billionaire. But Katie was also logical, and she knew there was always a catch to things like this. Nothing was perfect—it was just the nature of life. Still, she'd enjoy it while in the moment.

He pulled up next to the large driveway fountain, parking behind a topless corvette. From the darkness of the evening, Katie couldn't tell the color.

She wondered how many vehicles George had owned. A successful and wealthy man like George, it wouldn't be unreasonable for him to own a few.

The home was lengthier than it was tall. About five thousand square feet Katie guessed. She figured this had to be the home George had raised his family in. Clearly, it was a lot of space for just one person.

Her attention was abruptly hijacked by the sudden sound of an open door.

"I guess I'll wait here?" Katie suggested, watching George prepare to climb out.

He shook his head. "Come on in. I insist."

The ring camera announced they were being recorded when they approached. George turned the key and opened the door to three teenage boys standing in the hallway.

Katie instantly recognized one of them as George's son—same features and hair on a youthful face. The other two, she assumed were school friends since they were all dressed as if they'd just come home from an elite prep school: wearing matching khakis, striped ties, and navy-blue blazers, each with a symbol of a roaring lion on the pocket. The letters HC were engraved underneath.

George hung his coat on the rack, and then reached out for Katie's.

As she wriggled out of hers, she wondered how long they would be here. Surely it wouldn't take an hour to get a wallet.

"Boys," George said, hanging up her coat. "This is Katie."

Mini-Geroge smirked, while the other two beamed, greeting her simultaneously. Katie had already indulged in her game of guessing, naming his son, Andrew.

"Katie, this is my son, Caleb," he pointed to his mini-me.

Rats. Wrong again.

"This is my stepson, Landen," he pointed to the tall slender boy with pale skin and chin length hair. "And their friend, Mathias."

Mathia's smile was captivating, the same as his overall look. With a sharp jawline, light brown skin, beautifully shaped eyes, and short curls, he had quite the model-like appearance.

"Hello," she greeted.

They all smiled.

"Very pleased to meet you," Landen said. Katie noted his use of the words, "Very pleased," rather than "Hey" or the typical "Nice to meet you."

Judging from what she'd just heard, and their uniforms, Katie figured these weren't normal teenage boys.

Katie smiled, "It's a pleasure."

Caleb nearly pushed Mathias out of the way. "The pleasure is all mine," he said, grabbing her hand.

Landen slapped it away before he could kiss it. "You'll have to excuse him. He has a brain I promise. He just doesn't use it much."

Katie just nodded.

"Alright alright time to go guys," George said, urging them toward the door.

Landen picked up a pair of spotless leather coats off the rack, handing one of them to Caleb. As Caleb maneuvered his on, Katie caught a glimpse of the shiny Rolex on his wrist. She wondered just how often these boys came around and how much George spoiled them.

Mathias nodded toward Katie. "It was great to meet you."

"You too," Katie replied. But his back was already turned, headed toward his schoolmates outside.

"They seem lovely," Katie said once the door had closed behind them.

"Most of them," George said, but Katie couldn't tell if it was sarcasm or not, or which boy was the odd one out.

He took out two wine glasses from the cabinet and placed them on the center island. Four bottles of different kinds of wine sat below the cabinetry.

"Merlot?" he asked, raising the wine bottle.

"I don't drink," Katie replied.

She evened out her navy-blue polka dotted dress before sitting on the couch.

"How about water then?"

"That works. Thanks."

Katie scanned the dark blue walls. It was clear a man had lived here—a rustic living room with a deer head above the stacked stone fireplace. There was another deer head above the glass door, and a taxidermy mallard duck that stared at her from the coffee table. Her boots were standing on a brown bear rug spread out on the floor.

Katie wasn't sure if it was real or fake, and she didn't want to find out.

"You really enjoy hunting," she observed.

"Told you that. We should go together sometime."

Katie wasn't sure she wanted to, but before she could respond he'd come out with their drinks.

He took a seat beside Katie, closing any possible gap between them.

He slipped the remote from off the table. When he pointed it at the black sound box, sensual music began to play.

Katie already knew what this was setting up to be—a dark room, close proximity to each other, an attempt to give her wine, and now jazz music. Katie realized George hadn't really forgotten anything at home. This evening was planned. Katie hadn't exactly suffered from sexual frustration, rather she'd lacked the urges altogether. She hadn't experienced that satisfaction since college, and she swore her next would be within marriage.

"Do you have the time?" she asked him.

George dug inside his pocket for his phone. "It's 6:25."

"I should go," She said.

Katie was reminded of how little she knew about George. He was handsome, successful, and owned a business. He had one biological son, a stepson, and an ex-wife. He lived alone and he loved to hunt. But she hadn't known the more important things about him—such as whether or not he was mentally sound. Did he have stalker-like tendencies. How would he respond to hearing the answer "no"?

He hadn't raised any alarm bells before, but something about this night bothered her. If he'd wanted an evening alone with her, why not just ask for it instead of making up a story about his wallet? Katie wondered what else he'd faked.

She shot up from the couch. "I'd like to go home please."

"Is something wrong?"

"No," she said. "It's just getting late, and I'd like to go home."

George hesitated, staring at his wine glass. His silence caused Katie's heart to pound a little harder. Her palms began to sweat. She was stuck inside a stranger's house, and as of right now, she was at his mercy. She watched him closely, studying his every move. A sigh escaped his lips, and then he looked up at her. "Okay."

Chapter 8

Instead of cooking at home, Katie drove herself to a local fast-food restaurant, picking up her lunch. Her phone chimed while she drove. A text from Daphne appeared on the screen. As her eyes glanced back on the road, the oncoming traffic light was now red. Katie slammed on the break, causing her purse and Caesar salad to slide toward the edge of the seat. She'd caught them both just in time. When she looked up out of the passenger window, she saw the side profile of Jay, driving a U-Haul truck.

Katie swiftly turned away. It was happening. They were moving. Her heartrate began to pick up pace. In her peripheral vision, the lane beside her began to move.

The light had turned green, and she began traveling in sync with traffic, her eye never leaving the speeding U-Haul.

Its right turn signal had come on, heading for a narrow road. Katie discreetly followed, allowing vehicles room to disguise her.

She parked several feet away from the home that Jay had pulled up in.

She watched him lift the trunk. She sank back in her seat as she watched a woman and the girl she'd recognized as Beth, unload boxes from the truck.

Her heart raced. She wondered why he'd move so close. This street was just minutes away from her apartment complex. Katie feared what would come of this entire thing. Her teeth clenched. This was her home. Nobody asked Jay to move here.

She decided that she'd seen enough. She tapped the gas, and slowly drove away, hoping she remained unseen.

****

In the evening, Casper watched as Katie poured cat food into his bowl.

After her own meal, Katie grabbed her laptop, signing in to zoom. Max's face appeared on the screen a moment later. Her curls puffed from her high ponytail, and her reading glasses that Katie barely saw her wear, sat aligned at her eyes.

"Hi, my favorite sister!" she squealed with a large smile.

Katie chuckled. "I'm your only sister, Max. How's Stockholm?"

"Oh gosh it's so cold! It's beautiful but COLD."

"Yeah, Max. For someone whose favorite season is summer, are you sure Sweden is for you?"

"For the time being," she said.

"Are you making friends at least?"

She shrugged. "It's a little hard. People are really reserved here. They're sweet though."

Katie nearly felt envious since she'd never been out of the country herself before. Max had though, studying abroad in Spain while in college. She had told Katie that it was at that point in her life that she wanted to pursue a career that allowed her to travel, and it came as no surprise to Katie that she'd found it—being so young, and adventurous.

Max took a bite out of the meal on her plate.

"What is that?" Katie asked.

"Raggmunk. It's like a potato mixed with a pancake with bacon and jelly. It's actually really good."

Katie nodded. It didn't sound appetizing to her, but she wasn't surprised by Max's answer. There simply wasn't much that Max didn't like.

"So, how's life, Katie?"

Jay's gift he'd given her the other day came to mind. The envelope sat unopened on her dresser. There was so much she could've done with it—burn it, fold it into a blunt, or place it in a bottle destined for the ocean. She didn't need Jay's help to buy her dream office, and she didn't need Max interfering either.

"You know, the strangest thing happened," Katie said.

Max's smile broadened, "What?"

"I saw Jay the other day."

"Oh, yeah?"

"Yeah, he came by my apartment to pick up his daughter. And what's even stranger is how either one of them knew where I live."

Max's fingers reached the nape of her neck, as her face read guilt.

"Back off please, Max. This isn't your fight."

Max's shoulders dropped. "Well should it be yours? How long are you going to keep this up, Katie? He's trying to make an effort. Why don't you let him?"

Max didn't understand. Max *couldn't* understand. She simply hadn't experienced the same Jay that Katie did so many years ago. Jay had done this many times before. He'd acted one way, and then he'd switched character so easily it was as if he'd become a completely different person. It was eerie—out of this world creepy. He was dangerous, devious, and a very good manipulator to the point where even when you knew he was faking, there was a part of you that'd believed him anyway. Still, Katie had wondered why he'd go this far just to mess with her. What would be in it for him besides cruelty which he could do to anyone at this point? After all, they weren't children anymore, and Katie wasn't the only target in his life.

"I don't hate him, Max. There's just some things you don't understand."

Max nodded. "I understand that my therapist sister needs to practice what she preaches."

Katie was silent, unsure how to respond.

"I should go to bed. It's after 11 here," Max said. "Goodnight Katie."

The next morning, Katie woke up to a text from George, asking to see her again. She wasn't sure she wanted to after their last interaction. She didn't appreciate what'd happened on their last date. She suspected that she had been set up for an evening of fun that she hadn't agreed to. It was sneaky. Katie hated sneaky.

She ignored the message and turned on the TV while she prepared for work. It was the typical morning news that'd played nearly every day.

As she entered her walk-in closet, the news anchor announced the disappearance of another young woman, Sofia Accardi, a 21-year-old college student. She'd vanished late last night on her way home from a friend's house. Katie approached the TV with a long black dress in her hands.

As they displayed her picture, Katie took note of how young she looked. Her face was so innocent, and likely completely unaware of the danger that would befall her. The reporter stated she was fun, and full of life according to her family, a girl with hopes and dreams of her own. According to the news report, she was last seen in Belle Haven, a town just a few miles away.

Katie's phone vibrated off the bed again. The screen revealed George's number. She'd let it ring until it eventually stopped. It vibrated again after a moment, a single alert, indicating he'd either left a voicemail, or a text message.

Katie grabbed a towel from the linen closet and headed for the bathroom, the TV still going.

****

In the breakroom at work, Katie opened her lunch bag, taking out her dinner leftovers from last night. As she waited by the microwave for her food to heat, Harold Dyson walked inside.

"Good afternoon, Katie," he said with a smile.

She greeted him kindly.

He grabbed a coffee pod on the counter and began placing it in the Keurig. "How are you today?"

She shrugged. "Same as usual. Been seeing you a lot lately."

"There's always work to be done. Work that never sleeps," he sighed. "Life of a business owner."

She nodded. Her mind went straight to her owning the abandoned building for rent on Windsor Street. The sweet memory was short lived as she remembered her student loans she'd likely still be paying well into her 50s.

She imagined her brother, Jay, and the conversation they'd had that day in the park. He'd given her an envelope that still sat on her dresser. Katie wondered how much money was inside of it. A few hundred? One thousand? She nearly slapped herself for thinking about it.

Her phone chimed a text just as Harold had left the breakroom. It was a message from George, asking if she was alright since she hadn't answered his call or messages yet.

Katie hadn't decided on ghosting George yet, rather she was still figuring out how to respond to him. She hadn't wanted to come off as completely uninterested, there was a part of her that still hungered for a satisfactory explanation. However, she didn't want to come off as totally fine with what'd happened either.

She began typing out her answer, but before she could send, he'd sent another message.

I'm sorry if anything that happened the other night was uncomfortable for you. If you'd like, Landen's celebration dinner is tonight at 'Isabella's'. I'd love it if you'd join us.

Clearly, he'd known Katie was uncomfortable that night, and the invitation to a family dinner felt a bit too soon. She wondered, though, if taking him up on his offer would help or hurt the situation. It was just dinner after all, and at a public restaurant. She'd talked it over with Daphne earlier, Daphne agreed his actions were a little odd, but there wasn't much concern in her tone. She'd said George was weird, not in a dangerous way though. He was just unconventional, she'd said.

Katie texted him back, agreeing to the outing, and praying under her breath the night would have a pleasant ending.

****

Rather than George picking her up, she'd agreed to meet him at the restaurant just to be on the safe side. Unlike the restaurant George had taken Katie to, this one was more casual.

Katie was dressed appropriately for the occasion, ankle jeans, and a dressy top.

The long table held seven people. George, Mathias, Caleb, Landen, and three new faces that Katie hadn't recognized. Next to Landen, was an olive skinned, silky haired girl with cute, slanted eyes and a beautiful smile. The boy between Caleb and Landen was brown-skinned with hair that was clean shaven. The middle-aged woman across from them had a slight tan, light brown hair in loose waves at her chest.

George stood up as Katie approached, waving her over as if she hadn't already seen them.

"Katie," he said. "Welcome, please have a seat."

He pointed to the empty chair beside him that he'd clearly reserved for her.

"Hello, everyone," she said, before taking a seat.

Most of them greeted her with matching smiles.

"Katie, this is Lydia," he pointed to the tanned woman, "Landen's mother."

He pointed to the young girl beside Landen, "This is Hina, Landen's girlfriend."

And finally, he pointed to the brown skinned boy, "This is Bryant, Mathias's brother."

They all greeted each other in unison.

"We're celebrating Landen's acceptance into Dartmouth," George proudly announced.

Landen's widening smile revealed nearly all his white teeth.

"Congratulations, Landen," Katie said. "That's a huge accomplishment."

Caleb shrugged; his arms folded at his chest. "It's pretty low on the scale of the Ivy league. Just saying."

"Caleb," George warned. "Don't start."

Landen reached for his glass. "It's okay, George. We can celebrate him too. Caleb, what community college did you say you got into again?"

The default sound of a ringtone chimed, sending Lydia, George, and Mathias in a search of their belongings.

"Hello?" Mathias answered. "Yes, hang on."

He lowers the phone from his ear. "Excuse me, I gotta take this."
"I'll bet you do," Bryant said, folding his lips to keep from laughing.
Mathias lightly punched Bryant's arm just before he'd gotten up.

Nobody spoke, but Caleb's arms seemed to have tightened just a little.

The table flooded with conversation soon after Mathias had left.

Hina seemed sweet, and quick to laugh and smile at just about everything. Bryant interjected with jokes every so often, Lydia, seemed supportive in whatever her son's endeavors would be, while George bombarded Landen with guidelines on how to navigate the Ivy league. "Excellence runs in the family," he'd said, gripping Landen's shoulder.

Caleb's eyes darted to George. Katie remembered that Landen was only his stepson and not blood related. But apart from their obvious physical differences, it was hard to tell that was true based on the way George spoke.

George stared proudly at his stepson all night. Nearly everyone had, except for Caleb. He'd held the same position of folded arms and blank expression for most of the night, unfolding his arms only to eat and drink. There was something familiar about the way he'd looked. The rage within him that he didn't work hard to conceal. Katie scanned the table, knowing that she couldn't possibly be the only one who'd noticed.

At the end of the meal, George walked Katie back to her car. The night air was slightly cool, sweater weather, Katie thought to herself.

"So did you enjoy tonight?" George asked.

Katie nodded. "I did. Sounds like Landen's got a great future ahead of him."

She opened the door of her car.

"Will I see you again?" George asked, as she sat inside.

Katie's mind revisited the events of tonight. There was nothing too alarming or out of the ordinary. Every family has its share of drama. It wouldn't hurt to see him at least once more.

"I don't see why not," she said.

George smiled.

With that, she closed the door and headed home.

****

In the morning, Katie arrived at the desk of the therapy center. Gianna handed her the steaming mug of coffee. Katie thanked her and proceeded to walk down the narrow hall, taking sips as she passed her associates.

Colin was her first client of the day, and again, their session started out the same way it always did, Colin hadn't spoken a word.

There in the red bean bag chair, his eyes scanned the room as if he'd never been inside before. Katie wondered if it was an act, though she knew not to show her suspicion.

"Colin," she said.

He looked up but didn't speak. He stared at her, seemingly waiting for her to continue. Something was different. His body wasn't as closed off as it had been in previous sessions. His eyes held a layer of innocence mixed with fear. It appeared he wanted to speak but he held back. Something was waying heavily on Colin's heart.

"You know this is a safe place. You can tell me anything."

He stared at her. His lips were tightly shut. He'd gone back to scanning the room again, his fingers intertwined in his lap. Katie had a hunch of what his silence was and what was causing it, but she needed to be sure before she could let Angela or Reed know.

"I hear you have a birthday coming up."

His eyes met hers again, and again, there was silence. However, since he'd looked, Katie clocked that as a positive sign.

"You'll be seven. What are some things you like to do for your birthday?"

He shrugged, his eyes dropped back to his fingers. They found their way back to hers though, just as she'd suspected. Katie leaned forward, her heart picking up pace. Her eyes studied Colin even more closely. She held her pen and pad close, determined not to let this moment slip away. "You don't know what you want to do? Birthdays only come once a year, and they're supposed to be fun.

Don't you like to have fun?" she asked, smiling. Colin looked up at Katie. The two of them stared at each other wordlessly, as if it were a challenge of some sort. Katie keenly watched his lips. In a hushed tone, he said, "I'm not allowed."

Chapter 9

The rain splashed against the window of Katie's room as a series of bright flashes cut through the sky. Casper, the cat, climbed up the chestnut dresser in Katie's room. He flinched at the blaring rumbles of the storm.

"Casper," she called. "Come on. Get off."

Before she could reach him, he'd stepped over the white envelope at the end of the desk, sending it to the floor.

There it was, the envelope from Jay that Katie never opened. She picked Casper up with one hand, the envelope in the other.

She walked to the living room couch, placing Casper down beside her, but he hadn't stayed there long. He'd jumped down and climbed his tree tower on the opposite side of the room.

Katie sighed as she stared at the envelope in her hand. She figured it must've been a check since it was thin and light as a feather. She remembered the abandoned building on Windsor Street. She saw her future clients, and her future clinicians employed there. Her eyes dropped back to the envelope in her hand. Surely, it wouldn't hurt to simply look at what was inside.

Slowly, she tore the top until it'd completely detached, pulling out what was inside.

A check for ten thousand dollars sat between her fingers. She read and re-read the number, struggling to believe her eyes. Her jaw dropped—her thumping heart picked up pace.

The check slipped from her fingers, landing backside up on her knee. She quickly picked it back up. Suddenly, Katie didn't know how to feel. In her hand was the beginning of her dream coming to life. She should be excited, however, how had Jay come up with this much money? He had a high paying job according to Max, but he did have a family to support, and possibly some student debt to pay off. Why had he given this money to her instead of his own family? Why had he done this? Why did he want her forgiveness so badly?

What could he be up to? She thought. Katie knew there wasn't too many other ways that Jay could get her forgiveness—nothing that could really open her heart to him, except through this, paving the way for her lifetime goal to finally come into fruition. Katie picked up the opened envelope, dialing the numbers on the center.

As it rang, her heart bounced inside her chest. She'd played over the initial contact with her brother in her mind. Katie imagined what he'd say. Was he already regretting what he'd done? Had he been drinking while writing the check, accidentally adding one zero too many?

"Hello?" he answered.

"Um, hi, Jay…it's Katie."

"Hi, Katie, what's up?"

She could hear his smile through the phone.

"Jay, you gave me ten thousand dollars. Did you mean to?"

He chuckled. "Of course. I know what you're trying to do, and I want to help you do it in the best way I can."

Katie's lips folded shut. She could feel the tears swelling up in her eyes.

"I don't know what to say. I really don't."

"Just say you'll take it—and give us a chance."

Neither Katie nor Jay spoke.

Her hand cupped her mouth, the tears that trickled down her face met her fingers.

"Katie?"

"Yeah," she eventually answered. "Yeah, we can."

Katie didn't see any other way. She didn't know how to refuse someone who's just given her ten grand.

"Great," he said. "I'm really looking forward to this, Katie. It'll be amazing, you've got to believe that."

She stumbled over her words. So many images and thoughts had played through her mind like flipped channels on an old television set.

Whatever Jay was up to, whether well-intentioned or perilous, he'd known what he was doing, and he was determined to do it.

****

The clock inside the cat on the wall ticked seemingly quicker than normal. She was on her last client of the day already, a shy 14-year-old who suffered from chronic anxiety.

The session with her had gone progressively well, as it had for weeks. Katie mostly stayed silent as the girl laid out everything she was feeling, personal things and struggles that she hadn't disclosed to others. It always gave Katie joy to be helpful in such a way that others may not be able to. It was a blessing to be in this position, and she was thankful for it.

Before leaving the office, Katie gathered notes from the muted pink filing cabinet, reviewing the treatment plan of her last client of the day. She then pulled out Colin's chart. She already knew the questions she'd ask his family. He hadn't disclosed enough on their last session, but what he had said gave her insight into what was happening at home.

She set the papers neatly inside the drawer, before closing it back and heading out.

As she walked the semi-populated sidewalk toward her apartment, she'd looked up to find those familiar bluish gray eyes staring back at her. He held a shopping bag with the Book Café logo on it.

"Hi, Katie," Ian said.

She hadn't seen Ian since the bar fight at *Molly's Tavern*, and after losing his number somewhere in her apartment, she didn't think she ever would.

"You didn't call me," he said.

"I didn't. I um, lost your number. I apologize."

"Not a problem," he said, taking out his phone from his back pocket. "How about this time we make it a little harder for you to lose it."

It took Katie a moment to realize he was waiting for her response. "Sorry," she said, clearing her throat. As she gave him her number, she wondered how long he would manage to stay in her life. She wondered if this would be promising, or just another bump in the road. The two of them stood on the sidewalk staring at each other for a moment.

"Do you want to get coffee?"

Katie was technically just casually dating George. The two had never agreed to be exclusive, so why not?

"Okay," she answered.

Ian led her down the street to a local eatery. It was lightly populated inside, which slightly surprised Katie since it was evening time.

When their food was ready, they headed over to a lone table in the corner of the restaurant. Katie sat directly across from Ian.

"So," he said, as he leaned forward. "What've you been up to since we last met?"

"A lot," she said, taking a sip of her bottled water.

Ian just stared at her.

"Um…my brother gave me a check for ten thousand dollars."
Ian's eyebrows shot up. "Wow. For what?"

"I've had my own dream of opening up my business, and he was just helping me do it."

Ian stared at her. His eyebrow raised. "Are you gonna tell me what kind of business or…"

"Sorry. My private practice," she said. "I'd like my own therapy center. You know the building for rent over on Windsor Street?

"Yeah."

"I want it."

Katie knew she needed to perfect her conversational skills if she wanted to keep a relationship going. It was so much easier listening to other people, their motivations, and their desires. Since she hated digging up her past, she simply felt safer when the focus was off of her, and on to someone else.

"I've had this goal since college," she continued. "And I'm so close."

Katie began taking a bite of the large chocolate chip cookie she got at the counter.

"Your brother must love you."

She coughed several pieces of it into her napkin. "Sorry," she said in a hushed tone.

"What does he do?"

She met his eyes, her fingers still holding the napkin to her mouth. "Excuse me?"

"It's not every day that people have ten thousand dollars just lying around to give to their sister. That's huge."

"Right. He's an um—Algorithm engineer," she remembered from Max.

He nodded. "Nice."

"So, what's new with you?" she asked, hoping to shift the conversation elsewhere.

He shrugged. "Working. I did mention I don't do much but work. You and I both have that in common remember?"

His smile was infectious, and Katie mimicked it.

"So, it's just you and your dog?" Katie asked.

"Yep."

"How has that been? And for how long?"

"It's been alright," he said. "And for three years."

She waited for him to expound—possibly mention a past wife or a girlfriend, but he didn't.

"So," she said, leaning forward. "What has been your longest relationship?"

"Probably my last one. Five years."

Her suspicions that he hadn't wanted to talk about his past relationship were now confirmed.

"You're doing it too, you know," she said.

"Doing what?"

"You seem reluctant to give me information. Don't tell me I've influenced you already," she said, just before taking a sip of her drink.

Ian chuckled. "Maybe."

He stared at her intensely, almost as if he could see through her skin and straight into her bare soul. It'd matched the way he'd looked at her back in the bar, as if she were the only woman there.

"What?" she asked.

"Sorry. You just remind me of somebody I once—"

"Can I get you two anything? A refill maybe?" A man asked, glancing at Ian's cup. He seemed to have popped out of nowhere. The hat he wore sat tight on his head, revealing his chestnut-colored eyes.

It took Katie a moment to recognize him as part of the staff. He hadn't been to this table since they sat down, and now it was time to leave.

"We're good here," Ian said. "Thank you."

The man said nothing, bowing his head and then walking away.

They both finished their meal at the same time. Ian picked up the tray with their trash and dishes, emptied them, and placed the tray on top of the trash lid.

"Did you want to do this again, Katie? Not this place of course, but did you want to see me again?"

There was so much she still didn't know about Ian, and there was a part of her that was curious. He looked at her as if he'd known her much longer than he did. It had given her a feeling that she couldn't quite understand.

"Yeah," she said, smiling. "I'd like that."

****

Katie spent the next few days talking to both George and Ian. She hadn't juggled two men she'd had interest in since college. They both had something about them that'd intrigued Katie enough to keep the relationships going, though she'd known eventually she'd have to let go of one in favor of the other. She wondered if she too was also one of several other women they'd both entertained.

As she drove from the parking garage of the therapy center, her phone lit up from the mount on the dash.

At the stop light, she read it.

We still on for today?

Katie sighed before typing back her reply. She couldn't believe she'd done it. She'd actually agreed to hang out with Jay. She wanted to put her past behind her, the way she had while still in school. Harsh memories had occasionally popped up through certain triggers in life, but for the most part, prior to Max's going away party, Katie hadn't felt dragged down by the drama with Jay.

Katie fed Casper when she'd gotten home. She then went to her closet and put on a casual T-shirt and ankle jeans. It was quite unbelievable what Jay had done. Katie knew right away the envelope held a check inside, but she never imagined it would be for so much money. How could she refuse him after he'd given her 10 thousand dollars to start her life's goal?

Later in the evening, Katie stood outside of her car. The parking lot was crowded, which was to be expected on a Friday night. She scanned all passing cars in search of Jay's silver Elantra.

Mini golfing is what Jay had planned for the evening. It was one of Katie's favorites as a child. She wondered though, had he known she'd grown up already? She hadn't played this game in years, not since her 11th birthday.

A silver Elantra turned into the parking lot, and even though Jay's windows were tinted, Katie recognized him right away.

He parked and rose from the driver door. Katie waved him over to her location. He walked towards her with his hands in his pockets, taking his phone out to glance at it.

"Hi, Katie," he said, stopping in front of her. "You ready?"

Katie and Jay joined the long line toward the course. Thankfully, it seemed to be moving quickly.

Jay intermittently looked back at her, as if to make sure she hadn't slipped away.

"You ready for this?"

"Ready for what?"

"Winning. You know how you used to get when you'd lose."

Katie gave him a disapproving glare. "You mean those hissy fits I threw when I was a kid?"

"Hey, some things never change."

"But a lot of things do, Jay."

He shrugged at her before turning away. Quickly, he turned back. "By the way, thanks for agreeing to come today."

Katie nodded, "Sure."

When they'd collected all of their golfing supplies, they headed over to the course. The weather was beautiful for an outing like this one. There was slight wind, but the temperature wasn't cold. The sun would be visible for at least another hour or two.

Katie searched her brain for the last memory she'd had of her golfing. It was the last time she'd done anything with the family that included Jay. She didn't exactly win that day, but she'd still had fun.

"I'll go first," he said, when they reached their destination.

Katie watched as he hit the little ball into the ground. "That's one for me," he said, smiling.

It was her turn to go next. She aligned the club against the ball, tapping it lightly before she swung. The ball soared down the synthetic grass, completely missing the intended target.

Jay's lips folded, holding back his laughter.

Katie's competitive nature was starting to come out. For some reason, it was important that she outdo him in this.

They walked together toward the next hole. Jay aligned his club with the ball, striking it forcefully. It raced down the grass and into the hole.

Katie rushed her turn, aligning the ball with the club. When she struck it, the ball soared past the hole. Katie's blood began to boil. She hadn't remembered ever being this bad, she couldn't have been, because had that been the case, she wouldn't have enjoyed it so much.

"Don't worry," Jay said. "I'm sure you'll get it next time."

Katie placed her hand on her hip. "Don't patronize me."

"No really. I'm sure you'll eventually get it. You can't miss 'em all."

Katie snarled.

"There you go," he said. "There's my competitive sister."

Jay swung the golf club, striking the ball straight into its destination. He looked over at her, but Katie struggled to look his way.

"Come on, Katie. It's not that bad."

"I didn't say it was," she said, her tone slightly harsher.

Katie prepared her golf club, lightly tapping the golf ball. It was a close enough distance away, so Katie could almost feel the celebration she'd have when she finally made it in.

Katie struck the ball with more force than she'd meant to, and the ball traveled down the grass, completely missing its intended target.

Katie cussed the loudest she had in years, causing the group nearby them to turn and look.

Instinctively, she covered her mouth, but it was too late.

Jay laughed to the sky. Katie held her unwavering expression until it'd crumbled, and she'd joined in laughing with her brother.

"Okay," Katie said. "I think we know who's won this round."
"Yeah," Jay said, as he bent to retrieve the ball. "If only we were playing for money."

Katie remembered what Max had told her about Jay's occupation. Katie figured that as an engineer, winning money from a silly golf game would hardly benefit him. Still, she knew she'd be a fool to agree to that considering the way this first round was going.

"Hey," Katie said, "We still have the rest of the game to see what happens. Things may take a turn."

Jay chuckled. "We'll see."

****

They both finished up the game with Jay winning by a long shot.

Katie stood behind Jay as they waited in line to return the ball and clubs.

"Don't make that face, Katie," he said, handing the clubs to the staffer.

Katie's jaw had dropped. He'd said it as if he had eyes in the back of his head.

"How did you—"

"I can tell by your feet."

Katie looked down at her pink Keds, which a moment ago had been impatiently tapping against the pavement. She'd indeed showcased all of the signs of annoyance after losing to him, just like Jay had predicted.

"Have a good evening," the teenage employee said.

"You too," Jay replied.

They walked side by side toward the parking lot. Katie's arms loosened just a little. A slight smile had worked its way onto her face. It was surprising the way Jay had remembered things about herself that even she had forgotten over the years. It was equally as nice to spend an evening outside of her apartment doing something she hadn't done in years.

"Thanks again for coming out tonight, Katie," he said, slowing down.

Katie's pace matched his until they'd both stopped.

"You're welcome," she said. "But next time I'll pick the activity."

Jay's eyes widened.

"What?" she asked.

"You said next time."

"Yeah, well—*if* this happens again, I mean."

Despite her attempt at a cleanup, Katie could see Jay holding on to the slightest bit of hope he could get.

Smiling, he said, "Have a good one, Katie."

Katie watched him as he walked toward his car. Something deep within her began to nudge at her.

"Jay," she called.

He swiftly turned around. "Yeah?"

"I—" She struggled to get the words out. However, Jay didn't speak; he only stared at her, a smirk forming at his lips as if he already knew what she was going to say.

"Thank you. For tonight…and for the money. It really means a lot."

"You're welcome, Katie," he said. "I'll see you."

Chapter 10

Katie rushed inside the therapy center as if she were late, though she technically wasn't. However, Katie often felt that early meant she was on time, and on time meant she was late.

As she zoomed past the clients and their families in the waiting room, she noticed Angela sitting in the corner.

She looked much more put together today. Although still very slim, her hair was done neatly, and she wore clothes that looked more presentable.

Right on schedule, Gianna held out Katie's cup of steaming black coffee.

"Good morning, Katie," she said, her smile extra bright.

"Thank you," Katie said, taking it from her. "And same to you."

After heading down the narrow hall, Katie reached her office. She unlocked the filing cabinet and sifted through the files. When she reached Colin's, she pulled it out and reviewed it.

He was now seven years old. After careful consideration, and much observation of him over the sessions, Katie had reached her conclusion about his condition.

From the last session they had, Katie had gathered that Colin had suffered from extreme anxiety—possibly brought on by someone in the house.

Colin hadn't explicitly told Katie everything—that she knew would come later. Rather, he'd given her an idea of what may be going on inside the home. She took her folder and headed back out.

The waiting room was quiet, with nearly everyone either reading magazines left out on the tables, or they were occupied with their phones.

"Colin," Katie called.

He approached slower than before, allowing Angela to pass him.

"How are you both this morning?"

Colin was silent, but he maintained eye contact with her, which was an improvement.

"We're fine," Angela answered. "Thank you."

There was a certain glow to her this morning that wasn't present before. She'd done her make-up well, and her eyes were cheerful. Her clothes were tidy and sat neatly on her body.

"He talks a little bit—here and there," she said, smiling.

Katie nodded. "That's good news. Let's get started."

"Um, Katie," she called.

Katie turned to her. "Yes?"

Angela hesitated; her eyes dropped slightly. "I know I agreed to be in the session today, but I won't be able to make it... I've... got a meeting I have to get to."

She turned away from Katie without giving her time for a response. It wasn't Katie's desire or authority to demand Angela attend the session, even though children often fared better with at least one parent involved; however, Angela had rejected the offer in a strange way, and it had left Katie bewildered.

The room was silent, with Colin sitting opposite Katie in the red bean bag chair. The clock inside the red cat ticked loudly, as Katie and Colin stared at each other.

Katie leaned forward. Her smile was sweet and welcoming. "So, tell me how your week was, Colin."

He looked up at Katie as he massaged his fingers. He displayed a simple shrug at her.

"Did anything happen out of the ordinary?"

There was silence in the room, apart from the audible ticks and tocks from the clock on the red cat on the wall.

The things Colin had told her during their last session had Katie alarmed, but it wasn't enough to bring anyone else up on charges.

She was legally obligated to report abuse if she had "reasonable suspicion" of it. However, Colin simply hadn't revealed enough. He'd stayed silent after that until the end of the session—as if he'd said too much.

"Colin, about our last session—"

He looked up at Katie.

"Do you want to tell me more about that?"

His eyes lingered on her for a moment, and then they fell to his lap.

"I know it may be hard—and you can take all the time you need. But as I've said before, if there's something you need to tell me, it's important that you do. You can tell me anything."

He stared at her once again, but no words had made it out of his mouth. Katie held her tongue. She didn't want to appear too forceful, as it would likely backfire. Instead, she'd just stared back, giving him a chance to reply.

Katie had several clients who had been abused in the past. Most of the signs weren't easily missed. It was clear Colin was suffering from extreme anxiety; however, she wasn't certain of the culprit.

"Okay," he said, in a low tone. "But you can't say anything."

"Why not? ... Why not, Colin?"

After a moment of silence, Colin simply shrugged.

"Colin. You can tell me."

Colin began massaging his fingers like he always did during their sessions. Katie wished she could jump inside the boy's mind—exploring the depths of his brain until she'd gotten what she needed. Instead, though, she'd done the next best thing—she'd studied his body language. He was more open this time around; his eyes were focused on hers as he leaned forward. She waited for him to say something—anything, but there was nothing. She found herself leaning forward and then leaning back several times over the course of their session.

He hadn't disclosed any further information by the end of it, which admittedly frustrated Katie. However, she'd already had her hunch of what was taking place, and an email to Colin's parents she'd already thought of.

On Friday evening, Katie entered the elevator of her apartment complex.

"Wait, wait, wait!" A cheery voice shouted behind her. "Hold it please!"

Katie reached her arm out—holding the elevator door.

"Thank you, Katie" she said, smiling."

Annabelle White was a short woman with light brown hair and an attractive smile. She and her husband, Ron—a quiet man who mostly kept to himself—had been at the apartment complex ever since Katie moved in. Unlike Ron, Annabelle was lively and almost always out either walking their dog or running an errand; Ron, Katie barely ever saw.

She reached for the item in Katie's bag—a slightly rude, but foreseeable gesture from Annabelle. As she'd done it, Katie glanced at her middle finger. She wore a green and blue ring of an abnormally large size. It was mesmerizing—both very ugly and somehow beautiful in a unique way.

"Hot chocolate," Katie said. "It's a definite need on a night like this."

Annabelle nodded. "Certainly. I haven't had any in a minute though," she said, holding her stomach. "Down thirty lbs. now."

"That's highly impressive, Anna. I've noticed you slimming down recently."

Annabelle pulled up her pants. "Thanks. But it's both good and bad. Nothing fits anymore."

Katie just smiled.

Annabelle hummed as she scanned the elevator walls. "Can you believe it's going to be freezing all week? I remember back in Maine—"

Katie didn't intend to, but she ended up zoning out. Annabelle was indeed sweet, but her superfluous nature of conversation was bothersome.

"—and that's what I always tell my husband," is what Katie had caught.

She simply smiled at her.

The doors opened to Katie's floor. Annabelle lived on the 6th.

"Well, have a good night, Anna," Katie said, smiling.

"You too, Katie."

When she got to her unit, she settled down with a mug of the hot chocolate she'd just bought. She leaned back on the couch with a throw-blanket and warm fuzzy socks. Casper climbed up the couch and relaxed by the armrest.

A news alert interrupted the program she'd been watching. Another young woman had gone missing. Like the others, she was by herself when she was ambushed. According to the news report, this incident happened a few miles closer than the last reported vanishing. Katie's heart thumped just a little harder. Was there a serial kidnapper lurking in the shadows of unsuspecting women along the east coast? Who was the killer's target demographic and who was considered safe? Katie clicked out of the news report before she scared herself further.

She'd settled on a silly romantic comedy while she reviewed the notes of her clients. She read and re-read everything that'd happened with some of her clients in the week—Cedric, the child with anger issues, Noelle, the child struggling to heal from neglect, and finally, Colin who was a rare mute.

With her laptop in hand, Katie wrote an email for Colin's parents. Consent was obtained before the start of the session with Colin to disclose whatever Katie felt necessary. Rather than a direct quote of what Colin said, Katie pushed for further clarification of his home life. However, there was a part of her that felt she wouldn't get it.

Just as she'd finished typing the end of the email, the news came on once again. Katie glanced up from her screen, watching the news anchor report on the latest update.

The vehicle description of the suspect was a silver sedan with very tinted windows. License plate unknown.

Chapter 11

Katie had another date planned with George, which she'd realized she couldn't do. It was poor planning on her part, swamped with work from her clients'. Once again, overwhelming herself. She'd texted George earlier in the day, canceling their plans. He hadn't replied.

In the evening, as she stood over the stove of steaming hot tea in a kettle, a message appeared on her phone screen.

So, you can't come... Are you sure? The text from George read.

Katie's fingers swiftly typed, `yes`.

A moment later he typed, `Are you alone?`

Katie felt a shiver run down her spine. She wondered if George realized the nature of his text, given the circumstances of the missing women, Katie felt he should've known better.

She put the phone down on the counter beside her. She poured the kettle of hot tea into a white mug from the cabinet. After thinking a moment, she typed, `Why?`

`I could come over and keep you company while you work.`

Katie suddenly felt cold. Almost like the feeling one would get when a ghost has just entered the room. She poured the tea into a tall mug and sat at the table.

No thank you, she typed. *I'm alright. Have a good night.*

Katie stared at the empty chair opposite her. George suddenly appeared there. He casually took a gun out from his lap and pointed it at her. She was shot before she could even gasp, her body slumped over in a pool of blood spreading across the kitchen table.

She shook herself awake. Sitting upright, the table was clear. She was still breathing, and the chamomile tea from the mug was still steaming. Intermittently, she glanced at her phone as she sipped her mug—listening out for the chime that signaled another text from George, but it'd remained lull even after she'd finished.

****

"Katie!" Max squealed, just as she appeared on the screen of Katie's silver laptop.

Katie's heart bounced inside her chest. "What?! What happened?!"

The light in Max's eyes revealed whatever it was, wasn't at all alarming. Rather, it had to be good news.

"I met a guy."

Her folded lips struggled to contain her impending smile.

"Oh?" Katie asked. "What's his name?"

"Klas, and he's so amazing."

Katie wondered what'd made this man cause Max to soar all the way up to cloud nine. It'd never been hard for Max to notice men or for them to notice her. She was always the fun pretty girl that both men and women migrated to. She had her pick of the litter of men, but oftentimes she hadn't settled down for long with just one, nor been this excited about anyone since her first boyfriend in middle school.

"He's a family man, and he's completely gorgeous, Katie."

"So, what does he do?"

"He's a plastic surgeon."

Katie's eyebrows furrowed. "How old is he?"

Katie didn't know much about plastic surgery or how long it would take to become one in Sweden, but she figured it was safe to assume this man was nowhere near Max's age. Max's cheerful expression quickly erased, as if she'd known Katie would disapprove of the answer.

"Um…"

"Max," Katie said. "How old?"

Max's fingers reached the nape of her neck and lingered.

"He's…42."

Katie's shoulders dropped. "Max."

"He's a good guy, you know."

"You just met him."

"How do you know? I didn't tell you that."

"Exactly, and if you'd met him weeks ago, you already would have."

Max's eyes rolled in defeat.

"Look, Katie, age is just a number, alright?"

"And prison is just a room."

"I'm not underage," she fought.

"No, you're not, but something tells me that if it was legal, this man might not mind if you were."

"Katie, how can you be a therapist and be this judgmental? You don't even know him. Gosh, can't you just be happy for me? You're not mom you know."

Katie suddenly remembered Ruth. She wondered how Ruth was doing right about now. Was she even more frail and weak than at Max's going away party? She had to have been. She hadn't had much longer to live.

"Also, Katie, I really don't think you're the best judge of what a relationship should be."

Katie's eyebrows furrowed. "What's that supposed to mean?"

"It means your relationships never last. There's always something wrong with everyone you date."

Katie slowly blinked. "Let's just change the subject. How's mom?"

Max sighed.

"Mom's the same as when you last saw her. I just finished talking to her before I got on here with you. She's worried about you."

Katie nearly chuckled. "Worried... About me?"

She's worried about me now?

Max nodded. "Yeah, Katie. She said there's a stalker in your neck of the woods, which you didn't tell me about."

Katie had nearly forgotten about the scare that happened with George. She figured it wasn't worth telling Max about. There wasn't enough evidence or cause for any concern that George was a danger to her or anyone else, and she didn't want to possibly frighten Max for no good reason.

"Well, nothing's happened here yet. Casper and I are fine."

She smiled. "What's that little furball up to lately?"

"Nothing. He's lazy as always."

Katie glanced at the time on her phone. "It's getting late. I should go."

"Isn't it only five there?"

Katie sighed. "Yes, but there's something I have to get ready for in a little bit."

Max's expression changed. Her smile was an indication she'd already known what was up.

"Ready for something, huh? Could this be…A date?"

Katie sighed. "Goodnight, Max."

"Give this one a chance!" She yelled just before Katie closed the laptop.

Katie knew she'd have to prepare answers for the questions Max was guaranteed to ask next time they spoke. Max wasn't wrong though. Katie did in fact have a date planned for tonight. She and Ian had been texting back and forth ever since they'd run into each other on the street.

This would be their first official planned date together.

`2 minutes away`, a text from Ian appeared on her phone.

Katie grabbed her bag off the kitchen chair. She checked her hair once more in the oval mirror above the hall table.

She'd placed one final bobby pin near her left temple, completing her look.

The temperature outside was cool—63 degrees on a quiet March evening.

Katie waited beside the large logo of the apartment complex. The sidewalk was just as busy as it normally was on a Saturday night.

It was filled with couples, singles, and school-age kids enjoying their weekend of freedom.

Katie watched the cars in front of her pass back and forth. A black sedan slowly passed by her. A few minutes later it'd come back around. Shortly after that, it'd approached again, this time, stalling at a nearby gas station. Katie peered at the dark-colored sedan, despite its deeply tinted windows. It just lingered there. Nobody entered in or got out. She then thought about all the recent disappearances lately. However, the car that'd been reported suspect was silver, not black.

Katie shook her head. All the reports lately, and Max and Ruth's concern was starting to mess with her mind. It was just a parked car—probably somebody lost and simply pulled over to check their phone for directions. No reason to worry.

A blue car pulled up next to her. For a moment, her heart sank just a little. The passenger window rolled down, and relief had filled her face. Ian widely smiled at her. "Hey," he said. "Hop in."

Ian drove just a few miles down the street. Katie recognized the neighborhood immediately. She'd passed it by several times on her way to the interstate.

He pulled into the driveway of the last unit at the corner. It was a modest-looking townhouse from the outside—brown brick exterior and light blue shutters. With a Christmas wreath still adorned at the door in mid-March, Katie wondered if Ian was lazier than he'd let on. It wasn't unusual for men to try and present themselves to a woman in the best way possible—even if it meant telling a fib or two.

She followed him up the stairs to the porch. A barking dog went ballistic as he spied the sidelights of the door.

"Hey hey hey! Shut up!" Ian snapped, holding the golden retriever back. He looked back at Katie, who was still on the porch. "He's friendly I promise."

Ian cocked his head, signaling Katie to come inside.

"Hope you don't mind dogs," he said, smiling.

Katie nodded. "You can let him go. It's fine."

It wasn't that she disliked dogs. She'd never liked the idea of taking care of one though. They were hard work, and they demanded a lot of attention that Katie simply couldn't give them, so she opted for a cat.

"Easy, Sammy," he said, as the dog greeted Katie with both forelegs. His tail hadn't stopped wagging since she'd entered in.

"Can I get you anything?" he asked.

"Water would be nice," she said, fighting Sammy's weight.

Katie followed toward the kitchen. Sammy trotted closely behind her. Her eyes scanned the open living room as she walked. A small brown coffee table sat beside the cream-colored couch. A chess set was in the middle, and a Rubik's cube was at the end. With all of these things, coupled with his invested interest in the world around him, Katie knew she was dealing with a man of intelligence.

The setting in the kitchen was quite romantic—the lighting was surprisingly dimmed, doing its job in setting the mood. It was more than she'd expected for a first planned date, but somehow it wasn't off-putting.

Three covered dishes sat on the center island. Katie could only guess what the meal was going to be since Ian wanted to surprise her. She looked around as she stepped in further.

The kitchen was beautiful with maple wood cabinetry. Three mini chandeliers aligned above the faux décor granite countertops. The marble black tile flooring was spotless and looked recently mopped. Little kitchen figurines were aligned under the cabinets, and the overall space was very clean. It was hard at first to believe that a single man lived here, but then Katie remembered that Ian was a designer.

"Your kitchen is beautiful."

"Thank you. Please, make yourself at home."

Sammy chose a spot near the table, knowing they were about to eat.

At the end of the center island was a small square gift box wrapped in baby blue wrapping paper. A dark blue bow sat at the top. Katie felt a little awkward at the gesture. Ian had already bought her a gift. She tried to conceal her skepticism before taking a seat at the center island.

Ian took the gift off the counter and handed it to Katie. "This is for you," he said. "I think you'll like it."

"Thank you, Ian. Can I open it now?"

"I'd feel awkward if you didn't."

Katie chuckled. She tore into the wrapping paper, shedding it off the box. Inside was a purple and black snow globe of *The nightmare before Christmas*.

Katie glanced up at him, smiling widely. He'd remembered. He'd remembered their short conversation about her favorite movie and what she loved to collect, and he'd given her a gift of both. Even though she'd had many *Nightmare before Christmas* themed snow globes at home already, Katie was still flattered. It was always the thought that counted.

"Ian, this is beyond thoughtful. Thank you."

"Turn the bottom," he said.

Katie wound the bottom, and the light sound of the theme "This is Halloween," began to play.

Her smile grew even wider. "This is cool, Ian. Where'd you get it?"

"I made it."

Katie's jaw dropped.

"Nah, I'm kidding," he said, before Katie could compliment him. "I wish. A buddy of mine and his wife actually make these and sell them online. When you mentioned you liked snow globes, they were exactly who I thought of for this."

Katie's smile slowly faded at the sudden thought of an ex-boyfriend from college—the one who'd love bombed her until she'd given him what he'd wanted. Katie knew deep down it wasn't fair for her to label Ian negatively because of that, but the thought had lingered in her mind regardless.

"Well, this is truly sweet," she said. "Thank you again."

"No problem. Let's eat."

Ian uncovered the dishes, revealing Texas toast, brown butter pasta, and broccoli florets. Looking at the delectable meal made Katie remember how hungry she really was.

Ian took two glasses down from the cabinets and placed them both in front of two empty plates.

He took a seat opposite her and smiled.

"This looks amazing, Ian. Really."

"Thanks. Please, dig in."

Katie took the tongs and picked a little of everything. She planned to eat less than she normally would in front of Ian.

"So, how's work been?" he asked, before taking a bite of pasta.

She shrugged. "It's been alright, a little more challenging lately. I've got a child with intense anxiety, and I'm not particularly used to such an extreme form of it."

Katie was careful not to directly use the word mute, as it was too much of a potential identifier because of its scarcity.

"Do you know what you'll do?" he asked.

She shrugged before taking a bite. "What I always do. Work until I find a solution."

"So… Last time we talked about things you like. Anything you don't like that I should know about?"

"Socks with sandals."

Ian nearly spit up his drink.

Katie snickered. "Is that funny?"

"Something I didn't really expect," he said, wiping his mouth. "You mean people who wear socks with sandals?"

Katie nodded. "It's not exactly horrible. It's just not my favorite fashion choice."

Ian shook his head before taking a drink. In the moment, she wasn't sure if he found her idiotic or humorous—or both.

"Anything else you don't particularly like?"

Katie searched her brain. There were a ton of things she didn't like, such as abuse, too much negativity, spiders, and the word "moist."

She peered at him. "I don't like it when I can't crack a code on someone—when they hold things back from me that I can't figure out."

He hesitated, and then said, "Oh?"

Katie nodded. She knew not to pry too much, not with her clients or anyone else, but Katie was curious about Ian's life. She was curious about his romantic past, as any potential partner should be. Was it so wrong to seek answers?

"You never told me about your past relationship," she said.

Ian watched her as he gulped the last of his juice. "No. I guess I didn't."

She waited, fighting with herself on whether to push harder or let it go.

"I was married before," he said, ending Katie's inner dilemma. "Divorced?"

Just then his cell phone rang.

From the nature of the conversation, Katie assumed it was work-related. The conversation was quick, before too long he'd hung up. Katie stared at him.

"Work," he confirmed, answering a question she hadn't asked. Katie nodded, waiting to see if he'd pick up where they'd left off.

"Anything else you don't like?" He asked.

Just like that, he was off the hook. The phone interruption was perfect, a bit too perfect, as if God himself was on Ian's side tonight. Sighing, she replied, "I don't like scary movies…Or anything with horror."

"Yet your cat's name is Casper, and your favorite movie is *The Nightmare Before Christmas*?"

"Neither are horror…Right?"

"Rated G if they are." He shrugged. "I just wouldn't expect a person who's against horror to have their favorite movie be anything that starts with the word nightmare…or have their favorite holiday be Halloween."

Katie nodded. "That's fair. Although I wouldn't say I'm against horror necessarily. I like the innocent cutesy stuff—but when it comes to horror—like actual horror… I've just experienced enough of it in my own life. I don't need to watch it on the screen as well."

Ian slowly nodded.

"Is that something you're into?" she asked, before he could reply. "Horror?"

"I was big on it in my younger years, but I don't watch too much of it anymore."

"How big?"

"Any decent scary movie that came out from the 80s to about 2014 I've seen."

"All of the zombie films?" she asked.

"Seen most of 'em."

"Clowns?"

He nodded. "Seen 'em."

"Ghosts?"

"Seen 'em."

She snapped her fingers. "That old movie with the doll and the boy."

"Child's Play," he clarified, "And yes I've seen it."

"Well, what about—"

Ian chuckled. "Anything you name I've seen it…Especially the popular ones."

"Well, I'm not exactly a horror buff so the populars are all I got."

There was silence between them. Ian stared at Katie intensely.

"What?" she said, picking up her glass. "What are you staring at?"

She expected him to say an old, tired compliment about her eyes or smile, however, instead he said, "What's your middle name?"

Katie flinched. "That's random. Why?"

Ian shrugged. "Curiosity. It's just another thing about you I'd like to know."

"Brianne. And yours?"

"Andrew."

"Nice," she said, taking another sip.

The room had fallen silent again. Ian's stare had indeed made her a little nervous. Instead of looking away though, she decided to stare back.

"So... Can I know more about your relationship?" she asked.

His eyes fell back on his plate. "Sure, but why?"

She shrugged.

Looking up again, he said, "Not that much to tell."

Katie stared at him, waiting for him to continue. Instead, though, he said, "How's the food?"

Katie had already commented on it earlier. Clearly this was a distraction.

"Good," she replied.

She watched him when he wasn't looking. In the dim light, his face was even more inviting. She watched his hair, taking notice of how sleek and well-groomed it'd looked.

Katie took a bite of the bread and followed it with the pasta. It tasted heavenly. The noodles were cooked just right, and the bread was still warm. Ian had placed mango flavored juice on the table, which Katie had washed her meal down with.

After dinner, Ian and Katie were still seated across from each other at the table. Their eyes remained on each other.

"So, can I have a look around?" Katie asked.

Ian smiled. "Sure."

He got up after her, following her upstairs. Regret suddenly built up inside her. Hopefully Ian hadn't interpreted that as a sign to jump into bed. It wouldn't be the first time she'd inadvertently given a guy hope...or blue balls.

"It's not much," he said once they reached the top. "But it's good enough."

The flooring was carpeted a smooth cream color. Three doors besides the bathroom occupied the hallway.

Katie had searched the two bedrooms and took a quick look inside the bathroom. It was small, but still nice like the rest of the home.

She came to the last room, placing her hand on the knob, but it wouldn't turn.

Ian came up behind her.

She turned toward him. "This one's locked," she said smiling.

A sly smirk crossed his face. "It's off limits."

Katie waited for him to explain further, but his face was now emotionless. Curiosity undoubtedly struck her, but she decided not to pry.

"Well again, your place is nice."

This time, he hadn't said anything back. The way he stared at Katie wasn't threatening, nor was it sexual. His eyes read intrigue and pleasure, as if she said all the right things to impress him, but it wasn't her intention. She was simply being herself.

A smile formed on her face. Her heart felt a tad bit lighter than before. She realized in this moment; she'd felt something with him that she hadn't felt with anyone in a long time. She'd felt something real and authentic. She'd felt chemistry.

Chapter 12

Katie's work week went by quickly. She'd gained one new client, Hanna, who suffered from emotional neglect. She'd come in shy at first, but then softened up throughout the session.

Casper stood in the kitchen, staring as Katie refilled his water bowl.

"There you go," she said, setting it on the ground next to him. As Casper drank, Katie checked her phone. A text from Jay appeared.

Five minutes away, it read.

Instead of miniature golfing, they decided on a shopping center twenty miles away. It was something Katie had been looking forward to since she'd recently gotten paid.

When Jay texted that he was outside, Katie got her purse and closed the door behind her.

Brooke, a baby-faced twenty-something who lived on the 6th floor, approached her. "Hey, Katie," she said, joining her through the lobby.

"Hi, Brooke, how are you?"

"Busy," she said. "Lots of homework tonight. Did I ever tell you how much I hate college?"

Katie smirked. "Once or twice."

"What've you got going on tonight?"

Katie pointed to Jay, who stood leaning on his car as he waited. His head was deep in his phone. "I've got plans with my brother."

Brooke peered at him through the glass. "Cute brother."

Katie chuckled.

Brooke smiled. "Have a good evening, Katie."

Jay slipped his phone in his pocket as Katie came out. His face appeared tired, as if he'd just woken up. "You ready?"

"I am. But...Are you okay?"

"Great," he forced a smile.

Jay walked around to the driver side while Katie opened the door of the passenger.

A high-pitched ring erupted from Jay's pocket as he buckled in. He maneuvered his phone out, answering, with an exhausted, "Hey."

Katie heard the voice on the other end of the call lower into silence. She people watched as Jay conversed. A pale skinned pregnant woman controlled the stroller in front of her. Dozens of professionally dressed people crowded the sidewalk, most of whom Katie assumed worked in the buildings of downtown.

"Why didn't you tell me?" She heard him ask; frustration was clear in his voice.

Even though he hadn't hung up, he was quiet. His face held every ounce of irritation he'd held in just a moment ago.

Katie thought back to her time when they were kids. Jay didn't get angry in the traditional sense one may think of. Yelling at the top of his lungs or cussing someone out wasn't much his style. The danger would always lie in his silence; when his anger, or any dark feelings would fester and metastasize into action. The way he would look at you if you'd wronged him was the embodiment of *if looks could kill*. Jay lived in isolation inside his room, doing God knows what. It would smell sometimes inside. His explanation when Ruth would ask about it was "experiments." What kind though, Katie had never known.

She shook herself out of her own thoughts. That was then, and this was a new day. Jay was older, and wiser. There was no need for him to torture her as if they were still children again. Jay had never done anything for her that he didn't need to do or that he couldn't benefit from. Despite all that, he'd been good to her recently, and he even helped to give her own business a jumpstart by giving her thousands. What would be the purpose in that if he hadn't changed?

After hanging up, he put his phone on the holder on the dash, sighing to himself.

"Is everything okay?" she asked. The typical question to someone's obvious distress.

"Just some stuff at work. Don't worry about it," he said, shifting gears. "He'll learn."

Katie said nothing. She looked out of the window as Jay began to drive away.

They reached the interstate without much conversation other than how both of their work weeks had been. The video from Jay's Veestream app on his phone had ended. Autoplay had then jumped to the news. The report was on the latest disappearance in Virginia. This attack happened in Cedar, thirty miles away from Sperry.

The description of the girl was the same as what Katie had last heard. Young, pretty, and a college student.

She shook her head. Jay took notice and looked over.

"What?" A sly smirk rested at his lips; a gesture Katie did not expect.

"The poor girl. She's so young."

"They usually are."

It was a normal response to the obvious, but something within his tone and demeanor was bothersome. After the report, Jay played music on low as he picked up speed on the highway.

****

The car ride wasn't exactly short. Even though Jay sped down the highway, it still took them nearly forty minutes to get there.

Thankfully, it wasn't too crowded outside. Katie watched the giant water fountain in the middle. Pocket change lay spread out inside.

"Where should we start?" Jay asked.

Katie scanned all the stores that were attached to one another. There was both a first and a second floor beyond the fountain. Her arm extended once she'd locked eyes and her favorite store. "There," she said. "Let's start there."

****

Katie came out of one of the stores holding an additional shopping bag to the three she'd already had. Jay stood quietly waiting for her. He held a small bag from a shop unfamiliar to Katie.

They walked together on the second floor of the outlet mall. The slight breeze cooled her cheeks as they walked.

"So, what have you been up to all these years, Jay?"

"Already told you," he said.

"Yeah, but can we go just a little deeper?" she asked. "How was your reform school?"

Jay was sent off to Eagle Crest Academy after a year of living with their grandparents. Katie always wondered what Allen and Ruth thought an elderly couple could do about Jay. Perhaps it was a change of environment they thought would work. Obviously, it hadn't.

"It was okay."

She stared at him… "Just okay?"

"Yeah," he said.

"Was there lots of rules? Lots of fun? Did you make good friends?"

Jay snickered. His voice lowered. "Not really."

Katie playfully nudged him. "Oh, come on, Jay. Let's hear it. What changed you?"

He stared back at her. "Absolutely nothing."

His already dark eyes somehow got darker. A sharp chill shot through her body. There was something in his look that was eerily familiar.

"You coming?" he said, looking back at her.

It took her a moment to realize she'd stopped in mid traffic.

Slowly, she approached. They both reached a crowded escalator. Katie followed Jay. Neither of them spoke.

She watched him closely as she fell behind him. The mood had clearly changed. And Katie was now ready to go home—both because she had spent too much money and she was no longer enjoying herself.

"Where to now?" he asked, looking around.

"Home," she said, swiftly. "I want to go home."

Jay nodded. He dug in his pockets for his keys.

They parked far away from the shopping center. Katie realized how uncomfortable it would be to walk far in the dark with her brother, whom she now felt uneasy around.

"Katie," he said. "Are you coming?"

Once again, she'd zoned out. "Yeah."

She felt light drops of rain splash her skin, seemingly coming out of nowhere.

Both of them were quiet on the way home. Katie wondered if Jay had regretted what he'd said to her or the way he'd said it. However, there was no way to know. She was reminded of this happening so much as a child. Jay would always apologize, earn her forgiveness, and then revert back to his old ways. She hadn't known whether to comment on it or to leave it as it was. What would talking about it do?

Jay pulled up to the same location he'd picked her up hours earlier.

He placed one hand on the steering wheel and turned to look at her. Once again, it was the same look he'd given at the outlet mall. "Thanks, Jay," she said, grabbing her purse. She'd given no time for his response, nor did she look at him.

She expected him to stop her, say something to make her feel at ease and not overwhelmed or influenced by the past, but Jay had said nothing.

Closing the door, Katie had kept her focus forward, never looking back.

****

Katie's work week was flying by quickly. The days were fast, and the hours seemed short. She'd kept herself quite busy with plenty of paperwork from the therapy center. Jay had reached out every now and then, as if he hadn't noticed Katie's changed mood that night at the shopping center. She couldn't help but think he was playing with her. He couldn't have suddenly been that oblivious. Something within her grew furious at the thought. She shook her head out of the memory and returned to her paperwork, studying her client's notes. She sent an email over the weekend to Colin's parents, requesting a deeper dive into his home life. It'd gone unanswered for days.

Casper climbed on the couch and laid beside her as she planned her next big step in life.

Her pink floral planner was on her lap. Since it was only March, the majority of the book was full of empty entries.

Katie wrote down the date she'd make a major move for the abandoned building on Windsor Street. She'd definitely need more than what was in her own savings combined with Jay's 10-thousand-dollar donation. But at least now her dream was starting to feel more real. Therapy was something she'd become deeply passionate about—helping children specifically through things that others may not be able to understand. She'd made it her ultimate purpose in life.

The waiting room of the therapy center was full. Katie came in at her normal time and got her coffee from Gianna.

Most of the day had gone by quickly. Her newest and youngest client of the day, Hannah, had just recently lost both her brother and her mother in a car wreck. The thought of such sudden devastation had nearly caused Katie to cry along with her in the session. It was never easy to take in the tragedy and heartbreak of her young clients, no matter how many times she'd faced it. However, seeing them progress along the weeks, gaining hope and strength and happiness again had made it all worth it.

As she walked the narrow hall to the receptionist desk, Katie checked her phone. A new message appeared on her screen.

Are you free tomorrow? Jay texted. Katie stared at the message, unsure of how to reply. Normally, Jay would apologize excessively and then flip back into an evil character on their next interaction. This time was different. Jay hadn't addressed what'd happened at all, and it left Katie partially curious. She pondered what to do. She didn't want to live in perpetual fear or paranoia. Maybe it wasn't what she'd thought after all. Maybe she was wrong in what she'd thought and how she'd taken his words that night. What would

Jay be after now? What would his motivation be in wanting to harm her? And wouldn't he have done it already if that was his goal? She was genuinely confused, but she didn't want to go back into a pit of fear and anxiety again. Not again.

She took her phone out once again, writing, `Sure`.

"I'll see you in a half hour," Katie told Gianna at the desk.

"Have a good break, Katie!" Gianna said.

Katie usually brought lunch to work or she'd simply walk home to eat, but today she opted for one of the local eateries around town.

She walked the crowded sidewalk, passing by the familiar conjoined buildings along Main Street.

At the crosswalk, the big orange hand appeared—counting down the time for pedestrian crossing. A black sedan approached her, slowing down nearly to a complete stop.

Again, the windows were so deeply tinted Katie couldn't see who was inside. She grasped her hand, her chest tightened just a little. No way there would be an abduction in broad daylight. People these days were more emboldened, but such an act on a busy street would be truly outlandish.

The car picked up speed down the street once it passed her. She watched the license plate, struggling to remember what it was. She took her phone out to copy it but could only make out the first three letters. Quickly, she typed them in the notes on her phone. VHS.

Her reflection appeared on the glass of a recently established coffee shop a half a mile down. *Coffee by Irene*, the title read.

Inside the glass doors, the line was thankfully short. She'd gotten a sandwich and a pastry and took a seat at a lone table set for two.

Ian suddenly popped into her mind. She wondered how long things with him may last. Was he truly what she'd said she wanted all this time? Surely there were skeletons in his closet, as there were with everyone, but would she be able to handle what they were? Was she willing to stick around long enough to find out?

A man dressed in business attire got up to dump his dishes. His seatmate, dressed similarly, cleaned his glasses with a napkin as he glanced at his friend's action. She named them Pete and Russel—realizing a moment later it was the full name of a celebrity. She wondered about their life. Were they both married? Did they have children? Were they polite and committed family men? Or were they the type to live a double life? Coming home to a wife and kids hours after snatching people off the street in a black car.

Katie shrugged at the thought before taking another bite of her pastry. However, someone indeed was snatching people off the street. And it could be anyone, anywhere. And even though both men appeared friendly, the one thing Katie had learned well over the years was that evil has no face.

****

What's up Katie? George texted. Clearly, he hadn't taken Katie's delayed responses as disinterest like he was supposed to. She wasn't ready to block him just yet though. There was a side of her that wondered if she'd overreacted a little to what he'd texted her. It wasn't necessarily inappropriate after all, rather a little unnerving considering the circumstances. Also, her growing interest in Ian had taken the focus off of George almost entirely.

In the evening, Katie walked through the foyer of her apartment complex. Thadeus, Annabelle's large German Shepherd, led her forward. She rotated the ugly ring on her index finger, as she struggled to keep up with Thadeus. Katie would not forget the way it'd looked. Out of all the rings Annabelle wore, that was indeed her worst. On the flip side though, Annabelle always dressed well, with her clothes often matching her accessories.

"Hi, Katie," Annabelle greeted with a smile.

Katie sweetly returned it. "Hey."

Mr. Jones swiftly came up behind Katie. Jokingly he said, "Are you walkin' that dog, Anna, or is that dog walkin' you?"

All three of them laughed. However, Katie didn't quite catch Anna's response since she'd just received a humorous gif from Ian on her phone.

After reaching her unit, Katie had settled in on the couch with Casper until it was time for her to leave with Jay. She'd gotten busy with notes from her clients to pass the time. As the time grew closer though, Katie stepped inside her walk-in closet. Thankfully, since it was just Jay she was meeting and not Ian, she didn't need to dress to impress. She'd taken only a different pair of shoes out—a comfortable pair of black flats.

When she returned back to the couch, she glanced at the time on her phone. It was twenty minutes before the time she and Jay had set to meet. Texting here and there in the morning hours, she'd heard nothing from him since. Not even after leaving an, *Are we still on for tonight?* text.

Ten minutes had passed—then 15—then 30. After two hours and three unanswered calls it was safe to assume she was staying in tonight. She didn't like being canceled on, and even worse, she hated being stood up. She wondered what Jay's excuse would possibly be. Was he busy with work? Did he lose his phone and that's why he was unable to call? Had he run out of gas? Or was he back to his lying manipulative old ways again? Katie seethed at the thought of it all. She grabbed Casper up from the couch and headed for bed.

Chapter 13

In the morning, Katie got ready for work. She entered her walk-in closet, stealing a work appropriate black dress off the hanger. As she slipped it on, she could hear the rain aggressively splash against her windows, which immediately set her mood for the day.

It didn't take her long to get ready after she'd poured cat food into Casper's bowl and replaced his water.

She was out of the door early.

A female cop smiled politely at her as she headed down the hall. Another cop had passed her on her way to the elevator. This one had kept his focus forward, seemingly in a hurry.

When the elevator doors had opened, Katie saw a litter of cops along the lobby. Onlookers watched them, talking amongst themselves.

Police lights flashed on and off outside the glass doors. Katie could see the rain pouring down just as hard as earlier. Cop cars were lined up behind one another along the curb of the building. Yellow tape surrounded it. Katie's jaw had dropped slightly.

Brooke cupped her mouth. Her red eyes were puffed behind her large glasses, tears threatening to spill at any moment.

"Brooke," Katie said, rushing over to her. "What happened?"

"It's Annabelle," her voice cracked. "Annabelle's gone."

"What? What do you mean gone?"

Brooke's fiancé, Mason, came up beside her with two coffees in his hands. He gave one to Brooke, nodding at Katie.

"It happened last night. She went out to walk her dog and then she never came back."

Mason put his arm around her, caressing her shoulder.

Brooke lifted her glasses. "I don't understand how this could happen here," she said, wiping her eyes as she sniffled. "You don't ever think it's going to happen this close to home…And then it does."

"We don't know anything yet, Brooke," Mason said.

Katie never thought—not really—that this would happen not only in her city, but in her own apartment complex. If this disappearance was connected to the others around Virginia, this would be the biggest news to hit Sperry in years.

Katie's heart broke for Annabelle. She was kind and always smiling. This was truly tragic. Katie hoped she would be found soon and safe.

"Where's Ron?" Katie asked.

"He's probably being questioned," Mason answered.

Brooke continued wiping her glasses. "I don't think he was home. I remember Annabelle saying something about him working late. I don't think he'll know anything."

"He may know nothing," Mason said. "Or he may know a whole lot of something."

"Mason," Brooke warned.

"What? I'm just saying. We don't know. We don't really know much about him."

"We know he's Annabelle's husband and he loves her very much," she nodded.

"Do we know that? How many times have you talked to Ron? How many times have you even seen him? He doesn't show his face, he doesn't smile, and he doesn't talk. You gotta admit, the guy's a little weird."

"I see him sometimes," Brooke said. "When he's coming back from work."

"Well yeah, they have one car," Mason replied, "And he uses it for work—and according to her he's always working. That's why we see her walking around everywhere and we never see him."

Kaite felt a little uneasy at the details Brooke and Mason shared about Annabelle's life. Was she the only one who had tuned Annabelle out when she spoke too much? Such a thing was already wrong and rude, but considering the recent circumstances, Katie felt even more guilty.

Brooke shook her head. "Just because he's a quiet loner doesn't mean he's dangerous. And you can't be married to someone like Anna and not love her. Whatever bad thing that might've happened to Annabelle, he didn't do it."

Her eyes lowered, and her expression shifted, as if she didn't fully believe her words. Katie wondered if Brooke could be thinking of her past interactions with him and realizing how little of Ron she knew.

Mason lifted his hands in defense. "Look, I'm not saying he did anything. I'm just saying he's weird and we don't know him."

Katie almost always saw Annabelle by herself—or Annabelle and Thaddeus, their German Shepherd.

Katie knew when a victim went missing it was always their spouse that was the first suspect, but in this case, she felt it had to be different. Disappearances were starting all over the state of Virginia. There was a good chance that this wasn't the average domestic dispute, and if it wasn't the work of the Virginia kidnapper, there wasn't enough evidence to label Ron as anything other than a now grieving husband.

Mr. Jones headed over from the throng of cops and onlookers. "Can you guys believe this?"

Mason shook his head. "I can't, man."

"Did you guys see anything last night?"

"We went to bed early," Brooke said, speaking for both she and Mason. "We didn't hear or see a thing."

They all simultaneously watched Katie, waiting for her response—or defense.

"No," she answered. "I stayed in my unit after I got off work in the evening. I never saw or heard anything."

A woman Katie sometimes saw in passing spoke with a police officer. Her arms appeared tightly wrapped over her chest. The alarm on her face had matched Brooke. A moment later, she turned away from the officer.

When the officer made eye contact with Katie, it'd caused her heart to sink just a little.

He walked over to them, watching each of their faces as he walked. Katie's stomach began to feel empty, even though she had no reason at all to feel nervous, she did.

"Hi, I'm Officer Chen. Can I have a word with you all? Separately?"

All of them acquiesce to his request.

"I can go first…If that's okay," Katie said to the group. They all agreed. Katie wanted to get to the bottom of this, and she wanted as much information about what happened as she could get.

"Okay," he said. "Let's talk."

The officer took Katie a few steps away from the others. Katie could feel their eyes on them though.

"Hi. Can I get your name?"

"Katie," she replied. "Mackenna."

"Hi, Katie."

Officer Chen was slightly shorter than Katie. He had a friendly face, and his smile was welcoming. From the pocket of his pants, he took out both a pen and a pad of paper.

"What floor do you currently reside on and what number?"

It wasn't a hard question, but for some reason Katie struggled to answer. Officer Chen looked up from his pad, waiting on her.

"Your floor and apartment number," he clarified.

"Sorry, I'm on the third floor, 311."

She wondered if maybe she'd made a mistake going first since she lived on the third floor and Mason and Brooke lived on the 6th, the same floor as Annabelle.

"What were you doing from the hours of 8p.m to 1a.m?"

"I was getting ready for bed."

Katie went on to explain exactly what she was doing from memory. She watched Officer Chen's pen glide on the paper as she spoke.

"Do you have any knowledge of what transpired here, Katie?"

"I heard Anna went missing," she replied. She could barely believe the words she'd just spoken.

"Yes, unfortunately she did. How well were you acquainted?"

"We were just neighbors who happen to live in the same complex. I would see her around occasionally."

He nodded. "Did you have contact at all with her prior to her disappearance yesterday?"

"That evening I saw her pass through here—she was on her way out to walk her dog."

"Can I get the exact time on that?"

Katie reflected on the time she usually got back from work. "It must've been around 7," she said.

"Officer Chen?" his pen froze as he looked up at her.

"Is this related to the disappearances of the other women around this state?"

"We're really not sure yet."

When he didn't expound, Katie looked around the room at the police and the residents. There was much confusion among them, and fear.

Katie felt a deep chill race through her body. This was really happening. Annabelle was gone. Katie hugged herself, fearing who could possibly be next.

Chapter 14

Katie never made it to the office the day of Annabelle's disappearance. She'd called in to work and explained her situation. No further inquiries were asked of her.

Jay messaged her later that day. His excuse was that he'd fallen asleep and then got busy with work. He told her he didn't contact her sooner because he knew she'd understand. That last comment was indicative of Jay's nature. Just when she'd thought he'd changed, he'd do something again that'd reminded her of his past. She should've known this was going to happen again.

****

Katie escaped to Ian's townhouse in the evening. Being home alone with so much going on hadn't felt as safe.

Both Ian and Katie settled in the living room. Sammy sat by the fireplace biting down on his chew toy. The roaring fire scorched the wood, creating the only light in the room, and for a while, the only noise. Katie bit her thumbnail as she watched the fire.

"Stop thinking about it," Ian said as if he could read her mind.

"I can't. It just happened today. It's all I can think about."

"I know, but that's not going to help."

Katie went back to biting at her nails. Her eyes watched the black TV screen as if it were on. "Where do you think she is?"

"Do you really want me to answer that?"

Katie thought better of it. "No."

"Maybe you should—"

"Watch the news?" She finished for him.

"I was gonna say get some rest."

Katie stared at him. "I haven't been here that long. It's not time to go yet."

"I meant here. You can sleep here tonight."

Katie stared at him. It would be a relief no doubt not to be alone in her apartment at a time like this, but at the same time, this would be the first time she stayed the night with Ian.

"I'll be okay," she finally answered.

"You sure?"

"Yes."

"I'll be sad to see you go."

"We'll see each other again soon," she said. "We always do."

"Well, what are you doing tomorrow?" he asked.

"I'm not sure yet. I'll probably be busy like usual."

"How much time before you're not busy?"

Katie stared at him. "I don't know yet."

She started to wonder if she was sitting in the presence of a clinger. Even though it wasn't unusual for a man to want to be around a woman he liked, there was something about this interaction that'd made Katie a little unsettled. Like George, Katie was reminded that she didn't know Ian that well either.

"You're really afraid, aren't you?" Ian asked, seemingly out of nowhere.

Her heart sank deep within her chest. She wondered what kind of question that was. Of course she was afraid. Someone had been taken from her own apartment complex, which meant whoever had done it, probably was scoping the area—studying Anna before he got her.

"Of course," she replied.

A silence emerged between them. Katie struggled to keep her mind going anywhere that was negative. She searched her mind for a happier subject, something sweet—something that may lift the current mood. However, before she could speak, Ian said….

"Do you have protection?"

"I've got my pepper spray."

Ian chuckled. "I was thinking something a little more effective."

"Like what?" Katie asked, though she suspected she already knew.

"Like a gun."

She lifted up from him. "Oh, I don't—I've never even held one."

"No problem," he said. "I can teach you."

Katie stared at him.

"You'll be bad at first, but I can help you through it."

"I don't have a gun."

"It's okay," he said, rising up. "Come on. I got something to show you."

Upstairs was warmer, but still comfortable. Katie wondered if he was going to bring her into the room that he'd once deemed off limits, but instead they passed it. The room at the end was a guestroom. It was small with a queen-sized bed and a night table on the side.

Ian bent in front of it and opened the doors. He rose up with two different guns that he'd set on the bed. He mentioned which guns would be ideal for Katie to use. She'd forgotten the names of them as soon as he'd said it. There was only one time that Katie could think of where she'd been in close proximity to a gun. Allen had kept one safely in her childhood home for emergencies. Although she'd known where it was, she'd never actually gotten hold of it.

"Since you live alone, and just in general you should be able to defend yourself," Ian said.

Katie considered it a moment. She'd always kept her pepper spray close, and it'd kept her safe while walking after the sun had set. However, she'd never considered a gun before—not seriously anyway. She'd always figured she'd freeze if ever a situation came up where she'd needed to use it. And so she opted to use her pepper spray as enough of a defense.

"When do we start?" Katie asked.

"Well, you're the one with the busy schedule. You tell me."

Katie pondered her workload, and her stress levels. "I'll let you know."

Katie left Ian's place a little earlier than she'd planned to, but considering there was a kidnapper on the loose, she figured stepping outside sooner would be better than later. Ian stood on the porch; his fingers rested in his pockets. She'd felt safe with him there watching her leave. As she pulled out of the driveway, her mind went to thoughts of Jay, and how he used to be. If he truly hadn't changed, then his actions likely would now have gone well beyond the things he used to do. She didn't even want to imagine it, but the thoughts had reached her mind anyway.

In the office of the therapy center, Katie was bombarded with questions about Annabelle White. Her colleagues had wanted to know every detail about the case. Katie figured some of it was out of genuine concern, and some of it she'd assumed was just gossip.

Katie's boss had told her that if she'd needed more time to herself, she could take it. However, Katie had wanted to return to work. It took her mind off of herself for a little bit—which is what she'd wanted.

Angela and Colin had come in the evening as usual. Angela had never answered Katie's request for more information about his home life. When they'd walked in, Katie noted Angela was unexpressive, and her pace was quick, as if she were late. Though they were early for the appointment.

"Hi, Katie," she said when they'd come up to her in the waiting room.

"Hello, Angela," she greeted. "Colin, good morning."

Colin stood quietly, and still as a statue.

"Katie, can we talk for a minute?" Angela asked.

"Sure," she nodded.

"Colin, go on ahead of us."

Without question, he headed down the narrow hallway alone.

"So, I did get your email, Katie. Our home life is fine. Why do you ask?"

"Angela, I believe Colin's hesitance to speak out may have something to do with his home life. To be honest, I think—"

"Everything is fine, Katie," she interrupted. "I'm glad he spoke to you last week, and that's what we've been hoping for. He talks a little at home as well. We're optimistic. Please just continue to do what you do."

With that, she walked away, leaving Katie staring after her.

****

At home, Katie prepared a late Italian dinner. She'd thought about giving Ian a call since it was nighttime, and she was alone. However, she'd kept to herself, going over her client's notes.

Little Heather, whom Katie met with more than once a week, was suffering from abuse, but she seemed to be improving pretty well. Colin's anxiety was getting slightly better, but Katie knew she had to figure out a way to find out more about Colin's upbringing. On the intake form that Angela initially submitted; such information was shallow, and Angela's appearance was quite peculiar that day.

Rising up, Katie decided it was time for hot chocolate. It wasn't freezing outside, but it was cold enough, particularly inside her apartment to make her want it. As her pink mug spun in the microwave, Katie paced inside the kitchen.

She thought about the events that'd recently taken place. Annabelle's disappearance was still something she'd had a hard time facing. How could someone so innocent and kind be snatched away so quickly under everyone's nose? And would she come back alive? Katie winced at the thought.

As her drink was still heating, she checked the blinds in the living room. A black car was parked rather awkwardly outside her apartment complex. It was positioned as if the driver were deciding whether to turn into the free parking space near it or to drive off.

Katie mumbled a swearword. Since it was dark out, she couldn't make out who was inside.

Katie's body suddenly felt cold all over. She crossed her arms after allowing the blind to fall back into place.

She wasn't sure what to do or where to go from here. She felt silly calling the police based on a hunch. Perhaps she'd been wrong the entire time and it was nobody stalking her. Perhaps it was just all in her head the entire time, and the reports of everything that had been happening in her state had caused her anxiety to skyrocket.

She checked the blinds once again, and this time, she saw something curious.

The driver's door was wide open. When the silhouette rose, Katie peered at it. The parking lot light allowed her to see well enough. Her eyebrows raised at what she was looking at. Instantly, she'd shut the blinds and raced toward the door. She hadn't bothered to bring her pepper spray or her purse. She'd simply picked up her phone on the way out and slammed the door.

Katie zoomed toward the driver of the car she'd recognized. He stood beside the car, his back was turned as he spoke on the phone.

"What are you doing here?" she asked, speeding to him.

He'd nearly flinched at her unheralded presence. His face was surprised and guilt-ridden.

"Hi, Katie."

She folded her arms. "Hi, what are you doing here, Mathias?"

"Um—"

Without giving him a chance to answer, she checked the license plate. Taking her phone out, she reviewed the license plate number of the car she felt was following her that day on her lunch break. She had checked the first three letters she'd caught, VHS. They were a match.

"I'll call you back," he said, ending the call.

"What are you doing here, Mathias?" she asked again, this time, her tone was slightly harsher.

His eyes searched for a plausible answer. "My car broke down. That's why I'm here. I can't move."

"But you don't live here, so why are you here?"

She didn't know if he lived at her complex or not, but she figured his answer would tell her the truth.

"No, I don't live here," he replied.

Katie folded her arms as she waited for more information. However, Mathias simply stared at her.

"Why have you been following me?"

His lips moved, but nothing came out of his mouth.

"Mathias," she repeated.

"It's George. George asked me to do it."

"What?"

Katie wondered why George would put someone else up to this—why he would allow someone else to do his dirty work, and why he'd even bother.

"Why?" she asked.

"He wanted to find out who you've been seeing."

"That's none of his business."

Mathias nodded.

"Has he had you do this to anyone else?"

"No," he said. "Just you."

Katie shook her head. "I think you should go."

He looked back at the parked vehicle behind him. "I would but—I'm kind of broken down here."

Katie shook her head. What was it about their potential relationship that George could not let go of? They'd only seen each other a couple of times, and mostly communicated over text—hardly anything to grow attached to.

His phone jingled inside his pocket. "Excuse me," he said, picking it up.

Katie chose that moment to walk back to her apartment. As she walked, she thought about what she was going to say to George. The fact that he'd gone so far as to put someone up to stalking her was baffling. In the moment, she was thankful she hadn't yet blocked him. Now she was able to tell him exactly what she'd thought.

Chapter 15

Katie went through the day constantly thinking about the events in her life. Annabelle and George mainly. Why would he have her followed? It was possible that he was using Mathias in order to distance himself from any potential crime he was planning to commit. Was he the one stalking and abducting women in the state of Virginia?

Maybe he was having her followed in order to gain information on where she lived so he could come and abduct her. The thoughts had consumed her mind all morning.

****

After grabbing a cup of coffee from her Keurig, Katie boarded the elevator alone. The numbers lit in red slowly counted down to the ground floor. As she headed for the glass doors she looked around the semi-empty lobby. One of the newest clerks, a small-framed woman with hair wrapped in a pristine bun, spoke with her hands to two potential tenants. Her stature was short—her head barely met the elbow of the man beside her.

"I don't know why anyone would want to move in at a time like this," a voice said.

Mr. Jones joined her, watching as she did, the trio converse across the lobby.

"Me neither. Maybe they're getting some kind of discount."

When Mr. Jones didn't answer, Katie wondered if that was an appropriate response.

"I don't know," he finally said. "But I hope they catch whoever got Anna. I haven't heard much more talk about anything—just from Brooke and Mason. What about you?"

"I didn't hear anything or see anyone."

"What about your brother? What did he say?"

"Oh, Jay doesn't live here. He was just here to pick up my niece that night you met him."

"But last week, wasn't he here?"

Katie looked at him. "What?"

"Yeah, last week"

"Where?"

"Here in the lobby. He was talking to Anna. Or at least…I thought that was him."

"What were they talking about?"

"I have no idea. I just saw them in passing."

She looked down; her mind became busy.

"Katie, are you okay?"

She looked up at him, a smile formed on her face. "Yes, everything's fine. I...just didn't know that."

He studied her face as if her response wasn't sufficient. Instead of commenting on it, he gave a sharp nod. "I'll see you later Katie."

****

At lunch time, Katie stood in the kitchen, waiting for her food to heat up in the microwave. As she scrolled through her phone, a message popped up from Jay.

Sorry again that I bailed. You free tonight?

Katie rolled her eyes. Jay had quite the audacity to not only ghost her but then request another outing together.

Her fingers typed a response and then she'd deleted it. She could barely believe that she didn't immediately delete his number, along with blocking him. However, something about this new version of Jay had grown a curiosity within her. She wanted answers to all the questions she'd now had about Jay. Who knows, maybe he'd expound on why he was back at her complex, talking to Annabelle, and never mentioning he was there. Maybe now she could get answers she needed. She responded with a simple, *Okay.*

As Katie approached the therapy center, her thoughts had gone straight to Annabelle. She'd passed by Anna in the foyer that day, smiling as usual while struggling to control the pull of her large dog. Mr. Jones had said something to her in passing, she'd responded back, and then, just like that, Katie never heard from her again. The thought was baffling, crazy even—how someone can be here one minute, smiling while walking their dog as an everyday routine, and then vanish the next.

Katie's last client lasted a full hour. She traveled the busy sidewalk home with a satchel full of paperwork. When she'd reached her third-floor apartment, Casper was drinking out of his water bowl by the wall. He glanced up at her when she'd entered inside.

"Hi, Casper," she greeted.

He looked up at her and then trotted away.

The screen of her phone revealed a text from Jay. `I'll see you in an hour.`

Katie sighed. This was very familiar. She wondered if he would somehow bail on her again. She didn't understand why he would. It would of course cause her to likely never trust him again. Katie tried her best to stay open-minded.

After shedding her professional clothes for something a bit more casual, she grabbed her keys and headed downstairs to the lobby. Brooke walked up in a blue overcoat. Her fingers were buried inside its pockets.

"Hi, Katie," Brooke said, stopping in front of her. Her nose was red, probably from stepping in from the bitter cold. "Have you heard anything else?"

"About what?" Katie asked, though she already knew.

Brooke's eyes widened, as if she couldn't believe Katie was either this unperturbed or this dense.

"About Anna of course."

"I haven't. But believe me I've tried."

The words Katie spoke made her feel like a detective, as if it were her own responsibility to find the offender. It technically wasn't, but the crime had happened in her apartment complex. How good of a neighbor would she be if she hadn't at least done a little research? Brooke adjusted her glasses. "I haven't heard anything either. I'm so worried about her. I'm worried about all of us."

"It'll be okay, Brooke. They'll catch whoever is doing this."

Brooke pursed her lips. "I hope so."

Katie was in no position to promise anyone's capture. However, she knew that serial abductors and killers were rare nowadays. They'd been on a massive decline since the eighties. New technology certainly made avoiding capture significantly difficult. Katie wondered though, was there any kind of police corruption since the perpetrator was still on the loose? Perhaps these types of people weren't as uncommon as she'd thought. She ruminated past random abductions and killings she'd heard about throughout the years—which cases were national news, and which weren't, and which cases were solved abruptly, and which had gone cold.

"Well, I should go," Brooke said, interrupting her thought. "Have a good night, Katie."

Katie walked through the glass doors of the lobby. A blast of wind had smacked her face. Thankfully, she wouldn't wait long since Jay's car pulled up a moment later, stopping in front of the entrance.

He waved her in from the driver's seat. Katie wasted no time climbing inside from the freezing air.

"Hi, Katie," Jay said.

"Hey. I see you made it out this time."

He nodded. "I did."

Katie guessed what would happen next, a half-baked apology of some sort. Instead, though, he casually pulled the gear shift into drive without a word. As he began to drive, Katie stared at his wrist. At first glance, she'd thought it was a rash, but the longer she looked the more they appeared to be scratches. "What happened there?"

His eyes followed hers. "Oh…" he said, pulling the cuff of his button-down shirt over them, "An accident."

Katie decided not to pry further. She leaned back and began staring out of the window.

They drove in silence for most of the way. Jay had his music of classic rock drowning out any chance for discussion. It wasn't exactly what Katie had expected of him, since he seemed to take any chance that he could get to talk with her.

Jay parked inside of a near empty parking lot. It was a semi-abandoned park. Not the one he'd taken her to before, but this one seemed a little smaller. After taking the keys out of the ignition, he turned to her.

"Up for a walk?"

Jay had already known the answer to his own question since he'd known Katie loved walks.

"Yes," she simply answered.

They walked side by side until they reached a bench. Katie sat down first, then Jay joined her. He set his keys down between them. Katie scanned the area. On a cool night like this, the park was nearly empty, making her surroundings even more eerie.

She turned to him. At first, she hadn't spoken. She just stared at him until he'd looked up and met her eyes. There was that look again. The look that had haunted Katie all her life. His eyes were empty and lifeless. Just then, Annabelle's face appeared in her mind. She wondered if whoever had taken her, looked at her this way. All of a sudden, Katie felt even colder in the already chilly evening. She remembered what Mr. Jones had told her. What was Jay doing at the apartment? And why was he talking to Annabelle?

"What exactly happened the night you were supposed to pick me up?"

"Huh?" he asked.

He turned away before Katie could respond.

"The night you didn't show up for me—what actually happened?"

"I told you what happened."

Katie searched her mind for what his original answer was. His excuse wasn't satisfactory. At all.

"I went home and fell asleep."

"That's it?" she asked.

"Yeah. And then I got busy with work."

Again, she was reminded of Mr. Jones words. If Mr. Jones had seen Jay on the same night she'd gone missing, it meant Jay was lying.

"The day that—your neighbor went missing I had a lot going on."

Katie's eyebrow lifted as she watched him. "I didn't know you knew about what happened at my apartment complex."

"It's been all over the news. How could I not?"

She shrugged. "Well, you never let on that you knew."

It was normal to check up on someone who was so close to a tragic event. They may not have been super close yet, but they were still siblings, and supposedly, Jay was trying to make an effort.

"I knew you'd be okay," he responded. "You always come out okay."

Katie's teeth clenched. She'd come out anything but okay from his abuse. She'd distanced herself all her life from everyone in her family except for Max, and she hadn't had a proper sense of safety and security in all her life. It was because of Jay. He was the cause of most of her trauma. Katie wanted to rise from her seat and leave, but she realized if she'd done it, she'd have no way home. With a prowler on the loose, now was not the time to walk anywhere alone.

"What does that mean, Jay?" she asked.

"It means I've never seen you not be able to handle something."

Katie grinded her teeth. "How would you know?"

"Huh?"

"You were gone most of my life. You were sent away by mom and dad, so how would you know?"

Her tone was icy, but it didn't seem to faze Jay. He just stared at her. She felt a sharp shiver shoot through her spine. She reminded herself to keep calm. What he'd said wasn't anything to go into a meltdown about. She assumed his presence, and the circumstances she'd found herself in were bringing up harsh repressed feelings.

His focus fell to the ground. He leaned forward. His hands rubbing together.

"What, Jay?" Katie asked. "You don't have anything to say?"

Katie's heart was very close to sinking. She imagined Jay stating a long well thought out line about how sorry he was, and how he could make it up to her. However, silence came, and it lingered. Katie's heart pounded harder. Her pulse was undoubtedly rising.

"No," he finally said. "I don't have anything to say."

Katie leaned back against the bench. Her arms folded tight around her chest. She watched the full moon perched in the sky. It looked darker than normal, a slight shade of yellow.

Katie looked ahead of her toward a young couple walking a large dog. It was Annabelle who'd been walking her dog alone in the evening, snatched away without a single witness. She turned to Jay, who was now leaned back against the bench.

"When did you hear about what happened?"

"Hmm?" he answered as if he hadn't heard her, but Katie figured that he had—loud and clear.

"When did you first hear about Anna's disappearance?"

Katie made it a point to keep her eyes glued on his face. Jay hesitated, and his eyes darted.

"When?" she repeated.

"Why?"

Katie shrugged. "It's just weird to me that you didn't say anything about it."

"I already answered that."

"And now I'm asking you what was the day you knew."

"It was—" he began, scratching the side of his head.

"It's not a hard question."

"I didn't say it was, and I don't really remember, Katie. Look, why don't we talk about something else?"

Katie pondered what he'd said. She wondered if she should play it cool for the time being.

As Jay began talking about an entirely different subject, Katie looked at the empty space the young couple were once walking in. Instead, she'd imagined Anna walking toward her. Anna, and her dog. She was walking slowly—her hair bouncing in sync with her movement. She was smiling as she always did. The image slowly dissolved in the air.

Katie grabbed Jay's keys from the bench. "I'm ready to go. Are you ready?"

She stood before he could answer. She could hear the sound of his phone ringing as she walked toward his car. Before she slid inside, she looked over at Jay, who raised his finger, signaling he'd be there shortly.

As Katie placed her purse beside her, it had slid between the passenger and driver seat—the contents of it spilling out of the open zipper.

Katie leaned over, feeling around for her lost items. She grabbed her pepper spray and her lipstick. Her eyeliner had rolled further under the backseat at her touch. She felt around for her items. Thankfully, the car light guided her eyes. She felt two objects between her fingers, one large, the other small. She lifted one of them up and brought it to her eyes. With the light from the car, Katie gasped.

The ring was large—with the blue and green colors Katie remembered. Annabelle's big and ugly ring was here…inside Jay's car.

She glanced at Jay, who was still on the phone. In a panic, the ring slipped out of her fingers. Glancing back at Jay, he was swiftly approaching the car. Quickly, she'd done her best to act natural in the moment. Her heart was beating so fast she could nearly feel its thumps.

"What's up?" he asked, staring at her.

"Nothing," she said.

He watched Katie's eyes as if she were hiding something. She gulped lowly as she stared back. Slowly he nodded, placing his hands on the steering wheel.

"Let's go."

Chapter 16

Casper meowed as Katie worked at her laptop. She glanced at him and then glanced back at the screen. Once more, he meowed.

"Wait a minute, Casper," she said.

Her eyes had trouble breaking away from her computer screen. They'd been glued to it since she'd woken up in the morning. She'd searched for any information she could find regarding the recent disappearances of the women in Virginia. Article after article she'd opened, but nothing that would give her the information she'd needed.

She'd searched up Jay's work as an algorithm engineer. It told her nothing that would point him as a suspect of any of the disappearances. Katie had to take a step back for a moment, and wonder if Jay was guilty as she suspected, or was this simply her own desire to see him live a life completely behind bars. In this case, she'd need to be objective. Still, if she were right, she'd succeed in helping put a monster away—a monster who should've been put away years ago.

Her phone chimed with a text from George. `Hi`, he said. When Katie hadn't replied an hour later, he'd sent another. `Can I explain?` he'd texted. Clearly, he'd known that she'd caught Mathias that night in the parking lot of her apartment complex.

Katie ignored the message and went back to her laptop. Casper meowed once more. Katie growled, closing the top of her laptop. "Fine."

She went into the kitchen, taking Casper's food from the cabinet. He watched her as she poured into his food bowl, digging in before she'd finished. Her phone chimed on the coffee table. She'd stood up straight and headed back into the living room.

`Hey beautiful. You free tonight?` The text wasn't from George, but Ian. Before she could reply, she'd received another. "I'd really love to see you," and another after that, "Let me know."

Katie sighed.

Although neither Ian nor George were showing particularly positive signs; both possessive and more than a little clingy, she wasn't sure if she should be glad that men were at least giving her attention still, or annoyed at the manner in which they were.

Katie's thumb hovered over the block button on her phone screen. A second later, Max's words had entered her mind.

"Your relationships never last. There's always gotta be something wrong with everyone you date."

Was Max right? Was Katie finding any excuse to get rid of Ian? Or were her concerns about him valid? She slid her phone back into her pocket. A night out with him might be what she needed right now anyway. Surely it would take her mind off of things, and possibly help her relax.

****

Katie arrived at Ian's house in the evening. As she walked up the steps, she noticed the Christmas wreath had finally been removed.

Just as expected, Sammy barked as he watched her from the sidelight window.

Ian opened the door.

"Hi, Katie," he said, smiling. He opened the door wider for her. "Come on in."

He had a fire going in the living room. Sammy had settled quietly beside it, sleeping on his back. Katie sat close to Ian, watching the dog's breathing rise and fall.

"You seem better," Ian observed.

"I am a little. Although my thoughts about the situation are never too far from my mind."

Ian nodded. "I get it."

As they sat in silence, Ian placed his arm around Katie, slightly caressing her shoulder. Slowly, she leaned toward him.

"I can take your mind off of things if you want," he said softly.

Katie turned to him.

As he leaned closer, his eyes dropped to Katie's mouth. Katie closed her eyes, and she felt the soft touch of his lips. Slowly, she felt his kisses become more intense. Before too long, her body was pressed against the couch.

This certainly wasn't the first time she'd kissed Ian. However, they'd never been quite this comfortable.

Suddenly, she'd come back to reality. This was the same man she'd almost blocked just hours ago—the man who'd showed signs of possessiveness.

Katie slowed her pace. Ian followed suit. Lightly, she pushed him back.

"Are you okay?" he asked.

"Yes. But I think I should go now."

Katie rose from the couch. Ian stared as she positioned her sweater back on herself.

"That's quick. You haven't been here that long."

"Nope."

His eyes dropped to the floor. "Maybe you could stay for a little longer?"

"I don't think so," she replied, grabbing her purse from the arm of the couch. His eyes lingered, as if to wait for Katie to explain further, but she didn't.

"You really don't have to leave," he fought.

"Look Ian, I have a life, okay?"

"Nobody's saying you don't."

"Why are you so pushy? Let's just let this play out naturally."

Ian's head dipped. For a moment, her anxiety intensified. It was a mistake coming here. It must've been. How is it that the men she'd been seeing lately were turning out to be stalkers or very clingy?

"You're right," he said. His head dipped as if he were about to pray. He didn't say anything else, which made Katie wonder what was on his mind.

"Are you alright?"

He nodded. "Yeah. It's just—"

"What?"

"I guess I do push a little hard sometimes."

Katie cocked her head. "Why?"

His sigh prompted Katie to take a seat beside him, placing her purse back down.

"Remember when I told you I was married once?"

It was clear before that he hadn't wanted to go into detail about what happened, so she didn't pry. However, now she was glad more was coming out.

"During our marriage, I don't think I was really the person I should've been for her. I don't think the marriage was really something I worked hard enough at. I wasn't there when I should've been."

Katie nodded. However, in the back of her mind, she wondered if this was some sort of manipulation to make her feel sorry for him—sorry enough to stay. However, there was another side of her that was curious. He had brushed off this information about his life before, and now, even if by way of manipulation, he was finally opening up.

"And—"

Just then, something on the TV had caught her eye. It was a report on the disappearances. According to the reports, a body had been found. It was the first report Katie had ever heard about it ever turning out this bad. This person wasn't mildly injured, nor were they missing, this person was dead. The news anchor reported it as a 23-year-old woman whose name has not yet been identified. She was young, and had her own family, friends, and a whole life ahead of her—ripped away, likely without her having any idea or warning.

"I'm sorry, but can you turn that up?" She gestured to the TV.

Ian's expression was unreadable. Katie couldn't see if he was disappointed that she'd been distracted, or relieved he didn't have to continue.

The reporter gave details about the victim. From the report, Katie got her age, where she'd lived, and her career goals. Ian watched Katie as if he were waiting for her to explain the nature of her request. The woman was strangled to death. The reporter stated the victim had put up a fight.

Katie's hands covered her mouth. The anxiety within her increased exponentially as she remembered the scratches on Jay's wrists.

"You alright?" Ian asked.

She looked back at him, unsure of what to say. Could she tell him she suspected her own brother? What would he think? Would he think she was crazy? Would he find her paranoid? These were the questions regarding Ian that she wasn't yet ready to find out. It wasn't like she'd had sufficient proof, nothing that would make Ian understand.

"It's sad, isn't it?" she replied.

"It is."

She stared back at him. "I should go. Really, I should."

Thankfully, Ian hadn't pushed further.

When she reached her apartment after work, all evidence of police presence had gone. Katie was relieved that she wasn't reminded of Anna's disappearance, but part of her felt a little less safe.

After changing out of her work clothes, she refilled Casper's food and water bowl and headed back out of the door.

Katie walked through the glass doors of the Sperry police department.

There were two officers at the help desk. The one on the left was a heavyset man with a receding hairline. The one on the right was a female with her hair tied up in a bun. Her face was clear of make-up, and she wore a friendly smile as Katie approached.

"Hi, I'm Katie Mackenna. I would like to talk to someone about the disappearances around Virginia, specifically the one that happened here in Sperry—the Sterling Pointe apartment disappearance."

"Okay," she said, sitting up taller.

"My brother, Jason Mackenna—Jay for short. I had plans with him the night that Annabelle White went missing. I live in her apartment complex— third floor."

"Okay," the woman nodded, waiting for Katie to continue.

"He canceled on me that night without a good reason why. I'm a little suspicious because my brother—when we were kids, he was very dangerous and abusive. He loved torturing things that were weaker than he was. And he loved seeing people or anything living, suffer."

The expression on the officer's face hadn't changed. Katie couldn't get a read on her. She figured she probably didn't sound convincing to the officer. She didn't know Jay, and she probably wasn't concerned with something that didn't directly tie into the events around Virginia or with what happened to Annabelle.

"The other night I went out with him," Katie continued. "He took me to a park. I found something in his car. It was a ring, I think it could be the same ring that was on Annabelle's finger...because it's so unique and weird looking. It could possibly be hers I think."

"Possibly" the officer slowly repeated. This time the look on her face was quite clear. Katie immediately felt self-conscious, and a fool for coming here.

"Look, I don't have solid proof he had anything to do with what happened to Annabelle or anyone else," Katie said, "But I just would like someone to look into it in case I'm right."

Katie wondered how many leads the police got—leads that'd headed nowhere. She wondered if this officer had expected this to be just another pointless report.

"As a child," Katie continued, "my brother was abusive to me a number of times, and animals in the neighborhood too. My parents sent him away, and he blamed me for it. He threatened to get me back for it many times. I know he's capable of doing much more than making empty threats. If he's changed now that he's older than great, but if not—"

"Please fill these out," the officer interrupted, handing her an official police report. "We'll look into it."

The officer's smile was shallow, clearly humoring her only.

Katie had to wonder how silly she must've sounded to the officer. There was nothing concrete that she could prove. The connection had made perfect sense in her mind, but to put her thoughts into actual words was arduous. This meeting with the officer, told her one thing, she would need hardcore evidence.

****

The next afternoon, Katie came through the doors of the therapy center, cradling the side of her head. She'd stayed awake very late last night with thoughts about Jay, and the information she'd given the officer at the station. She was so embarrassed by the officer's reaction, she neglected to mention the scratches on Jay's wrists. It likely wouldn't matter anyway.

She left the police station feeling that the only thing the officer would do was put the information she'd given her into the pile of other useless leads. She also thought about Mathias parked outside of her apartment complex. She wondered when exactly George had Mathias follow her, and why he'd even agreed to do it. Was she really the only person he'd stalked? Maybe she was wrong about Jay, and he had nothing to do with any of the disappearances. Could it be that George might've been responsible for the disappearances instead? She knew there was more to the story…There had to be.

The waiting room inside the therapy center was full, with nearly every seat occupied.

The office was filled mostly with adults and only a small handful of children. She prayed nobody could see the fatigue that was likely written on her face.

Katie's first client, Noelle, was a twelve-year-old home schooler battling severe depression. Katie met with her twice a week. Progress was slow, but she was steadily improving.

Noelle took a seat on the bean bag chair, and Katie sat comfortably across from her.

Katie leaned forward, forcing a smile. "How was your week, Noelle?"

She nodded. "It's okay...I spoke to my dad yesterday."

Katie's eyes gravitated toward one of the clocks strategically placed in the room. Only five minutes past one o'clock. It seemed as though time was moving extra slow today.

Jay's face entered her mind. Again. His dark eyes void of any warmth staring back at her. If he did take Anna, what would he want with her or any of the victims? Was he really capable of murdering people? He certainly talked about it before, but Katie knew it was one thing to talk about it when you're young just to scare someone, and another thing to actually do it. However, if he did do it, it would definitely be believable. Jay was cold and uncaring. She spent many days wondering and studying if he'd fit the profile of a psychopath. He was charming to those he wanted to impress, studious with human interactions, learning the ways to appear normal, and adapting normative behaviors and patterns. Lying had come so easily for him that Katie had to wonder if he'd convinced himself that the stories he told were true.

"So…" Katie said, her eyes leaving the clock. "Have you spoken to your father, Noelle?"

Her eyes lingered on Katie. "I just said that."

"Said what?"

Noelle stared at her as if she were mentally impaired. "I just…said I did Ms. Katie."

"Oh…Um… I'm sorry, Noelle. Please continue. What did he say?"

Jay's face appeared in her mind once again. She thought back to when they were kids, when she'd told Ruth about what Jay did to her. Each time Katie had come to her with the truth, Katie was always faced with the same kinds of answers such as "He's playing with you," and "I'll deal with it tomorrow," though tomorrow never came. As the horrific memories of Jay began to resurface, Katie felt her eyes beginning to water.

"And then he told me he's coming," Katie heard Noelle say. Immediately her pulse accelerated. Her stomach had churned just a little.

Her client had spoken, and she didn't listen. Once again, she had no idea what Noelle had just said about her father.

If only there was a way to replay the last sixty seconds again. Katie knew it would send a terrible message to Noelle that she had once again zoned out while she was talking. If Noelle noticed, it was going to look like she had little concern for her, which wasn't true. It wasn't at all true.

Katie nodded along while writing on her pad, switching to a different subject. Noelle hadn't appeared to react negatively, but Katie could only guess what she may have been feeling in the moment.

"Excuse me," Katie said. She shot up from her seat. "I'll be right back, Noelle."

Katie was never good at covering up her emotions. She'd worn them so blatantly on her sleeve her entire life. She hadn't wanted Noelle, nor anyone else, to see her in any way less than professional. She headed toward the bathroom near the end of the hall. Harold appeared at the corner.

"Katie?" he said, watching her distressed face.

Katie hadn't bothered to look up, as if keeping her focus down would somehow mask her feelings.

"What's going on? Are you okay?"

She could tell her face was probably bursting with emotion, nearly impossible to hide.

"Yes, I'm alright."

"Katie," he said, waiting for the truth.

"I'll be fine." She fought back oncoming tears as she anticipated the end of this interaction.

"Are you in the middle of a session?"

"Yes," she admitted.

The way he'd looked at her matched Ruth's expression whenever Katie was in trouble.

"Who?" he asked.

"Noelle McDaniel."

"Has she been waiting long?"

"No, I just left. I'm just going to run to the bathroom."

He stepped aside, allowing Katie to continue on. Her eyes started to water, and she'd hoped Harold hadn't noticed.

Katie rushed to the nearest stall, crying into her hands. She once again had the same feelings that she had when her niece, Beth, was on the couch in her living room. How could this happen here? How could she have allowed her feelings to rise to the point where it had interfered with her job? She knew she was letting her client down in one of the worst ways possible.

The bathroom door opened, but Katie hadn't heard anyone go into the stall next door. She held her breath, quickly wiping her tears away. She heard the door open and close again. She was unsure whether or not she was alone. Either way, Katie knew her time in hiding was now over. She imagined Harold standing outside the door, casually waiting for her. She imagined him calling her into his office to have "a talk."

When she'd opened the door though, the way was clear. Slowly, she'd exhaled, mentally preparing herself to walk back inside her office and professionally finish what she'd started.

By the end of her session with Noelle, Katie rushed inside the break room as if she were starving. She opened the fridge and dug inside for her blue lunch bag.

The break room door opened to Harold staring at her. "You alright, Katie?" he asked, entering.

"I am," she said, her eyes dropping to her lap.

He leaned against the counter below the microwave. His arms folded across his chest. "What happened?"

She paused, carefully considering how to answer his question in a way that sounded reasonable. She looked up at him, but no words made it out of her mouth.

"Katie, you gotta give me something," he said.

Katie ruffled her fingers. "It's my brother, Jay. I think he might have something to do with the disappearances."

Authentic concern filled his face. "What? How do you know? Did he attack you?"

"No."

"Did you see him hurt someone else?"

"No. I don't—I actually—don't have proof."

Her eyes dropped to her lap. When she looked up again, she was reminded of the female police officer at the station. Her expression had now matched Harold's.

"Well, I'm glad you're safe, Katie. But your clients need your professionalism. If you need time off—"

"NO!" Katie hastily objected.

Harold stood quietly, staring at her.

"That won't be necessary. I'll be fine, honestly."

Harold nodded. "You're a great therapist, Katie, but take care of yourself. We really can't have that happen again."

Katie's heart sank. Harold's words played back inside her mind, causing her to wonder what would happen if something like that did occur again. She shuddered at the thought.

She checked her phone at the table as the door closed behind Harold. A message from George was on the tiny screen.

She hadn't even considered what she was going to say to him. With so much thought surrounding Jay, what George did had floated all the way to the back of her mind.

How are you? is what he'd sent.

Katie was surprised he'd texted again.

She considered blocking him this time, but she wanted to hear what he had to say about the whole thing. Though there was something about George that'd made Katie uneasy. The night they had together at his house felt like a complete set-up. Katie knew she probably should've ended things that night. However, there was a side of her that was still curious about him…or perhaps she was desperate to have someone in her life. Katie feared the latter.

She'd shortened her last client's time with her today, which was something she'd hardly ever done. However, her client didn't seem to emotionally need the full hour, and so she wasn't going to give it.

She walked into her apartment complex keeping her head down. She simply wasn't in the mood to talk to anyone at the moment.

In her apartment, Casper was laying beside the armchair of her couch. She rushed past him, preparing for her night out with Ian.

They were going to the local gun range so Katie could practice her self-defense. Ian was a professional compared to Katie, and he could easily show her how to protect herself. Katie never would have imagined herself doing anything like this, but the time had come to where she may need to.

As she curled her hair in the mirror, she watched the article on her laptop. She was researching stories of serial killers from the past. She studied the double lives they'd led during the years of homicide. Many were male, and either in their 20s or 30s during their crime sprees. They had wives, children; some were active in their churches, and some took jobs in caring for others. The thought was scary, how many evil people exist among the population—people the average person may never have suspected. However, if Jay had anything to do with Annabelle's disappearance, he was probably responsible for the other disappearances as well. But why now? Why would he start doing this now? Or perhaps, it hadn't just started. Perhaps he'd started years ago, and it'd gone undetected, and now he may have faced some kind of trigger. Katie had gone through many speculations in her mind. But she couldn't think of a single plausible reason for why Jay should have a ring exactly like the one Annabelle was wearing inside his car. Katie didn't understand it.

****

Ian picked her up thirty minutes later. Katie flinched upon walking inside the gun range. Loud bangs erupted one after the other.

"It's okay," Ian said, walking beside her. "They're just doing what we're about to do."

"I'm fine," she said, slightly jumpy.

Ian chuckled.

The gun range wasn't very busy inside. There were a few people sprinkled in some of the aisles in the building.

Shelves were stocked full of all things gun related: to gun cases, every kind of bullet known to man, shooting earmuffs, and gun cleaning supplies.

She followed Ian to the middle-aged woman at the desk. She smiled at them both before offering to assist. Katie gave her ID and answered a brief questionnaire since she'd never been there before.

The cashier rang them both up for earmuffs, a stapler, and two splatter paper targets.

Ian hung the targets up with the stapler and placed them twenty-five yards away.

Ian placed the gun in Katie's hand and explained to her about gun safety. He inched closer to her as he spoke, his body pressed against hers. Katie slightly blushed as a small smile formed on her face.

"Go ahead," he said. "You got this."

Katie closed her eyes as she fired. The sound loudly went off, but when Katie's eyes opened, she'd missed her target almost completely. The bullet pierced the lower right end of the splatter paper.

"It's okay. It's your first time. Go ahead and try again."

This time he came up next to her, watching keenly.

Instinctively, her eyes shut. The gun went off, and this time she'd completely missed her target.

"Don't close your eyes. You don't ever want to do that while firing a weapon."

"Sorry," she said.

The action wasn't exactly voluntary, but since she'd never handled a gun before, it'd felt quite automatic.

"Just try it again. You'll eventually get it."

Katie pointed the gun slightly higher, struggling to keep her eyes open. The gun went off again, and this time the bullet had pierced closer to her intended target, but still nowhere near it.

Ian smiled. "See? You're improving already."

Ian went over to his own separate lane as Katie continued to shoot in hers, missing every shot. The closest she'd gotten was a bullet that'd gone through the abdomen of the figure on the paper target. Eventually she went over to Ian's lane, watching the bullets run through the splatter paper, hitting the red dot at least twice.

"How long have you been doing this?" she asked him. She raised her voice over the loud banging in the room.

Ian stopped shooting. He placed the handgun down and faced her, lowering his earmuffs.

"I've been coming here for years," he said. "My grandfather taught me when I was a kid."

Katie nodded as she continued to watch.

"Don't tell me you're through already."

She shook her head. "I'm not, just on a break."

Judging by the look on his face, Katie figured he didn't buy it. "Did you want me to come back over and help you?"

"Nope, I'll go back in a minute."

Ian studied her pensive expression. "Something on your mind?"

"There's this guy I was seeing before you," she replied. "His name's George. He had me followed the other night."

"What?" he asked.

She nodded. "Yeah."

"For what?"

"He doesn't like the fact that I've been seeing you and not him."

He nodded as if he were familiar with this. "So, you've got yourself a stalker."

"It would seem so."

"All the more reason to be here," he said.

Katie nodded. "Guess I'll head back over. See you once I'm out of bullets."

When they'd finished, Ian drove her home. The moon had set in the sky, and the streetlights had come on. The two of them sat inside his idle car, talking about the recent events going on in Sperry.

"Have you heard anything about your friend?" he asked.

"What friend?"

"The one who went missing in your apartment."

"Oh," she nodded, "Annabelle."

Katie felt guilty for not realizing he was talking about Anna. The reality was that Katie spent a lot of time in her own thoughts about her life, thoughts that circled mostly around Jay. And it was only getting worse.

"I heard the police have questioned Ron, her husband, but as far as I know there aren't any new suspects."

"Do you think he might've had something to do with it?"

"I have no idea. I don't know Ron. Nobody really does. He's very quiet and he always keeps to himself."

"Okay," he said. "Questionable."

They both chuckled simultaneously, which Katie felt an immediate spark of guilt for doing.

The car had gotten quiet. Katie wanted to tell Ian what'd happened with Jay, but something held her back from speaking.

Ian's eyes dropped to his lap.

"Are you okay?"

"Yeah, I'm great," he answered. He placed a hand on the steering wheel.

"I'm just thinking—are you going to be okay by yourself considering everything that's happened? Because if not, you can stay with me tonight."

Katie wondered if this was his clinginess popping up again or genuine concern. Or perhaps he was like George—a stalker who apparently wasn't ready to be rid of what he and Katie had. However, Katie sensed sincerity in his voice.

"Okay," is what she ended up saying. "Let me get my stuff. I'll be right back."

She rose from the passenger door and walked back to her apartment unit on the third floor.

Quickly, she grabbed a pair of night clothes and her toiletries, loading them all in her duffel bag. She'd come back out a moment later, returning to Ian's car.

It didn't take long for him to pull out of her apartment complex. Since it was dark out, traffic was on the lighter side. They arrived at Ian's home shortly after leaving Katie's apartment parking lot.

To Katie's surprise though, Sammy hadn't come to the door with hysterical barking.

Ian took the gun case from Katie's hand. "I'll be back," he said, in a butchered Arnold Schwarzenegger impression.

Katie chuckled, "Okay."

Ian walked up the squeaking stairs with both gun cases in his hands.

She could hear him pacing upstairs. Shortly after, she'd heard the opening and closing of the gun cabinet.

As she walked to the living room, she saw Sammy knocked-out on his back. She watched as he slowly inhaled and exhaled.

She put her purse down on the couch, digging inside of it for her tiny container of perfume. She ran it across her collarbone, leaving a sweet scent on her skin.

When Ian headed back down the stairs, Katie swiftly placed it back inside her purse.

"So," she said, turning to him, "guess I'm on the couch?"

"Well, you could be if you really want to, but I figured you'd want the guestroom since you're you know—a guest." They both chuckled simultaneously.

"Makes sense," she said, recovering.

"Want to see it?"

"Sure."

Katie followed Ian upstairs and into the room at the end of the hall. The door was slightly ajar. Ian opened it all the way, signaling Katie over.

It was very plain inside. The walls were white, and the queen-sized bedding was cream-colored.

"Whose room was this?" Katie asked.

She remembered Ian didn't always like talking about himself or his home life. The two of them had that in common, which sometimes made for a difficult interaction. However, silence between the two of them wasn't necessarily awkward the way it could be with other people. She'd always felt a level of comfort with Ian, and it didn't matter if they had a deep conversation, or they'd said nothing at all.

"It was the spare," Ian answered.

Katie stared at him, waiting for him to expound, but he didn't.

"Have everything you need?" he asked.

It was a cold night. Katie's arms had already grown goosebumps.

"Can I get another blanket?"

He nodded. "Sure."

When he disappeared from the doorframe, Katie played her game of guessing. She wondered how many people they'd had come through this room. She also wondered about his wife. He'd never mentioned her name, and Katie hadn't asked. She assumed he would tell when he was ready to.

Moments later, Ian returned with a folded blueish grey fleece blanket. He handed the blanket to her and backed up to the wall. His lips formed a smile as he watched her.

She wondered if this was going to be the moment. She wondered if this was going to be the moment that they both share a bed—a night together full of deep passion that she hadn't had in years.

"Good night, Katie," he said, leaving the wall. "If you need anything, just holler. I'll be down the hall."

"Okay." Part of her was relieved, and the other part, in some way, was left slightly disappointed.

****

Katie woke during the night. She'd heard tapping somewhere outside her door. Katie grabbed her phone, checking the time of night. 3:31 A.M it read. She sat up and made her way toward the door. She cracked it open, revealing the open door of the forbidden room. Sammy's silhouette had just trotted out, holding something Katie couldn't quite make-out in the dark.

Katie walked inside the bathroom, pondering her growing curiosity. She didn't open the door herself. Sammy must've. She simply noticed it open. When she finished in the bathroom, she closed the door behind her, staring at the open door to the room Sammy was just in—the room Ian hadn't wanted her to see.

She wrestled in her mind the possible reasons why. Perhaps it was just simply messy inside at the time, and that was the reason he'd wanted her out. Or maybe she ought to be respectful enough not to enter a room she was told not to be in.

Curiosity had won the battle, though she did pay homage as well, deciding to simply close the door, and not enter all the way in. She got her phone from off the nightstand and approached the open door. With the flashlight from her phone on, she leaned to close the door, but something inside had gotten her attention.

On the night table were about three bottles of red wine. She wondered if he truly did live alone, and if he did, why was this room holding all of his wine and why was it not in his own?

Katie looked at more of the room. There were three shelves on the walls. They were full of office supplies mostly. However, when she'd come to the desk below it, she saw a stack of photos. She peered in closer to it. The first picture was an image of herself walking on Main Street. Katie began sifting through the rest; her open mouth grew wider at each one she'd picked up. Some of the pictures she realized were taken as early as last week, indicated by a particular picture of her wearing a green sweater she'd recently purchased.

Katie gulped. *What. The. Hell.*

Her heart began to race as she saw each picture of herself. She was horror-struck when she'd noticed that most of them were taken as she walked on Main Street, the sidewalk of her job. How long had Ian been watching her? How long had he been stalking her?

Katie put the photos back where she'd found them, and swiftly rushed out of the room.

As she slowly walked down the hall, she glanced at Ian's door. Her breathing had settled as she saw it was still closed and appeared undisturbed.

Katie tiptoed back to the room, quietly but swiftly collecting her belongings. Slowly, she crept out to the hall, where Sammy had apparently been waiting for her. Her breathing accelerated once again. She lifted a finger up to her lips. *Don't bark. Please don't bark.*

Sammy watched her as if he were deciding to obey or betray her. His wagging tail stilled. And just like that, he'd turned away. She quietly walked down the steps, walked out of the door, and then caught a surprisingly quick Uber ride back to her apartment.

Chapter 17

"I'm not sure what to do," Katie said, holding the phone to her ear as she paced her living room. "It's unbelievably creepy."

"So, they were *all* pictures of you?" Daphne asked.

"Yep."

"Whoa, be careful out there, Katie. Are you going to call the police?"

"And tell them what? That some guy has pictures of me in his house? That just proves I have a stalker."

"Uh, yeah. Considering the current circumstances, I'm sure they'd investigate it. It'd be irresponsible not to at this point."

Katie remembered when she'd tried to go to the police before about Jay. It'd gone absolutely nowhere, and Katie had felt like a fool for even trying. However, Daphne may have had a point. This was someone new that'd recently come into her life, and she hadn't known him as well as she'd thought, apparently. It may be worth looking into. Katie gasped at the wooden clock opposite her.

"Hang on," she told Daphne.

She peered at the clock once more to make sure her eyes hadn't deceived her. She swore louder than she'd meant to. "Oh gosh. I gotta go, Daph. I have a client waiting."

In her room, she swore under her breath for the fifth time as she zipped up her pencil skirt.

"What are you looking at?" she said to a gawking Casper at the doorframe. He meowed softly, his head dipping to the floor. She couldn't believe she'd done it. For the first time in all her years of practice as a therapist, she would be late for a client. It was shameful, embarrassing even. How could she have let something like this happen?

On her way out, Casper meowed as he followed her to the door.

"No, not this time, Casper," she said, maneuvering her sweater on. "I'll be back later."

And with that, she grabbed her keys from her purse and closed the door behind her.

Katie stormed through the doors of the therapy center minutes later.

She smiled at her client, Elliot, and his mother, neither of whom returned it.

She met Gianna at the desk.

"So sorry I'm late, Gianna. How long have they been waiting?"

"About twenty," she said, handling paperwork.

Katie rushed toward the narrow hall. Harold caught her as she walked. His stare spoke volumes. Katie felt a shiver run through her spine. She'd already known what was coming.

He didn't speak to her, though Katie was sure he'd wanted to. He'd known she was late, obviously. So instead, he'd let her pass, but not without giving her a look of disapproval. She knew she'd be forced to deal with him later.

She gathered her notes, quickly reviewing them. Without wasting too much time, she'd rushed back to the waiting room.

"I'm so sorry I'm late," she told them.

"We were waiting for twenty minutes," Elliot's mother complained, standing up.

"I understand. Again, I apologize."

"What happened?"

"Something unexpected happened. My apologies."

She waited for Katie to explain further, but she hadn't.

The woman shook her head, turning to Elliot. "Have a good session, Elliot. I'll pick you up in an hour." She turned away, without another word to Katie.

The session went by a lot slower than Katie had anticipated. Despite Elliot's progress, she couldn't cut the session short since she was late. Thankfully, nothing major had changed in Elliot's life in the week she'd last seen him. This allowed her to relax just a little, and take pride in the fact that she wasn't going to have any more added stresses.

At lunch, Katie walked inside the break room door to find it abandoned. She sighed a sigh of relief before taking her lunch bag out of the fridge.

As her food spun in the microwave, Katie took her phone from her purse.

Swiftly, she typed Ian's full name and occupation in the search engine. All social media related to the name had popped up.

Katie scrolled through tons of information, and tons of photos, but none resembled Ian, not the Ian she'd met.

The night she'd spent with him played over in her mind. What was he doing spying on her? If he were the town's kidnapper and murderer, was she going to be next on the list? Katie began to feel sick at the thought. She started to miss Max even more lately. She simply had nobody else to turn to. Daphne could help the best she could, but with a husband, twins, and a newborn, she was barely available.

Harold appeared at the lunchroom door. His stare had made Katie hold her breath.

"How are you feeling?" he asked, still at the doorframe.

"I'm fine, Harold. Really."

"You were late."

She nodded. "I know, and I'm sorry."

"Katie... what's going on? Is everything okay with your brother?"

She didn't know how to respond. Right now, it was about more than just Jay. Ian was now on her radar because of what she'd found in his home the other night. However, she was hesitant to share this information with Harold. She wasn't certain how he would take it, or if it would help her in this situation or hurt her even more.

"I'm not sure. I'm trying to get enough evidence against him."

"Do you still feel like you're in danger?"

"No," she blurted.

The honest answer was yes, but not only because of Jay. She felt nobody in town was safe, and at the moment, she wasn't sure who the perpetrator was.

"Katie—" he rubbed his eyes. "I don't—"

"Harold," someone called from the hallway.

He looked back at Katie before turning to leave. "We'll talk later."

Katie didn't like the way he said that, nor his expression. She knew it was a warning: a future conversation she didn't at all look forward to having. With everything that was happening, therapy was the one thing that'd kept it all together. It was her purpose in life, and so what life would she have left without it?

Her phone vibrated inside her bag. Another text was sent from Ian. It was one of five since she'd left his home.

Katie, why'd you leave? What's wrong? Is everything okay?

She read and re-read all his texts, acknowledging once again that she wasn't yet ready to answer. She wondered how likely it would be for multiple suspects to all be people she knew. Her life began to resemble a movie of some sort. Something that would make for good entertainment, but hell for anyone going through it in the real world, and now she'd had Harold to deal with to make things even worse.

Katie managed to avoid Harold for the remainder of her time at the therapy center. She wasn't sure if it was such a good thing though, considering she'd have to face him eventually, either in person next time, or perhaps he'd call.

She entered her apartment and flipped on her TV, turning to Veestream. In one of the suggested videos was live TV. An unidentified body was found near a lake a few miles south of Sperry. Katie gulped as she watched, praying it wasn't Annabelle.

Katie raced to her laptop, looking up every detail of Annabelle's disappearance and the news of the latest victim.

Article after article had come up of leads that'd gone absolutely nowhere.

"What happened to you, Annabelle?" she muttered under her breath. Her thoughts returned to her brother—the things he'd said to her as kids, and the things he'd done to other living things weaker than himself was enough to make anyone suspect he was capable of murder as an adult. She covered her mouth at the reemerging memories. She felt her eyes growing heavy, ready to pour tears at any moment.

The thoughts had consumed her. Perhaps she should give Jay a call. Maybe she'd catch him off guard again, and this time he'd slip up even more, providing Katie with damning evidence she could use against him.

Katie took out her phone and began dialing him. It rang until his voicemail came on. She dialed him a second time. Again, there was no answer. She tried a third time, and after that, she'd given up. Her phone buzzed on the pillow. Ian's number was on her phone screen. She watched the ignore option, considering ending the call. Perhaps it wouldn't hurt to at least hear his explanation. Though she couldn't think of a good reason why he'd have pictures of her at all, especially at a time like this. If he wasn't a psycho murderer, then he was an obsessive stalker—neither of which was any good. Still though, what would he say? How could a person defend something like that? If she didn't answer though, she'd never know the truth.

"Hello?" she answered.

Katie could hear the relief in his voice, and somehow, unbelievably, it managed to flatter her.

"Katie, are you alright? I've been trying to get in touch with you since you left my place. What's going on?"

She sighed. "I saw your spare room. I saw the pictures, and it scared me, Ian. Why do you have pictures of me in your home?"

An uncomfortable silence emerged between them. Katie deliberated hanging up on him.

"Katie," he said, before she did. "It's not what you think."

"What do I think?"

"Please meet with me tonight and I'll explain everything. If you're free. I promise it'll make sense."

Katie could sense the desperation in his voice, but instead of being turned off by it, Katie found herself curious. She wanted an explanation, and now she could get one. If it didn't seem believable, she could always escape.

"How about right now?" she asked.

"Trust me, Katie. Please."

She contemplated his request for a moment. It was only a talk, and of course she would request they meet in a public place. Still, she could hardly believe what she was about to agree to.

"Okay," she said.

As Katie prepared to see Ian, she had the news on, hoping to find out any new information about any of the missing persons or murder updates. There was nothing new as usual.

Conveniently, she hadn't had work today, allowing her the opportunity to speak with Ian. After what she'd discovered in his townhouse that night, she didn't think she'd ever speak to him again. But there was something Katie noticed. Every time she'd suspected she wouldn't see him again, something happened to have him resurface once again in her life. It was simply difficult to get rid of him, and curious as to why it was happening.

Katie and Ian agreed to go back to *Molly's Tavern* where they'd first met. It was loud inside at times, but Katie figured it would be crowded enough that she'd feel safe.

Once inside though, she saw the place was much less crowded than the last time she was there. She figured it likely had to do with the recent crimes around town. Nobody wanted to be the next victim, which made Katie question her own sanity, and why she was not only out at night with no protection, but why she was sitting across from a man who she'd known was watching and stalking her in a city where murders and abductions recently happened. Ian waved her over from across the room.

"Hey, Katie. Please sit," he said, gesturing toward the empty chair.

She pulled the chair out and casually sat. The two sat staring at each other. Ian leaned forward.

"I'm sorry for what you saw at my house. It wasn't supposed to happen like that."

Katie thought back to that night. There was a part of her that wished she'd never seen it. There was a part of her that wished things could go on the way they were before. Ian had made her happy and forgetful of the troubles surrounding her, and there was a part of her that dearly wanted to hang onto that. However, the other part of her, the more rational part, knew this was a good thing. If Ian wasn't who he said that he was, it was a good thing she'd found out before things had gotten worse.

"You look a lot…like someone I knew a long time ago…my wife, Amanda."

Katie's eyes narrowed. "You're married?"

The tone in her voice was stern and fueled by frustration. He shook his head.

"No, my late wife, I mean. She died four years ago."

Katie's shoulders dropped, and her body leaned back in her chair. Ian was hesitant to mention his romantic life before. As a therapist, she'd never forced any of her clients to talk about something before they were ready, and even though Ian wasn't her client, she'd still carried that same rule with her in personal relationships.

"I'm sorry to hear that," she said. "How did she die?"

Ian sighed as he leaned back in his seat. Clearly this was hard for him, but Katie remained quiet, waiting for him to continue.

"Covid," he blurted.

"I'm so sorry," Katie replied.

He nodded. His eyes watched the table, and then slowly looked up at her. "The first time I saw you, it was hard to forget you."

He dug in his pants pocket, taking out a black wallet. He showed Katie a picture of a woman who bore a striking resemblance to her. She'd had the same hair color, the same length, and she had very similar facial structures and features to Katie. The only difference Katie could tell was the hairstyle, Katie had bangs, and the woman in the photo didn't.

"When I saw you, I didn't want to let that image go. I didn't think I'd ever see you again, until I did. You walk Main Street; the same street I'm on when I read at the café."

She'd felt a little strange that someone was watching her, but considering Ian's explanation, she began to understand a little more. Katie nodded. He explained to her earlier that everything would make sense, and she admitted to herself that it was in fact starting to. She was quiet though, taking in everything that he'd said.

He closed the wallet, cutting off her view. He stared at her, as if to wonder what she was thinking, though he didn't bother to ask.

"Amanda was her name?" she asked, finally.

He nodded, "Yes."

"Okay. I get it."

Hope had filled his face. "So, I'm forgiven?" he asked, smiling.

"I have my eye on you, but I'm not upset. I understand. But you could have told me you know."

His head dipped. "I know."

Katie wondered why he'd kept it a secret. Obviously, it was part of his life that was hard for him to talk about. Though Katie figured that simply revealing that Katie resembled his former wife wouldn't have been major news. She wondered though, if it was truly her that Ian had an interest in, or just that she resembled his former wife. It was a scary thought, but at the moment, she chose not to address it.

"Thank you for understanding," he said, bringing her attention back to him.

It was nice having Ian around. Initially, she was close to cutting him off, confirming Max's assessment of Katie's dating life. However, as the more time she'd spent with Ian, the more she'd grown to like him. There was a side of her now that wasn't ready to let him go just yet.

"So…" he said, leaning back in his chair. "Are you busy this weekend?"

The smirk on his face signaled to Katie that he was sure he'd end up with an easy "Yes."

His arrogance should've turned her off, and maybe in the past it would've, but as of right now, his offer sounded almost good. She couldn't believe herself, and what she was about to say to a man who'd had dozens of creepy pictures of her in a secluded room in his house. She'd looked up at him, half smiling, "Nope."

Casper was in the same position on the couch he was when Katie had left—snuggled up by the armrest.

Katie took a night shower and proceeded to get ready for bed. Casper had come by the doorframe, meowing as he'd come in. Katie thought back to the events of her life. What reason did Jay have for keeping Anna's ring inside his car? He hadn't answered any of Katie's attempts to reach him either. She didn't know what to make of it, and any time she'd thought of it, she'd gotten just a little sick.

She picked up Casper from the floor and headed to the living room. Casper reclaimed his favorite spot by the armchair. Katie turned the TV on. As the Veestream advertisements aired, her anxiety returned. As long as the killer was on the loose, no matter who it was, nobody was safe.

A news report appeared on screen, capturing her attention. The report was of a masked man running from a fallen victim clinging to life. The victim was rushed to Sperry Medical Center where he remained in critical condition.

Description of the victim: Adult male. Age 18. Name: Landen Finley.

Chapter 18

Katie spent the morning researching all the events that'd happened in Virginia, the disappearances and the murders.

A message had popped up on Katie's phone. It was from George.

Katie, Landen was attacked. He's in a coma now. If you pray, please send your prayers our way. I'm sorry for everything.

Katie typed back, *Of course I can. I'm sorry about Landen. Do you have any idea who might've hurt him?*

I don't, he said. *If you're not busy tonight, I'll be at Sperry Medical Center with Landen. You're welcome to come. Have a good day, Katie.*

She considered this. She hadn't spoken to George in quite a while, and especially not since he'd sent Mathias to spy on her. However, his stepson was hurt. It wouldn't kill her to show up. She figured George may have wanted all the support he could get.

Of course I'll come, she texted back.

George texted back a smiley emoji.

Katie texted Ian next. A moment later, her phone chimed a notification. Her shoulders drooped when she saw it was just her feed, and nothing from Ian. She'd texted him two hours ago, asking what time he'd wanted her at his place tomorrow. He hadn't answered. It was unusual for Ian to go longer than fifteen minutes to reply. And if he did, he always let her know why. She didn't harp on it too much longer though, instead she started on paperwork from the therapy center.

****

In the evening, Katie came through the doors of the Sperry Medical Center. Two staff members sat at the long desk. The waiting room to her right was lightly sprinkled with people of all ages; some visibly sick, others displayed no signs or symptoms of anything other than fatigue on some of their faces.

The tall security guard held the lapels of his vest as he lightly swayed from side to side. He nodded as Katie passed by. Behind the desk, the plump sized woman in green scrubs perked up.

"Can I help you?" she asked. Her tone was lifted, as if Katie had finally given her something to do.

"Yes, I'd like to—"

"Katie," George said, walking toward her.

Apparently, he'd been waiting for her.

"How are you?" Katie realized the question was asinine as she'd asked it, but George didn't seem to mind.

"As good as I can be," he answered. He guided her down the hall of dull colored walls and matching floors. The rectangle shaped lighting above them seemed extra bright. Like the sun, it'd felt dangerous to stare too long.

"I'm so sorry, George" she said, her focus returning to eye-level. She shifted aside to allow a nurse in pink scrubs to pass.

He nodded. "Yeah. Me too."

"Do they know what happened exactly?" Katie asked. She remembered he said Landen was attacked, but she wasn't told any other details.

"The person who attacked him fled the scene. As far as I know it was a man running away. Witnesses didn't see his face."

George opened the door to a relatively large room with three different seats. The three faces Katie had met at George's house, and at Landen's celebration dinner were present.

Mathias looked up at them as they entered. Caleb sat slothfully on a chair by the large window. His eyes never parted from his phone.

And then there was Landen, comatose on the hospital bed. The ventilator that was hooked up to his mouth and nose hid his face. Katie watched his chest slowly rise and fall.

"They found him with his head on a brick," George said.

Katie shook her head. She remembered the report on TV. A witness had stated a figure was running from the scene, though it was too dark for proper identification. Clearly, this was no accident, but Katie decided now was not the time to discuss the possible suspects.

George claimed a seat beside his stepson, which Caleb had keenly watched him do.

Katie stood close beside him. "I'm so sorry," she said again.

This time he didn't answer her. His face wasn't watching Landen. Instead, he looked pensive as he stared out at nothing.

A middle-aged woman had entered the room, the same woman Katie had met at Landen's celebration dinner weeks ago. Katie felt an immense amount of guilt for not remembering her name. She walked in closer, a diet coke in her hand.

"I'll sit with him. You can all have a break," she told the room. Mathias and Caleb shot up from their seats.

"I'm good, Lydia," George said.

After a moment, she tried again. "I'd like a minute alone with my son please."

"Okay," George said, lightly patting her hand. "We'll go."

He gestured Katie to join him, which she'd done so immediately.

"What's she saying to him?" Caleb asked once George closed the door behind them. "It's not like he can hear her."

All eyes were on Caleb, but what was most surprising to Katie was that he didn't seem to care.

George's eyes had become hardened to Caleb's callous comment.

"What? What'd you just say?"

George approached him.

"I said—"

"I heard what you said," George interrupted. "Why don't you go home, Caleb? If you're not going to be supportive of your brother, why don't you just leave?"

"If I had my car I would've left a long time ago. And he's *not* my brother."

Katie watched Mathias. If Caleb didn't have his own car, she guessed that Mathias must've been the one that Caleb had ridden here with.

George stared at Caleb. "You did this, didn't you?"

Caleb's eyes narrowed. "What?"

"You attacked Landen, didn't you? You were the one who did it."

Shock and hurt filled Caleb's reddening eyes. In all the years of Katie tolerating Jay's abuse, she'd never once been accused of it herself, she emphasized immediately with how Caleb must've felt. "What? No, this is BULLSHIT!"

George gripped the collars of Caleb's dress shirt. "How is it that out of all my life's disappointments, you've become the biggest one?"

Caleb's red eyes lingered on George, as if to process what he'd just heard. His face scrunched as he pushed his father back. George retaliated with a very loud slap. Passing patients, and nurses gasped.

Mathias cut between them, holding Caleb back.

"Just go," George said. "Both of you get out of here."

"George—" Mathias said.

"GO!" he yelled.

Caleb roughly broke from Mathias's grip. He stormed down the hallway quickly, barely allowing Mathias to catch up.

Katie wanted to leave, but she'd felt that George needed comforting now more than ever, and she'd already forgotten about his possessive and borderline creepy behavior toward her.

However, she'd gone back to the waiting room with him. Now that it was just the two of them, Katie felt a little bit more relaxed. George sat leaning downward as he watched his phone screen. Katie, however, sat upward, watching the people in the waiting room.

A young couple with a small child sat closely together. The woman looked healthy, patiently reading a magazine from off the coffee table beside her chair. The little boy seemed to have a lot of energy, even though at this hour it was probably past his bedtime.

He'd said something lowly to his mother as he tugged at her skirt—something that Katie wasn't close enough to comprehend.

The man sitting beside them though, had looked severely tired. He cradled his head as he leaned forward. Katie assumed he had to have been the sick one of the family.

It was like that with nearly all of the faces in the waiting room—healthy looking people accompanying their sick family or friends.

"Do you want to go back?" George asked her.

"I don't know that we should," she answered. "Do you think Lydia is done?"

"I don't know," he said, rising up from his seat. "Let's find out."

There it was, George's pushy and controlling nature arising. She began to empathize with Caleb even more.

"I don't know, George…"

"If she's not done, we'll walk right back out."

"Okay. I'll be there in a minute."

He nodded and then headed back down the hall.

Already an outsider, and still pretty much a stranger to Lydia, Katie didn't at all want to come off as presumptuous. She wanted to wait longer before heading back inside Landen's hospital room.

She traveled the halls and asked a male nurse where she could find a vending machine.

He directed her to the closest one, where she'd gotten a coke and some potato chips.

She walked the plain hospital halls, tearing into her bag of chips. As she reclaimed her spot in the waiting room, she took her phone out. Finally, a text from Ian appeared on her phone.

Hi Katie. I'm going to have to cancel our plans for tomorrow. I'm not feeling well.

Katie's heart sank just a little. It was a blunt message and a very short explanation. She quickly texted back, letting him know it was alright and that she hoped he felt better. Just then, on the TV above, a breaking news story came on.

A body had been found by a nearby lake in Elwood Drive. It was found by two high school students, who Katie knew would likely suffer emotional damage from witnessing such a thing.

Whoever the killer was, it was clear that he'd made Sperry his resting area, with Elwood Drive being only minutes away.

Like usual, the police had no direct suspects and eyewitnesses that hadn't held enough detailed information for an arrest. Katie sucked her teeth at the report, disappointed this nightmare that'd haunted Virginia, Sperry, in particular was not yet over.

She sat, keenly watching the news report. Her heart pounded relentlessly against her chest. Her teeth were clenched together, a knot forming in the pit of her stomach. According to the report, the body was a white female in her thirties.

Please no, please no, please no. Please don't be Anna.

Katie's pulse tightened; the pace of her breath grew faster. Remembering what she'd found in Jay's car that night, had left her worried. The anchorwoman went on to mention the body hadn't yet been identified.

Katie's thoughts of Jay had quickly returned, his cruelty and his lies, all ruining the temporary pleasure she'd had from the junk food in her hands. Not wanting to hear any more of the TV, she'd gotten up and left.

Chapter 19

In the morning, her phone was clear of any responses from Jay. She'd given up, and dedicated her entire morning, staying in a continuous search of the recent events that'd taken place in all the cities of Virginia, and in Sperry especially.

All morning she'd waited for her usual text from Ian. But again, there was nothing. When she'd texted him first, asking how he was feeling it'd gone unanswered until noon time, with a simple, "I'm alright. Thank you."

Simple enough, yet Katie had wanted more, though she knew she wasn't going to text again. She knew that Ian should be the last thing she should be concerned about. She wondered about Jay, and what he might be up to. Ever since she'd left the hospital, he had taken up almost all space inside her head. Thoughts about how Jay used to be. He was no doubt a dangerous child, she could imagine what he could truly be capable of now.

October 31st, 2010

"He's going to kill someone," 18-year-old Katie said, laying on the recamier in Dr. Kumar's office.

Looking up from his notepad, his eyes locked onto hers. "How do you know that?"

"It's what they say isn't it? They say that serial killers always start off with animals—then they graduate to people."

"You've seen him hurt animals?"

Katie nodded. "I've seen Jay do a lot of things Mr. Kumar. Nobody ever believes me though."

Dr. Kumar went back to his notepad, writing quicker than before. Katie studied the dark wood grandfather clock in the corner. It stood tall beside the royal blue curtain. The hands inside were stagnant, which made Katie consider the clock was simply for show. The holiday decor sat closely together on the small glass table; a palm-sized pumpkin next to a witch-hatted snoopy holding a caldron.

"Has he threatened anyone that you know of?" Dr. Kumar asked.

Katie's eyes returned to him. "Nope."

It was a lie. He'd sent her messages throughout the years, threatening to get her if she ever told anyone…And threatening to get her back for sending him away. It'd never made sense why he'd blamed her for it. He'd allowed himself to get caught, choosing the moment he did to torture her while both Allen and Ruth were home. He'd simply done it to himself, why was she to blame?

"I wonder if maybe he might've just been playing a game," Dr. Kumar suggested.

Katie stared at him.

"I wonder if maybe he might've just been trying to scare you? And he won't actually hurt anyone."

"You don't know my brother. He likes hurting people. He likes doing evil things just because they're evil. He likes earning your trust and then betraying you—and he'd pay to replay that look of hurt in your eyes over and over again if he could."

She turned toward the wall that was painted dark blue. Her arms folded over her chest.

"Jay has no feelings and no remorse. He's a demon...or a sadist if there's a difference."

Katie began to feel empty as well. She was starting to feel like even Dr. Kumar wasn't ready for the truth of what Jay really was. What was she risking speaking about any of this? She'd come for some sort of relief, but in the moment, she'd felt even more despair. Katie struggled to get to her feet. In a well over 200-pound body, things like that were often a struggle.

Dr. Kumar leaned forward; his legs uncrossed. "We still have time, Katie. You don't have to go."

She shrugged. "I don't have much else to say."

"You can say anything you want here. Anything you need to say. Please Katie. Don't hold anything back."

She thought about all the stress and fear of what Jay could or would do to her if she wasn't careful. It wasn't worth it. She thought that by coming here, maybe Dr. Kumar could help make her feel better, but her anxiety was now at an all-time high.

"Please Katie," he urged. "Anything."

Katie looked up at him. "Happy Halloween Mr. Kumar."

****

In the afternoon, Katie sat on the couch in front of the black TV screen. Casper took his regular spot by the armrest. She held the folder full of her client's notes in her lap. As she scanned notes from her previous sessions, her eyes lingered on Colin's name. She read only one line before her thoughts had drifted to Jay...And then to Anna. Maybe there was more information on the case, something— anything she hadn't yet seen.

Just as she was about to leave the couch in search of her laptop, her phone rang.

It was a call from the office. She gulped just a little. She knew Harold would be in the office today, and she also knew she couldn't avoid him. Was this him calling to end her employment?

"Hello?" She answered with a lump clear in her throat

"Hi, Katie. I'm just calling to inform you that your 3:30 appointment has canceled last minute. Sorry about that."

Katie's breath slowed to a normal pace. Her shoulders dropped just a little.

"Thank you, Gianna."

"Have a good one, Katie. I'll see you when you get here."

Gianna hadn't provided a reason for the cancelation, and at the moment Katie was too relieved to care.

After hanging up with Gianna, Daphne's number appeared on her phone.

"Hello?" she answered.

"Hi, Katie, I finally have a free moment. The baby's sleeping and Carson's got the twins."

"Hi, Daphne. It's so good to hear from you."

"You too, sorry it took me so long to get back to you, but now that I have, what's going on with Ian?"

"Well, I went out with him the other night," she said.

Katie could sense the drop of Daphne's jaw through the phone.

"What?! But what about—"

"I know," Katie said, cutting her off.

She explained to Daphne everything Ian had said to her. Daphne was silent at first, but then her tone had lightened a little.

"So, what now?" she asked.

"Well, I was supposed to be seeing him tonight, but he canceled. It's weird, lately it's been really hard to get in touch with him. He takes a pretty long time before he responds to me. It's not really normal of him."

Katie thought back to her college days of dating. It seemed impossible to find a man worth her time. Many of the guys on her campus were down to sleep with her, but not many were looking for a committed relationship. And the ones that were, she'd often found herself, for whatever reason, unable to see those guys in a romantic light. It was undeniably frustrating.

"Well maybe he got…Busy," she offered. Though Katie suspected Daphne hadn't believed her own suggestion.

"I guess," Katie replied.

"Do you really believe he's innocent?"

"You mean do I believe he's not the Virginia killer?"

"Yeah."

"I don't know what to believe anymore. His explanation did make sense though. You should've seen her. His wife could easily be my twin…or clone."

"Okay," Daphne replied. "Only other thing I can say is just make sure he's not entertaining any of his female friends."

Katie pictured Daphne demonstrating quotation marks around the word 'entertaining.' She wasn't surprised Daphne had said this at all. As a freshman in college, Daphne started dating a guy who had fallen in love with his best friend, a girl he'd once told Daphne not to worry about. Despite her marriage to a different partner, and three kids later, Daphne never forgot it.

"I don't think he's cheating," Katie said. Ian hadn't given Katie any reason to suspect he were doing anything inappropriate with anyone else, and he seemed very worried about losing her.

"Maybe not," Daphne said. "But you never know with some of these men out here. Just be careful, Katie. Have you heard from Jay?"

Katie had worked hard to push the thoughts of Jay deep in the back of her mind. She wasn't particularly happy that Daphne had brought them back, though it wasn't her fault.

"I haven't," she said. "And I'm not sure I want to."

Surprisingly, Daphne hadn't replied. She was sure Daphne was going to encourage her to keep up a relationship with him, no matter how bad things used to be between them. Daphne often reminded Katie of Max, who was the same way. Max and Daphne always wanted to repair relationships. To them, whatever was broken always could and should be fixed.

When Daphne changed the subject, Katie's mind had stayed on Jay. She wondered what he could've been doing at this moment. She wondered what his plan was or if he'd ever had one. Her mind started thinking of a scene in her head where Jay was being escorted out by police. Similarly to when they were kids, and Jay was being escorted out of their childhood home by their father. In her vision, he'd worn the same smirk.

"Katie?" she spoke. "Katie are you there?"

Immediately she was bought down to earth. "I'm sorry, Daphne. Yeah." Katie said, returning to their conversation.

"No worries," she said, "The girls just woke up. I'll call you later."

****

Katie entered the office in the evening. It was at a normal capacity for this particular day and time. She made it behind the desk, grabbing her paperwork from Gianna.

"It's frustrating. I really don't understand why they haven't caught the guy." she heard one of her colleagues say.

Sheila, a tall and thin dark-skinned woman who'd been employed at the office longer than Katie was. She'd worked primarily with married couples, and she'd occasionally give Katie unsolicited advice on how to behave once she'd gotten married. Katie began to view her as somewhat of the older sister she'd never had.

Matt, pale skinned with shaggy hair said, "I bet there's some kind of police corruption."

Sheila rolled her eyes. "You and your conspiracy theories."

Katie froze, her heart plummeted as if she'd just been caught stealing something.

Once again, her mind had gone straight to Jay. She fiddled with her silver necklace she'd put on in the morning, as her temperature began to rise.

"Seriously though," he continued. "Who gets away with murder these days?"

"Are you okay, Katie?" Gianna asked, watching Katie fan herself.

"Yeah, thanks," she said.

Her colleagues continued to talk about their frustration at the lack of damning evidence, and the fact that the perpetrator was still on the loose. Katie had wanted to get away from it all. However, it'd triggered her anxiety enough that she'd had to excuse herself to the bathroom.

Looking at herself in the large mirror, she splashed water in her face, as if to wake herself up from the nightmare she'd found herself trapped in. While staring at her reflection, she said in a hushed tone, "Don't let any of this get the best of you, Katie. You're not the same helpless little girl you once were. You can do this. You've got clients waiting."

One of the stalls opened, and Cynthia, a newly hired marriage and family clinician, walked out of it, smiling at Katie in a way that signaled she'd heard every word.

Katie smiled politely, her face turning slightly red. However, nobody spoke a word.

Once the door had closed behind Cynthia, Katie took one last look at herself in the mirror, and then turned to walk away.

Amy was her first client of the day. Her body was turned away and her face had read boredom.

"Amy," Katie said. "How are you?"

Amy didn't bother to look at her. Instead, like so many children, her focus remained on the red cat on the wall.

Katie looked back at the candy dish on her desk. It was clearly close to empty. Katie made a point to stop at the store when it was her time to leave.

"Would you like some candy?" she offered.

Amy's eyes landed on hers. Slowly she nodded.

Katie took it from the desk and got up to approach her with it.

"Take any kind you want."

There were about five pieces left. Amy looked inside and took both a piece of taffy and a snicker mini bar.

"Thank you," she whispered.

When Katie sat back down, Amy had already switched positions. She was now cross legged in the bean bag chair. Opening the wrapper of taffy.

"Do you want to tell me about your week?" she said, her voice higher pitched.

Amy nodded. "I've been okay," she said. "My dad has been around me a lot."

Katie nodded, waiting for her to finish.

"It's been helping me."

Katie smiled at her. Again, waiting for her to continue. "Sometimes it feels like it's not really enough though."

Katie's head cocked to the side. When Amy got silent again, Katie said, "What do you mean exactly?"

Katie crossed her legs, getting more comfortable. Her notepad sat in her hands.

"We talk, but not about the things I want to talk about."

"What things do you want to talk about?" she asked.

"Well, he spends a lot of time watching the news. He thinks what's been happening might scare me a lot."

The silhouette of a man appeared in Katie's mind. He was stalking the streets of Sperry. As he'd crept closer, Katie recognized him as Jay. He was getting closer and closer....Her heart raced and her eyes became puffy as images of the abuse from Jay resurfaced.

Her head dipped to the paper in her lap. Instead of focusing on what she'd written, once again, Jay's face appeared. Sitting still,

Katie couldn't properly face Amy, past horrific memories had triggered her. Her fingers began aimlessly drawing across the note in her pad. She could feel oncoming tears.

A teardrop fell and landed right beside the nib of the pen. Amy had been watching her the entire time.

"Ms. Katie?" Amy called.

"Um"—Katie wiped her eyes— "Sorry, Amy."

"Are you okay?" she asked.

"Can you please give me a minute?"

Katie sat up before Amy could respond, though she had once Katie was up. She stormed out of the room, leaving Amy staring after her.

In the corner of her eye, she caught Harold watching her race from her office toward the bathroom. She knew her expression and tears were probably clear as day, and she knew she'd have to answer for it later.

They made brief eye contact before Katie glanced away. She checked underneath all of the stalls before sitting inside one of them.

No, she whispered. *Not again*. Her hands covered her wet face as she sobbed into them.

The bathroom door swung open.

"Katie?"

Katie recognized the voice as Olivia's, a young marriage and family clinician.

"Katie?" she called again. "Are you in here?"

"Yes," Katie responded, her voice cracked.

"Are you okay?"

"Yeah, I'm fine. I'll be out in a minute, okay?"

Silence formed between them. "Can you tell me what happened?"

"Who says anything happened?" Katie immediately felt stupid for saying that.

"Harold," Olivia responded.

It was enough for Katie to open the door. At the moment, there was nothing left to hide.

Katie couldn't believe what was happening. She'd just had a meltdown in front of her client, her colleagues and her boss. It was embarrassing no doubt, and horribly unprofessional. She could barely recognize herself in this moment. She was now stuck in a hole she had no way of crawling out of.

"Katie," she said, studying her face. "Please tell me what's wrong."

"There's so much," she said, sniffling. "It's everything that's going on lately. My brother, the murders and disappearances." She didn't want to go into detail about how she suspected her brother was involved with the events in Virginia with no evidence. She knew it would only make her look even crazier.

Katie came out of the stall. "Please Liv, that's all I can say now."

She stared at Katie's watery red eyes and hopeless expression. "I think you need a day off."

"I think I'm about to get more than enough. Only I don't think it'll be my choice."

She opened the door to Harold staring at her. "What's happened Katie? Are you okay? Are you with a client right now?"

It was clear which answer Harold cared most for, but regardless she'd answered with hesitation.

"I am," her voice quivered.

He sighed with closed eyes. "Okay. Come to my office."

He turned to Olivia. "Liv, can you notify Katie's client that the session is over and that her family won't be charged?"

Olivia nodded.

Katie mouthed a "Thank you," to her before following Harold toward his office.

She made a point not to look anyone in the eye. She'd kept her focus on the floor. Her heart had nearly stopped as she walked. She could feel the sweat forming on the palms of her hands. She was regretting this day had ever happened. It was the worst thing that could right now.

When they arrived, Harold said nothing, simply gesturing her toward the chair that'd directly faced his desk.

She'd only been inside his office to report the client's serious issues of self-harm or something similar that she'd had to report. He took a seat behind the desk that'd separated them.

"What's going on, Katie?"

"My brother—the crimes around my hometown, and my apartment complex. It's...."

She froze at the feeling of tears reemerging in her eyes. "It's been difficult...with everything."

He nodded. "Did you seek anyone out?"

"Sorry?"

"Anyone to talk to."

More tears began to fall down her cheeks. "No."

"We have a facility full of therapists, Katie. We have therapists who know other therapists. Why?"

"I..." She hesitated.

The truth was, Katie didn't want to face the fact that it was her turn to do the talking on the opposite end of the room. She hadn't wanted to face the realities of her situation. As easy as it was listening to her clients, it hadn't come as easy to speak her own reality.

"Katie," he said, before she answered. "We can't have you like this here. We just can't."

Katie's body lightly trembled, fearing what was coming next.

"I understand you're having a hard time, but that's something we never let our clients see."

He may as well have kicked her straight in the heart. Hearing those words reminded her of what just happened, and how horrendously unprofessional it was. She would give anything to take her failure back.

She nodded. "I know. I know. I'm so sorry. Trust me, Harold, it won't happen again. Please."

He said nothing. His hesitation and lack of eye contact had caused Katie's heart to plummet.

Katie was silent. She studied the floor as her hand crossed her torso, meeting her arm.

"I know this looks terrible, but I need to be there for my clients. I want to be here for them. They need me."

"Well, *I* need you to take some time off for a while."

Her heart pounded hard. Fear filled her body. Her motivation, her purpose, was slipping away right from her fingertips. "Please it won't be necessary. I can—"

"It's not a request, Katie," he said, firmly.

Her heart sank at his words. Tears began to fall down her face faster than before. *Failure. Failure. Failure*, she'd heard in her head.

"I can see you care for your clients. But this is no place for you right now. You understand that right?"

Her eyes dropped to the floor. She wanted to fight for her position here, but common sense held her tongue. Harold's words felt like a sharp blade piercing through her bare bone, but he wasn't wrong. She wasn't in a good place, and the truth was she didn't know when she would be.

She wiped her face, clearing it of her tears. "What about my clients?"

"They will be taken care of. I have someone else in mind."

She stood in front of him, more tears racing down her face than she could control.

Harold looked away from her, opening his desk drawer. He took a card from it and handed it to her.

"Her name is Heather. She's a very good therapist, Katie. I strongly suggest you don't waste this time off from here. Please see her, and please take care of yourself."

His breach of eye contact was Katie's cue to leave. She wiped her tears, though more soon followed. She took one more look at Harold, who began sifting through his paperwork.

Wiping her eyes, she walked away, hoping Harold would call her back, and give her another chance, but she'd heard nothing but the sound of the door closing behind her.

Chapter 20

Katie opened her eyes to a dark room. The rain had come down hard against the windows. She picked up her phone from the charger of the night table. The time read 10:30. She'd slept in longer than she had in months. Unfortunately, yesterday's events were no dream. Katie was no longer working. She'd just lost the very thing that'd kept her sane. Tears fell down her cheeks as she sniffled. Her hope of opening up her own practice, which was everything she'd worked for, now felt far removed from reality. Her reputation was tainted, and her life's goal was bleak. *I should've never gone back to Huntley*, she thought. *I should've never allowed myself to be in his presence. In what way would things be different? They never were, and they never will be.*

Katie grinded her teeth. Jay was always the source of everything negative in her life. Why did he have to creep up in her mind? Why did he have to be at Max's party? Why had she agreed to go? Everything had gone downhill ever since.

Katie reached for the tissue box on her nightstand, inadvertently knocking down surrounding used tissues to the floor. After wiping her tears from her face, Katie fell back in bed.

As she scrolled through the feed on her phone, Max's international number appeared on the screen. With a blank expression, Katie watched the phone until it'd stopped ringing.

A few seconds later, Max had called again. And again. Katie's voicemail notification had popped up when she hadn't answered. Katie planned to answer her later, but she hadn't planned when later would be.

Katie spent the majority of the day in bed eating soup and crackers, something she hadn't done since she was sick with the flu. She'd gotten up only to use the bathroom, and to replenish Casper's water bowl.

When she reached the cabinet for a sleep aid, she realized she was out. She was also running out of crackers. She sighed to herself, contemplating whether to order a delivery or go out and get what she'd wanted herself. Lying in bed all day was never something Katie enjoyed doing, not even when she truly was sick. It'd gotten old. Her mind was made up a second later. She'd collected her day clothes, jumped in the shower, and then grabbed her keys.

Katie stopped at a local grocery store and took a powerful sleep aid from the shelf. On the next aisle, she took a box of crackers. Ian had popped into her mind as she'd put it in the cart. He'd said he was sick. Perhaps crackers and ginger ale could benefit him just as much as it would Katie, likely even more. She'd made up her mind right there what she was going to do.

Katie took a can of chicken noodle on the next aisle. From the drink aisle, she took a two-liter ginger ale.

Thankfully, the check-out counter wasn't crowded, only two people stood ahead of her. The elderly white-haired cashier looked as though she'd wanted to be anywhere but at work.

When it was Katie's turn, she'd hurried to pay for the items in front of her, hurrying to slide her card in and out.

"Have a nice day," the cashier said, without making eye contact. "You too," Katie muttered. Though she wasn't sure how a day like today could possibly get any worse.

****

She pulled up to the driveway of Ian's townhouse. It was very unlike her to show-up anywhere without calling, but Katie figured Ian—or any sick person would love to be surprised with soup and crackers.

Katie knocked with three swift knocks. Sammy erupted in a barking fit, appearing at the sidelights of the door seconds later. Ian popped up above Sammy. His smirk had instantly dropped at the sight of her.

He opened the door ajar. "Katie, wht—what are you doing here?"

"You said you were sick," she said, scanning the inside of what Ian couldn't conceal. His face had looked quite normal. His tone was healthy and there was no sign of redness anywhere on his face. He looked like a perfectly healthy man.

"I decided to… surprise you," she said, lifting up the bag. "But you look fine."

"Uh, yeah," he said, touching the side of his head. "I'm uh feeling much better."

His eyes had trouble meeting Katie's, and when they had met, it wasn't for long. She'd been a therapist for years, and if there was one thing she'd become especially good at, it was reading body language.

Daphne's words had come back into her mind. "Make sure he's not entertaining any female friends," she'd said. Katie's heart started to bounce inside her chest. Anger began to swell within her. This *wasn't* the day.

Stepping closer, she said, "Can I come in?"

It wasn't a request, and Ian knew it. His eyes dropped, scanning the welcome mat that was underneath Katie's shoes. "Actually, Katie, I don't think you should."

Ian's face was guilt ridden. Daphne's words had hit her once again, this time slamming into her like an oncoming train. Was she right all this time? Had Ian really been hiding someone from her? She thought of the extra room that Katie had stayed in the other night. Of course it'd belonged to someone else. There were cans and bedding like someone had been living there a while.

"Who is it in there with you? What's her name?"

"No, it's not like that," he said. "It's just—"

"Let me see," she interrupted.

Sighing, Ian opened the door wider. She looked in and saw Colin kneeling on the floor. He was holding an extremely eager Sammy by the collar. He looked at Katie in surprise. The same look of surprise had emerged on her own face.

Ian looked back at Colin. "Give me a minute, buddy. I'll be right back."

He joined Katie out on the porch.

She walked to the stairs, slowly and dramatically sinking down on the top of them. Ian sat beside her.

Her eyes watched the peeled red polish on her fingers. "You two know each other?" Katie asked. "How do you two know each other?"

"He's my nephew," he answered. "I have him for a couple of days."

"Your nephew. Clearly you knew he was my client too."

He nodded. "I did."

Her head rested on the palm of her hand. Just when she'd thought this day couldn't get any worse.

Katie burst out laughing all of a sudden. Ian stared at her, his eyebrow rising as if to wonder about her mental state.

"You've got to be kidding me," she said shaking her head.

"I thought that if you knew we were related you wouldn't bother to see me. I know it's not exactly professional."

She shook her head, recovering from her laughter. "It isn't, and I wouldn't have—seen you if I'd known."

He nodded. "I know."

They sat in silence until Ian had broken it. "I was with my brother-in-law when I first saw you from the cafe. He told me who you were, and that you were helping Colin."

"Reed?" she asked.

"Yeah," he confirmed. She remembered Reed from when he picked up Colin from his first session. He hadn't said much, nor did he seem interested in the outcome of his son's session. Katie couldn't figure out if Reed hadn't known the gravity of the situation or if he simply didn't have faith in therapy. However, Katie hadn't spoken on it. One might ask why Ian had chosen Katie instead of pursuing someone who wasn't his nephew's therapist, but the answer was clear.

"I couldn't take my eyes off you," Ian continued. "You looked so much like her."

The first half of the sentence would've sufficed just fine. Words like that, though a little corny, would've made nearly any woman swoon if she'd truly believed them. Unfortunately, though, Ian hadn't ended the sentence there.

"Amanda," she said. "Your wife."

He nodded. "Yeah."

"I'm not her. I'm not Amanda. Yes, we have similar features but—"

"I know Katie, and this is probably coming out terribly, but it's the truth."

Katie studied the steps below her. It seemed like things were truly going from bad to worse. Ian had known her all along. Katie wondered just how long he'd been watching her. The more she thought about it, the less romantic it all seemed.

"Can you say something?" he asked her.

She stared at him. Ian was surprising her in all the wrong ways. She realized that she didn't know him the way she thought she did. Their relationship was built on deception. His intrigue, his interest, was all for someone else. There was a killer on the loose in Virginia. Her trust in people was wavering, and though she couldn't say that Ian was definitely the killer, it'd bothered her more that she couldn't for sure say he wasn't. She didn't know him well enough—she didn't know anyone well enough.

"I don't think I can do this anymore."

"What?"

She stood up from the porch steps and turned to face him. "I have a lot going on right now, Ian," she said, tears flowing down her face. "I'm not working anymore, there's a murderer here, and I don't trust you or anyone else."

"Katie—"

"It's over," she said, turning away. Ian called after her, but Katie kept her focus on her car, swiftly digging for her keys. As she struggled putting her seatbelt on, she was determined not to look up at Ian, though she could feel him staring at her. She backed up out of the visitor lane and sped away.

Chapter 21

Katie returned to her bed. She laid on her back, staring at the dust on the edge of her ceiling fan. Under different circumstances, Katie would've gotten up to clean it the moment she'd seen it. However, today she hadn't had the strength or desire to do much of anything.

As she rolled on her side, she felt one of the three different types of chocolate bars she'd placed on the bed. Chocolate was what Katie had always flocked to in times of distress, and it'd never disappointed her.

Despair swelled within her as she watched herself in the bathroom mirror, pondering her life. No job. No boyfriend. No clients. A dying mother, a possible murderous brother, a sickly father, and a distant sister.

Katie's white sweatshirt hung off one shoulder. Grape stains from the juice she'd purchased earlier was splattered near the zipper. Even though it was white, she hadn't cared enough to take it off and toss it in the washing machine.

Staring at her reflection of bloodshot eyes and a red nose, she barely recognized herself. Nothing felt normal. She wanted to disappear, or at the very least, find some kind of distraction. As she stood staring at herself, she decided then to do something she hadn't done in years.

Rather than drive, Katie walked outside of her apartment complex. Her destination was nearly a block away, and on a slightly warmer day than the rest, she knew it wasn't going to be an unpleasant walk.

"Hi, welcome," an upbeat employee greeted. His smile was large, and his eyes joyful.

"Can I help you find anything?" he asked.

"Vodka and a fireball please."

"We havin' a party?"

"Something like that."

He hesitated as if to wait for Katie to expound. When she didn't, he gestured for her to follow behind him.

He took her to the shelves which stored her requests. Without wasting another moment, she took her bottles to the check-out counter.

"ID please," he asked.

Katie had forgotten, both that she'd still looked young enough to have to show her ID, and that she was required to show it in the first place since it'd been years since she'd drank.

"That'll be 45.76 please," he said, after scanning her license. Katie dug inside her purse for her debit card, slipping it out and placing it in the card reader.

"Have a good day," he said, handing her the receipt.

"Thanks."

Katie slipped away quickly, as if someone she'd known had seen what she'd just done.

Back at home, Casper meowed on the couch as he sat watching Katie consume drink after drink. She began to feel elated all of a sudden, laughing at just about everything; to Casper's fur color, to what she'd seen on TV, and to the thought of the spelling of her own name.

Katie's phone rang beside her. She watched Max's name on the screen. Her hand hovered over the phone, stopping mid-air. If she'd answered the call, surely Max would give her some kind of lecture on why she'd chosen to start drinking again, after she'd gotten past the initial shock that is.

She decided to let the phone ring until it had stopped. Another new voicemail alert popped onto her screen. It was unlike Max to ever leave voicemails for anyone, and this was yet another one to Katie. This intrigued her just a little, however, not enough to call back.

Slowly, she laid on her side, watching the spinning room grow smaller until she faded into darkness.

Chapter 22

Katie woke up around noon, much later than she normally would've on her regular schedule. She'd ordered a large meal delivered to her door for lunch. It was a meal very high in calories she knew she'd later regret, but in the moment it was worth it. She'd done the same for dinner as well. Casper sat seemingly in judgment as he watched her binge both meals. Katie, however, was unaffected.

Her phone rang again, and this time it wasn't Max. It was Ian. Just like she'd done with Max, she'd watched the screen until the name on it erased. There was no new voicemail, and he hadn't tried to call again. Her thoughts of her newest ex-boyfriend hadn't lasted long. Her own brother may be the town's killer, her dream job and purpose for living was taken from her, and her good-hearted neighbor was likely dead. Now, she needed a distraction from everything she couldn't control, and she was determined to get it.

****

After dark, she decided to walk down to *Molly's Tavern*. Ian wasn't there this time around, and she was thankful. Inside wasn't as crowded on a weeknight. Katie sat down at the bar, but she hadn't intended to drink. She was on a mission. Carefully, she shed her thin sweater, revealing a black spaghetti strap dress she hadn't worn since college.

Within minutes, a dark-skinned man dressed in a salmon button down shirt walked over. He looked attractive and close enough to her age, possibly in his mid-to-late 20s. *Perfect.*

"Hi," he said, smiling with a beer in his hand. He had a gorgeous smile and very sweet eyes.

"How are you doing tonight?"

"I'm great," she said.

Katie began to lay into the flirtation extra thick. It was unusual for her, however, this was a stranger—nobody she'd intended on keeping past the night, so, bold was what she'd chosen.

"I'm Dave," he said.

"Katie."

He sat down beside her, and they proceeded to have small talk and their work lives, and interests. It hadn't taken long for Katie to suggest they both go somewhere more comfortable.

He agreed and proceeded to follow her out of *Molly's*.

They walked inside her apartment, nearly hitting Casper with the door.

"Can I get you anything?" she asked.

"I'm good," he answered.

His body language and eye contact revealed he'd anticipated the same thing Katie had, and there was no need for the mundane decorum.

The man standing in her foyer, the one whose name Katie had already forgotten, looked around the living room. "Nice place you got here."

Katie inched closer, tip toeing to kiss the stranger's lips. "Nice face you got here."

She nearly cringed at how corny that'd come out, but the man simply smiled and returned the kiss. It was more forceful, more urgent. Casper watched them as they swiftly made their way to her room. They made it inside and slammed the door behind them.

The man left in the morning, leaving Katie a note on the bed with a winking smiley face, and the word "Thanks."

She remembered the appointment she'd made with the therapist Harold had for her.

Her appointment was in an hour. It was the beginning of the week, and thankfully, Katie hadn't had any more to drink since her night on the couch with Casper.

She'd rehearsed everything she was going to say to her as she'd gotten dressed in front of her full-length mirror. She looked professional enough, dressed in a pink pencil skirt and a dressy white top.

Heather owned her own private practice, and she saw clients straight from her home, which is what she'd told to Katie upon scheduling their session.

Fortunately, Katie was able to slide in upon a recently canceled session.

Heather lived in a large home on the wealthier side of town. The surrounding houses had matched in size and beautiful exterior. It was a brick house two stories high, with a black SUV in the driveway.

Katie parked on the street, lifting her purse from the passenger seat.

She rang the doorbell, and a petite older woman, possibly pushing her early sixties opened the door.

"Please come in. You must be Ms. Mackenna," she greeted.

"Katie," she corrected. "And yes."

Heather's foyer was large, just like the outside structure. Her carpet was neutral and looked like it'd just been vacuumed.

She'd had a large statue of a lion near the wall. The curtains in the living room were red, reaching the floor.

"Follow me," she said.

"Your home is beautiful," Katie said as they walked.

"Thank you."

They reached a medium-sized room in the back of the house. A large fish tank was stationed by the wall. Katie peered inside. Her reflection was visible from the glass.

Different kinds of fish swam inside of it, beautiful colors Katie had observed. Unlike the fish she'd seen at the pet store, all of these had been alive and well.

"Please take a seat, Katie," she said.

Katie took a seat on the large couch. Heather sat opposite her, with her notepad in hand.

"So, Katie, you told me that you work in mental health yourself," she said.

Katie nodded. "I do."

"So, you already know a bit about how this process works."

"Yes."

Again, Katie nodded. It was strange to be on the opposite side of the therapy table. The hard part, however, was not that she was now the client, but it was that she'd have to talk about herself, and it was the one thing she hated doing.

"Today, since it's our first session together, we're just going to go over what your goals are and what you expect to get from these sessions."

"I just want my job back," Katie blurted.

Heather remained silent, her head cocked just a little, indicating she'd wanted Katie to continue.

"I was recently put on leave," she said. "I want my job back."

"I understand, Katie, did you want to talk more about that?"

"If we can come up with a plan to get it back."

Heather smiled. "I'm sure we can."

"Is there anything else you would like to work on?"

Katie thought about how she's been these past few weeks. She'd been scared, her anxiety on a level she hadn't recognized in years. She wanted it over. She wanted it to all be over, and to wake up from this nightmare. However, that wasn't something that was in Heather's control.

"I'd like for my spirit to be settled. My anxiety is through the roof—and lately when I'm alone, I get triggered by past memories." Katie thought of the stranger that'd stayed over last night, and left probably before sunrise. She wondered what Heather would say if she'd known.

Heather smiled warmly, nodding slowly. Her face was so kind; it'd put Katie at ease.

"So, you'd like to just talk," she said. "Get everything out to someone—a listening ear."

Katie nodded.

"Well," Heather said, smiling. "I'd say you're in the right place."

Katie returned it. "Yeah," she said, wiping the tears from her eyes. "I suppose you're right."

Chapter 23

"Hi, Katie," Max said, popping up on Katie's screen.

"Hi, Max," she replied.

Her eyes were tired and red—as if she'd been crying. Her face had looked like it'd missed several days of sleep. Before Katie could ask about any of it, Max said, "Did you get my voicemail? Any of them?"

"No, what's up?" Katie convinced herself that it wasn't exactly a lie. She received a notification, but she hadn't opened it. She wasn't going to mention the latter part.

"Mom's in the hospital. They think this is it."

Katie thought back to Max's repeated calls to her that she'd ignored, feeling immediate guilt.

"When was she admitted?" Katie asked.

"Yesterday. I'll be there Wednesday," she said. "Are you coming?"

The way she'd asked it, Katie knew it was expected of her.

"How was mom the last time you spoke to her?"

Max shook her head. "Not good," she said, wiping her eyes. "I'm not ready for her to go. I'm not ready to lose our mom."

Katie waited until Max had gotten her feelings out before she replied.

"I know. I don't think anyone ever is. How's dad taking it?"

She sniffled. "He hasn't left her side from what I hear."

"What time is your flight? I can pick you up. I'll head to the house tonight."

"Are you sure? What about work?"

"Don't worry about it."

Max hesitated. Concern filled her eyes. "Are you okay?"

"Yeah. I'll explain later."

"It's a fourteen-hour flight. I'll be getting in at 11 in the morning your time on Monday. Thanks."

"You're welcome. Listen, I'll see you soon, okay?"

Max smiled. "See ya."

Katie was prepared to get as far away from Sperry as she possibly could, and she didn't care that she was about to embark on a spontaneous four-hour trip to Huntley.

After quickly packing, Katie dropped Casper off at the local kennel. She'd packed more clothes than might be necessary, but she didn't know how long she'd be away.

The trip back to her hometown wasn't long. Katie found herself speeding down the highway. Thankfully though, she hadn't at all been pulled over. The only time she'd stopped the car was to fill up on gas, and to buy snacks and coffee. She hadn't had the time or the patience, nor the sufficient attention span to listen to another audiobook. Instead, she'd kept herself calmly entertained with loud music, both to help keep her awake and to help her mood.

When she'd pulled up to the house, it was emptied as to be expected. Allen was still at the hospital with Ruth. When they last spoke, he informed Katie that the key was under the mat, as if she hadn't known—having lived in the house for eighteen years.

She opened the door, and this time she hadn't felt any type of anxiety. She flipped on the light, and it'd come on to an empty hallway.

Allen told her she'd be taking the guest room again, formerly Jay's room. Max would have her old room back, which Katie knew wasn't top priority or concern at this time, but she'd likely still appreciate.

Lights lit up into the house from the outside. Katie peered through the blinds. Her father rose from the car, limping toward the door, just as he had when she'd last seen him for Max's going away party.

Katie held the door open for her father. She came down the porch stairs, attempting to help him up, but he'd shooed her away.

"It's alright," he said, "I can make it, Katie."

"How's mom?" she asked when he'd closed the door behind them.

His head shook. "She's not responding to treatments anymore. She sleeps all day. She doesn't eat."

Silence emerged between them. Things were just as bad as Max had described. She wondered then how Max could've been feeling at the moment.

"I came home to get a few of my things, and then I'm heading back to the hospital. I'll see you tomorrow, Katie."

He turned his back, heading up the stairs.

"Wait," she said.

He turned toward her.

"I'm coming with you."

The hospital in Huntley was much bigger than the local medical center in Sperry. Katie had gone to the hospital in Huntley a number of times; for a broken leg, a dog bite, and a high fever.

It was just like she'd remembered. Elevators, dozens of vending machines, and two food courts.

Katie followed behind Allen to Ruth's room. She was on the sixth floor of the hospital. As they walked, Katie locked eyes with a handsome male doctor or nurse, she couldn't quite tell his profession.

She felt a twinge of guilt for noticing the staff while her mother was dying alone in her hospital room, but she'd quickly brushed off the feeling and caught up with Allen.

Allen opened the door to Ruth lying on the hospital bed. She seemed to be asleep. She was even skinnier than Katie remembered months ago.

She was hooked up to all sorts of wires and machines. Her breath was slow but steady.

Allen bent over her, "Katie's here."

Katie shook her head. "Dad, there's no need to wake her."

Ruth's eyes opened. "No. I wanted to see you, Kate."

Kate. Nobody had called her that in years. Katie was her preferred name, but in the moment, it hadn't bothered her.

"Sit down, Katie. I'll be back," Allen said.

Katie sat down close to her dying mother. Ruth held her hand up, it quivered just a little. Katie's emotions were now all over the place. She could feel her eyes beginning to puff. They must've resembled red she was sure of it.

Katie intertwined her fingers with her mother's. Not knowing what to say, she stayed silent.

"I'm sorry, Katie," she whispered.

Katie shook her head. "It's fi—"

"No, you need to hear this," Ruth said, cutting her off. She proceeded to break down in a fit of hysterical coughing.

It was a lie Katie was about to tell anyway. Nothing that happened when she was young was fine. But Katie didn't like to talk about her past, nor face it. It was always easier to say the typical reply to an apology than to elongate the conversation of a difficult topic.

"I've been a terrible mother, I know," Ruth said.

Katie just watched her. She knew her mother didn't want her to interrupt. She knew she'd wanted her to listen. She had a lot to say, and Katie wondered how long this must've been in the making.

"The way Jason treated you," she said. "I didn't want to believe it, and your father wasn't around enough to see it. Please forgive him—and me."

Ruth's coughing had started up again. Katie sat still, watching her until she'd settled.

"I knew. I knew that something wasn't right with Jay. I knew," she said, nodding. "I didn't want to face it." Her eyes returned to Katie's, "And I let you suffer for it."

Images of Katie's childhood with Jay began to play in her mind. He was so sneaky and so manipulative. He was the biggest liar she'd ever known, and he had nearly everyone else fooled due to his good looks and charisma. Speaking of Jay though, he wasn't at the hospital. Ruth was dying, and he wasn't here.

"Where's Jay, Mom?"

She shook her head. "I don't know," she said, returning to her coughing fit. "I haven't heard anything from him. Neither has your father or Max."

Katie wondered what was up. If he could show up to Max's farewell party in North Carolina, he certainly could make it to see his mother's final moments. It wasn't as if it were a Sunday dinner or a family Easter service he was missing, his mother was dying, and he was nowhere to be found.

"Katie," Ruth said.

Katie's full attention was back on Ruth.

"There's something you should know."

Katie's heart sank just a little as she looked up at her mother. She didn't know what exactly Ruth was going to say, but whatever it was, she feared it.

"I love you very much," Ruth said, her voice shaky. It was customary to mimic the words back after a declaration of love from a family member, but Katie's mouth was sealed shut. Her head was bowed. It had been difficult to maintain eye contact with her mother before, however now, it was nearly impossible.

When Katie had glanced up, Ruth was still watching her. "I'm so sorry, Katie"

"Stop," Katie interrupted, in a shaky tone. "I understand, Mom."

Ruth stared at Katie. Her head slowly fell back onto the hospital pillow. She raised her arm slightly over the railing, reaching for Katie. Katie stared at Ruth's weak and quivering hand, but she remained still.

"Please forgive me, Katie" she whispered. "Please."

Just as Ruth began to retract her hand from the railing, Katie caught it.

A small smile made its way onto Ruth's face. A glimmer of hope rested in her eyes.

"Would you please do me a favor?"

Katie nodded.

"I want to be cremated. That's what I want. Can you tell Max and dad?"

She stared at Ruth. "What?"

Katie knew Allen must've already started funeral plans. "You heard me. No funeral. Just cremation. And I want to be taken home."

Just then, the door opened. A nurse came through, explaining to Katie the medication she was about to give to Ruth. Allen came in behind her.

She joined Allen by the wall as the nurse did what she'd come in to do. Katie watched the nurse, knowing full well that this type of treatment wouldn't heal Ruth, but simply make her more comfortable.

"Thank you," Allen said to Katie in a low tone.

She looked up at him, "For what?"

"For…coming here," he said, his voice shook. "And for getting your sister tomorrow."

Katie looked down at the hospital room floor. She could feel her eyes growing puffy. She glanced up at Allen, whose attention was back on Ruth. Was it right that he was thanking her for coming to see her own dying mother? Something about that had bothered her. Even though some might say the distance she'd put between her and her family was justified, and well within her right; in the moment though, Katie couldn't have felt more wrong.

Chapter 24

Katie arrived at the airport right on time. She texted Max that she was outside, among a string of cars in front and in back of her, parked outside of the terminals. Minutes later, Max had come out. She walked dressed in a long-sleeved black and white striped shirt; on top of it was her unzipped sleeveless burgundy vest. She slothfully hauled her wheeled luggage behind her and held her carry on and what appeared to be a puffed black jacket closely.

Katie rose from the car, taking her bag. "Good to see you, Max."

Her face was make-up free. Her hair was wrapped in a weak bun, with fly-away hairs loose. To be expected, her cheery smile wasn't present. Her eyes were red and baggy. She looked one blink away from falling asleep either standing up or collapsing to the ground. Katie peered at her.

"You didn't get one wink of sleep on that flight, did you?" A fourteen-hour flight from Sweden to the U.S, must've been exhausting.

She shook her head. "Too much on my mind."

Max let go of her luggage and hugged Katie tightly, burying her face in Katie's shoulder as she sniffled.

Katie held her, lightly patting her back. Max wiped her face, smiling what little smile she could muster as she pulled away from Katie.

"Let's go."

On the highway, Katie changed lanes at the sight of an approaching state police car. Max looked out the passenger window, studying people in their cars. She sighed to herself before turning to Katie.

"So, tell me about work. They understand that mom is…. Not doing well, right?"

"Yep."

"Did they give you a set time to go back?"

"Nope."

"Are you supposed to call them when you're ready to go back?"

Katie sighed, "Do we have to talk about this now?"

"Yes," Max swiftly answered.

"If I don't talk, I'll think about mom, and if I think about mom I'll start crying and I don't want to do that…So, yes."

"Okay, Max. Fine. I got temporarily let go."

Max's head dipped; her jaw lowered. "What?"

Katie nodded. "Yes, and as of right now I don't know when I'll be back."

"What happened?"

"Meltdowns. Some at home…and others at work."

"In front of your clients?"

Katie nodded. Her focus, still on the road.

"Wow. What were your meltdowns about?"

"A lot of things going on in my life."

Katie was careful not to mention what she suspected of Jay. With everything that was going on with Ruth, Katie figured it would simply be too much for Max to handle.

Katie dug inside her purse as she drove, pulling out her mint flavored gum.

"Can I have some?"

With eyes still on the road, Katie handed it to her.

"Have you talked to Ian yet?" she asked, opening the gum's wrapping.

"He tried calling, but I didn't answer. I don't know if I'll see him again."

Max sighed as the car approached the oncoming red light. "That's not surprising. I knew this would happen."

Katie turned to her. "He thinks I'm his wife, Max."

"No, he doesn't. You remind him of her. There's a difference."

"And that's his motivation for getting to know me."

"So? Everyone has a motive for pursuing someone. This sounds like a classic case of you looking for something bad enough so you can avoid a relationship."

"So how are things going with your sixty-year-old boyfriend? Do mom and dad approve?"

Max rolled her eyes. "He's 42, and I know you remember that. Mom knows. Dad doesn't. And he won't…Not until…."

Max abandoned her sentence. Allen would never approve and now would not be the time to tell him. After Ruth's passing would be the safest, both for Max and for Allen.

****

When they arrived at the house, Max dropped off her luggage inside her childhood room.

Katie prepared lunch for both of them. Allen was still at the hospital with Ruth.

Max sat at the table texting someone as Katie was at the stove.

"Has dad talked to you about funeral arrangements?" Max asked.

Obviously the time of her not wanting to talk about Ruth was now over. Katie took the food away from the stove, pouring the chicken and rice onto Max's plate.

"We're not having one. Mom wants to be cremated."

"What?"

Katie nodded.

"Why?"

"I didn't really have a chance to get down to why exactly, but it's what she wants."

Max stared at her as if she weren't just speaking English.

"Everyone has funerals," she whined.

"'Fraid not. I guess mom just wants to do it because it's cheaper."

Max sighed and shook her head. Putting her phone down, she began to eat. "Thanks for this."

Katie watched as Max began to stuff her face. "Have you heard from Jay? Where is he?"

"No, but I'm sure dad has. I know Jay's on his way, Katie. He wouldn't miss this."

After lunch, Katie drove Max to the hospital. Max quickly followed Katie to Ruth's door. Her hand covered her mouth as she watched Ruth lay helplessly on the hospital bed.

She immediately broke down, hugging her mother. Katie watched them, wondering if she should give them a moment.

Instead, she walked closer. Ruth ran her fingers through Max's noodle-like strands, picking one of them out of the bunch. "I'm so proud of you," she said. "You became a traveler."

She nodded. "Yeah…I guess I did."

Ruth had looked so tired even though all she'd been doing was laying in the bed. Her body had managed to get even skinnier than what Katie had last seen.

"Mom," Max said, amongst her sniffling. "You can't die. You have to see me get married."

"I will," she said. "Maybe not from here, but I will."

Max started bawling her eyes out. Allen placed his hand on her shoulder, comforting her.

Katie had stepped out for a moment to collect her thoughts. She contemplated everything that was happening all at once. Her once gratifying life had now become One. Big. Mess. Her mother was at death's door, her brother may be the town's killer, she'd started a forbidden relationship with a client's family member, and she was now unemployed until further notice. She'd slept with random men and even started drinking again—something she'd once vowed she would never do again. She wasn't sure how she was going to navigate these next few days, but somehow, she'd have to find a way.

****

They'd stayed inside the hospital room with Ruth until the nurses had to clear the room to treat Ruth. At this point, it was close to dinner time, and nobody had heard from Jay.

Max looked for a vending machine, Allen was in the food court, and Katie decided to explore the gift shop.

It was quiet inside the small shop. A heavyset woman with a pixie cut leaned on the glass checkout counter, turning the page of a magazine as she chewed her gum.

Katie scanned the many shelves inside the shop. Bears holding Get well cards, candies of different assortments, and Angels with well-meaning and encouraging phrases on them.

One item in particular caught her eye. It was a fish on display amongst an oncoming tide, with the words, "Make waves in your health. Get well soon." '

Katie wasn't sure if it were appropriate since her mother was sure to die at any moment, so she'd opted to leave it alone. Even though she was almost certain Ruth wouldn't want to eat, she'd bought a candy bar anyway.

Katie headed back to the elevator, passing several doctors and nurses on her way. Some looked fresh and ready to continue on their shift, others looked half dead, running on nothing but coffee fumes.

When Katie had come back into Ruth's room, everyone had returned. Both Allen and Max were by Ruth's side. They'd all turned to look when the door opened.

Katie came in on the other side of the bed. "Hi, Mom," she said. '

"I got you some chocolate. I don't know if you're in the mood for it."

"Maybe a little later. Thank you."

Katie took a seat beside her. "I also saw a fish in the gift shop. It made me think of you."

Her eyebrow lifted. "And you didn't get it for me?"

"I didn't like the phrasing."

"I do," Ruth said. "Whatever it says, get it. I want it."

Katie wasn't about to refuse a dying woman's wish. She nodded at her, and then proceeded back out.

She rushed back to the gift shop that was set to close in only a couple of minutes. Thankfully, there were still no customers inside. She'd collected the fish, paid for it quickly, and then headed back out. A group of people, clearly not part of the hospital staff walked up past her; two women and a lone man.

"I really hope they catch the monster," one of the women spoke. She was large in size, compared to her neighbors.

"There hasn't been a serial killer in how many years?"

"I know," the man said, "I'm surprised he hasn't been caught yet."

As they passed, Katie assumed they had to have been talking about the Virginia disappearances, and it'd only fueled her concerns. Whether Jay was involved or not hadn't made the nightmare and fear of living in Virginia with a killer less scary.

Katie reflected on what it would be like back in Virginia. If she did end up fired, would it be beneficial to move close to her lone father? Allen had no other family living in the state. He'd be by himself completely. Katie considered it for a moment, but the thought hadn't lasted long. The elevator doors opened to her mother's floor. As she approached the hospital room, she could hear Max's loud cries. Katie rushed to the door.

Max was leaned over Ruth's frail body, sobbing hysterically.

Allen looked up at Katie as she entered, his eyes red and glossy. "She's gone," he told her.

Katie slowly sat in the empty chair Max had abandoned. Allen put his hand on Max's shoulder. Slowly she rose up and hugged him. Among the tears in his red eyes, he looked over at Katie and reached his hand out.

Katie hesitated, watching his hand for a moment. Allen looked as she stood up and made her way over. His hand covered her back as she joined them, hugging near her mother's now lifeless body.

This was it, her mother, the woman who'd given birth to her and who she hadn't had a relationship with for most of her life, was gone.

It was quiet in the Mackenna house. Allen had been on the phone on and off. Max was in the living room watching TV.

Katie stood in the hallway staring at Max watching the TV. She was sitting on the couch, holding the red throw blanket close. She looked over at Katie as if she could sense her presence.

"How could he?" she asked. "How could he not come? Mom's gone and he didn't come." It was too dark to see the tears in her eyes, but her quivering voice gave it away.

"He hasn't answered any of my texts or calls, and he hasn't answered any of dad's."

Katie came in closer, taking a seat next to her. Max's head rested on her shoulder, as Katie rubbed her arm.

"I hope he's alright," she said.

Katie flinched. It hadn't even crossed her mind that Jay could be in any danger at all. Katie always imagined him causing suffering, but never the victim of it. Was it possible that he to had become a victim of the killer's crimes? It was unusual to say the least, for someone truly innocent to not only miss their own mother's final moments, but to also ignore all contact from relatives leading up to it. But if he were in a position where he couldn't contact anyone—that would make sense. Perhaps his wife, Jenna, knew something. Katie wondered if anyone in her family had tried contacting her.

"What are you going to do, Katie?" Max asked, interrupting her thought. "I mean when you leave here?"

"Go back home."

"But what if you don't get your job back?"

"I don't know, Max."

The thought of never getting her job back was something too terrifying to face, though it was a possibility.

Katie disclosed to Max her job situation the day they rode home from the airport. She'd told her that life stresses and frustration were the cause of her meltdowns. She'd made sure to leave out her suspicions of Jay, and the trauma that'd come with it.

"Do you think you should move back here?" Max asked.

Moving back to Huntley did cross her mind earlier, but it wasn't a serious thought. There would be no good that could come from living in Huntley again. In the back of her mind though, she had considered her aging and unhealthy father living alone, and four hours away from the nearest family member. It did make Katie feel slightly uneasy.

"I don't know about that, Max. It'd be really hard to imagine myself doing that."

"I know," she said, "So if you don't, I will."

"Max—"

"He doesn't have anyone else, Katie."

"Now is not the time to overthink anything. You have your entire life ahead of you in Stockholm, and dad can still function on his own. He's not bedridden."

"Not yet," Max chimed.

"You have a good heart, but dad will be okay."

"What if he won't?"

"Then we'll cross that bridge when we come to it. But let's not stress out about a problem that doesn't exist yet…And you're not leaving Stockholm."

Katie felt her blood pressure rising as she waited for Max's rebuttal. However, Max simply nodded.

Katie subtly sighed at her sister's surrender. Both of them had sank to the couch, continuing to watch TV together in the dark.

*****

In the morning, Katie prepared waffles and eggs for the house. Max walked down the squeaking steps in checkered pajama pants and a thin thermal. Her eyes were tired, and red. Her thick hair was too much for her scrunchie as it was slowly bursting out of it.

"Morning," she mumbled as she approached the kitchen. She took a seat by the round table.

"Hi, Max. How are you holding up?"

Max kept her focus downward and shrugged.

Katie chose not to push any further. "I made your favorite. Waffles."

"Thanks," Max said dryly.

Katie took a clear glass from the cabinet, filling it with milk. She handed it to Max.

Allen hadn't come down. Katie figured he was probably sleeping in, remembering it was a common habit among older people. However, she'd made a plate for him anyway.

"When do you head back to Stockholm, Max?"

Max's head slumped hidden in her arms. Clearly, she was in no mood for small talk.

"I'll be here until Monday," she blurted. "I don't want dad to be alone."

Katie reluctantly nodded. Max gave of herself so willingly to help Allen. It was admirable, but Katie couldn't help but feel uneasy. Max was the youngest, not the oldest, it simply shouldn't be her responsibility to give so much.

She nodded. "And you too, right?"

"I can stay as long as I'm needed, Max."

Without a job, Katie didn't have an urgency to leave right away, and no reason why she should.

Max smiled. She took her plate of food into the den, turning on the TV. Katie caught a flashback of Max as a child watching cartoons on a Saturday morning with a bowl of cereal. The thought made Katie smile.

She began to put the food away, washing the dishes and putting them in their proper place by memory.

"Katie," Max called. "Isn't this your apartment building?"

From the kitchen, Katie looked at Max, who stared back at her as she pointed at the TV screen. She was right. The screen displayed her apartment building, mentioning the disappearance that'd happened there. A body had been found.

"A white woman in her thirties," the news anchor reported.

No, Katie thought. Her heart plummeted.

—with brown hair and hazel eyes."

No.

"The body has been identified as 35-year-old Annabelle White."

Chapter 25

Katie stood in front of the full-length mirror, once again in Jay's old room.

She soothed down her black dress from the waist to the hem, sighing to herself. Ruth was gone, and now she'd known for sure that Annabelle was too. One death after another. It seemed like she was surrounded by it.

"Why don't you just use an iron?" Max suggested at the doorframe.

Max's dress was shorter, long-sleeved, and black laced. Black flats on her feet. Her hair was loose and newly straightened, the ends resting at her chest.

"It's not wrinkled enough for that. This'll do."

"You look good, Katie."

"Same to you. Are you ready to go?"

Max approached Katie at the mirror. Resting her head on Katie's shoulder, "I can't believe she's gone." Katie reached for Max's shoulder. "I know."

After a moment of shared silence, Max said, "Can I have some of your gum?"

Katie nodded. Her eyes remained glued on the mirror, making sure she was presentable from head to toe.

"You're...Drinking again, Katie?"

Katie swiftly turned around. Max held the small bottle of liquor Katie had forgotten was inside her purse.

"Well...I needed something to numb my nerves. I haven't seen our relatives in a while you know."

Max said nothing. However, her face read disappointment as she leaned to put it back.

"The gum should be in the front compartment," Katie said.

She took it out and got a piece. Quickly, she put it back.

"Thanks," Max said, rushing out of the room and avoiding any eye contact with Katie.

Katie returned to the mirror, sighing at her own low, miserable, and pathetic reflection.

Even though Allen agreed to honor Ruth's request of cremation, he still wanted to put a ceremony together, with Katie's help. They'd planned a small gathering of Ruth's friends and some family members in the backyard of the Mackenna house. It would be exactly what Ruth would've wanted; Allen figured.

Katie followed Max downstairs. Family members on Ruth's side of the family were seated together on the couch. They all looked up at them as they approached. Simultaneously, they all greeted them.

Katie and Max joined them in the living room. Story after story they shared about Ruth. Stories from her last years on earth all the way back to when she was a child. Katie struggled with her feelings. It was like they were describing a stranger who shared DNA and a house with her for eighteen years.

She nodded along as Aunt Becky, Ruth's sister, talked about everything she and Ruth used to do as children. It was mildly intriguing to hear what Ruth was like in her childhood years, some things Katie had heard before, and other things were new.

Katie could feel her mouth getting dry. She'd ignored it a few times earlier until it'd become irksome.

"Excuse me," she said, standing up.

Three pictures of Ruth sat on the long table with green cloth. Katie stopped at the very last photo. Ruth was standing on the sand with a life jacket on, smiling as she held a paddle. She was wrinkle-free and looked to be quite carefree as well. Katie guessed she was probably somewhere in her twenties.

"She was so beautiful," a voice behind her spoke.

Katie turned to find Aunt Becky watching the same photo she was.

Katie nodded.

Aunt Becky's hand ran through her loose dark curls. "Are you doing okay?" she asked.

"I'm alright," Katie replied without considering the question.

"Katie, can I ask you something?"

Katie's heart sank just a little. She turned to face her, "Sure."

"Where's Jason? I keep asking around, but nobody seems to know much more than I do."

Aunt Becky didn't appear to shy away from sensitive topics. Any information she wanted, she pursued it.

"I don't know, Aunt Becky. None of us do."

She shook her head. "How could he miss his own mother's ceremony?"

"Maybe something happened to him," she said, remembering Max's concern.

It appeared Aunt Becky struggled to keep her eyes from rolling. "Oh, he's around."

Katie's eyes narrowed. "What?"

"Katie, he's got an active social media. And according to Jenna he's been a little down in the dumps, but if you ask me, that's no reason to skip out on your mother's death *and* her ceremony."

Katie's teeth clenched. Her blood pressure began to rise. A rage grew within her. She hadn't known what to believe or expect anymore. Nothing was making sense, and everything was changing. Before she could reply, people had started moving outdoors.

"Guess it's time," Aunt Becky said. "Let's go."

The weather had matched the mood perfectly. It was cloudy outside, but with no rain.

Uncle Rudy, Ruth's brother, gave the eulogy. Just like Aunt Becky, he told stories about his sister growing up. He spoke of her praises and the funny things she'd done throughout life. Still, Katie struggled to smile or laugh authentically. What Aunt Becky had said still lingered inside her head, and she'd had trouble getting it out. If Jay had been unharmed and ready and able to come to Ruth's ceremony, why didn't he? Why wasn't he at the hospital? Where had he been?

Katie stared at the brown urn that'd held her mother's ashes. At the hospital, Ruth requested to be taken home. This must've been what she'd meant. The final resting place, here at the home she'd shared with her family. It was surreal that Katie was not only facing the death of her mother, but now it was clear what'd happened to Annabelle. It was so unfair. Life seemed so unfair. It was the complaint of many of her clients since she'd been in therapy. At least now she'd known what happened to Annabelle, as hurtful as it was, but what did that mean for Sperry? Will there be another victim? Would the killer strike again in the same area? Who was next?

Katie felt a raindrop fall on her hand. Instinctively, she looked up at the sky. More raindrops had landed on her face.

Her eyes returned to her mother's urn. She was surrounded by so much death, and she was far more involved with it than anyone could ever want to be. She played the images of her mother, Annabelle, and all the other deaths inside her mind. Staring at the urn, Katie made a promise in her mind, that no matter what happens, or how hard it may be, she would get to the bottom of the crimes in Sperry.

****

It was dark outside by the time all the guests had left. Max went to her room, and Katie decided to watch TV the old-fashioned way. Instead of streaming from her phone, she'd made a place for herself on the couch, with the TV on in front of her. No further news about the crimes in Sperry had come on, nothing that she hadn't already known.

Katie heard the creaking of the steps. Allen froze near the bottom of them, staring at her.

"You've always liked sitting in the dark." He spoke. Katie could only make out his silhouette from the light of the TV.

"Yeah," she replied.

Katie grabbed the remote when he entered the room, pressing the mute button. He carried Ruth's urn snug by his side as he walked.

"She wanted me to give you this, Katie," he said, after sitting beside her. His eyes still studied the urn as he held it in his lap.

"She did?"

He nodded. "It's yours if you want it."

Katie hesitated. She couldn't refuse her mother's ashes even if she'd wanted to, but her mother's request for her to have them was something Katie did not expect.

"Why me?" Katie asked.

"You're the one she wanted."

"I don't know why."

"You don't have to take it if you don't want to."

Katie wondered if his suggestion had meant he'd secretly wanted her to reject it.

"How could I refuse it?" she asked.

Allen didn't answer. Instead, he'd simply nodded.

"Max tells me things are going well at work," he said at random.

Katie was aware this was his way of making small talk, which he rarely engaged in. Katie wondered though, how long-ago Max had told him this, since she'd just been suspended, which Max had known about.

"Work is work" she replied.

Allen watched her as if to wait for her to continue, but she didn't. Once again, silence had taken over.

Katie watched the urn in his hands, wondering when he was going to give it to her. Her eyes traveled up to him. What was going on inside his mind? Was he thinking about Ruth? Was he thinking about his own absence from the lives of his children? Had he regretted it?

What kind of parent isn't there for their children when they're needed, Allen with all of his flights around the world, neglecting his family. Sometimes, when Katie would think of all this, she would get angry with many outbursts of rage. She'd dealt with these outbursts all through-out college. However, sitting here with Allen, the way he stared at the urn, Katie could feel nothing but sympathy. At present, he wasn't a neglectful man who never showed her protection. He was an older man with a debilitating illness who'd just lost his partner of over 30 years.

His eyes had met hers. "I'm really…glad you made it back here, Katie. I know, Mom—we" he corrected, "appreciate it."

Katie nodded. Again, there was silence. As she began to get up, Allen looked over at her. "Katie," he said.

She froze in place, watching him.

"We could've done better, as parents. I could've done better… with everything."

Katie forced a smile, knowing it was Allen's way of apologizing—the best way he'd known how.

Katie patted his shoulder. "I know. Goodnight, Dad."

Chapter 26

The drive home had filled her head with thoughts of her mother. She didn't regret coming back to Huntley, nor had she dreaded her departure. Seeing Ruth during her final moments had made Katie feel less angry. There was no benefit and no need to stay bitter at someone who was no longer alive. Ruth apologized. There were things Katie had still wanted to discuss with her mother, though it would be alright left alone. She had felt at peace with thoughts of Ruth, which was something she hadn't experienced in a long time.

Katie was just an hour away from home when Daphne had called. "I know you're going through a lot right now, Katie. I'm so sorry about your mom and your neighbor," Daphne said. "And I wish I knew how to help. I really don't know what to tell you."

"And I don't know what to do," Katie said.

"Did you want me to come over when you get back?"

Katie shook her head as if they were communicating face to face. "No," she said. "Your family needs you."

"And you're included in that, Katie. You're family too."

Katie smiled at her words. "Thank you, but I'll be fine."

"I know you don't do God, Katie, but—"

"It's not that I don't do God, Daphne, it's that I don't do God's people remember?"

Daphne chuckled. "I know I know, but we're having something special going on this Sunday. If you want to come, you're invited."

"Thank you, Daphne. I'll talk to you later, okay?"

****

After picking Casper up from the kennel, Katie went back home to her apartment. All was just as she'd left it. Only it was very cold inside. Katie turned the heat up just a little. She'd prepared a hot chocolate in her favorite pink mug.

Casper snuggled up next to her as she watched a random TV show she hadn't seen in years. It was an old comedy she'd hoped would lighten her mood and take her mind off of all the things that'd happened lately. However, she'd found the episode boring, and ended up turning it off before the half hour mark.

She'd wanted to get out of the house, but considering there was a serial killer on the loose, Katie didn't feel it was a safe, nor smart decision. She gathered Casper up from the couch, turned off the living room light, and headed for bed.

George texted her the next afternoon, *How are you*?

Katie took her time getting back to him. She was unsure if she'd wanted to keep contact with a man who'd stalked her. She knew his son was in the hospital, but that didn't mean he wasn't a suspect in this ongoing investigation, and in the moment, Katie hadn't trusted anyone.

Katie walked back into the lobby with her duffel bag from Huntley.

She slipped her phone from her purse as she walked. She'd received two missed calls from Ian; calls she knew she wouldn't return.

As she looked up, she'd locked eyes with Ron, Annabelle's husband. He walked with his head down, either to pretend nobody else existed or to watch the ground.

As they came closer though, he looked up at Katie. Uncertain of what to do, Katie simply shot him an apologetic look.

His face was clear of any response or emotion at all. He'd wore the same face he always had on the rare occasion that Katie saw him. "I'm sorry, Ron," she said, stopping in front of him. "I'm sorry about Anna."

He was much smaller than the last time Katie had seen him—almost malnourished. He looked tired—either drained by the day, the week, or the year. His beard had grown out, with slight particles webbed inside. Unkempt was an understatement, but Katie knew it was out of line to judge a man who'd just lost his wife. He broke eye contact with Katie, and then awkwardly brought it back.

"Ron, I know this is probably a stupid question… But…How are you?"

Katie's heart sank just a little as she waited for his response. It'd been so long since they'd spoken, Katie wondered if Ron had even remembered her name. All those quick glances and semi-polite nods they'd exchanged through the halls had substituted for actual conversation.

"I'm doin' as well as I can."

His voice was low and impatient, but somehow not rude. It was a short enough response. Katie figured he probably didn't want to speak, but before she could step aside, he'd said, "I see her everywhere I go. I think I'll probably leave town for a while...When I can."

Katie wondered if the last portion of his sentence had meant if he were allowed to leave. It was quite normal for police to suspect the spouse of the victim in these kinds of cases. Though Katie felt it was safe to assume Ron was not involved in his wife's murder.

"I'm so sorry, Ron," Katie replied.

As she studied his face, she was reminded of Allen. Though they differed greatly in appearance, they'd both worn the same look of mutual grievance for the recent loss of their spouses.

He said nothing. Instead, he'd given Katie a simple nod before stepping away.

Katie decided to take a walk down the sidewalk of Main Street. It was perfect weather in early April; either a light sweater or a simple T-shirt would suffice.

There was no need to figure out her destination, Katie had already known before she'd left the house.

She walked through the doors of *Molly's Tavern* and claimed a space near the end of the bar table. Within minutes she'd locked eyes with a handsome stranger. They'd been playing eye-tag until the mystery man decided to turn away from his friend and come over. Katie wondered what they must've said to each other before he approached. Was his friend giving him pointers? Were they discussing the best pickup line to use? Katie figured it didn't matter. After tonight, she didn't plan on ever seeing him again.

"Hi," the stranger said. He flashed a wide smile at her. It wasn't as impressive as the last guy's smile, but it wasn't bad. This man looked older, probably not a day younger than forty. He was paler skinned with parts of his dark hair slightly gray, and his smile revealed laugh lines. Again though, Katie figured none of it mattered. "Can I buy you a drink?" he gestured to the bar.

Before she could answer, Max's face appeared in her mind. What would she say to Katie if she could see all this? What would she do? The look of disappointment on Max's face when she found Katie's liquor had haunted her ever since. Max would be beyond upset to see her not only slipping back into old alcoholic habits, but to also see her sleeping with random men. Still, as shameful as the thought was, it wasn't enough to compel her to stand up and go home.

He sat beside Katie and the two began conversing. She forgot the man's name as soon as it was uttered. They left the bar an hour later, on route back to Katie's apartment.

"So, this is nice," he said, walking closely beside her. The night air was just as cool as it was upon going in. There weren't many pedestrians traveling Main Street on a weeknight, so they were able to walk close without being separated.

Katie didn't respond. She was busy wondering if she still had leftover condoms in her dresser back at her apartment. If not, he would have to provide them, and if for whatever reason he couldn't, Katie would be back at the pub soon after.

"So, I can't believe someone like you isn't taken yet."

"Such is life," she replied in a low tone.

Katie felt the urge to roll her eyes, mostly because the compliment didn't feel authentic. He'd complimented her seemingly about thirty times before they'd left *Molly's Tavern*, an obvious form of love bombing, Katie thought.

"So, before you mentioned that you were back in town," he said. "Where did you go?"

"I went home," she replied.

They stopped at the crosswalk intersection. Katie watched the orange hand ahead of them. When the last car passed, they continued walking.

"Home is…?" he continued.

"Where the heart is," she finished.

Katie didn't want to dive into a conversation about her home life. She was afraid it would lead to thoughts of her mother, and Max, people she didn't want to think about at the moment.

"That's cute," he said. "But I meant where is home located?"

"Why is it important?" she asked.

"Why is it complicated?"

Katie's blood began to boil, seemingly out of nowhere—similar to the rage she had when Aunt Becky talked about Jay.

"I just don't want to talk about it is that okay?" she said harshly.

The man didn't respond. Instead, he turned the other direction.

"Where are you going?" she called.

He turned to face her. "I've already dealt with one crazy hormonal woman today; I'm not in the mood to put up with another."

Katie wondered who the other crazy woman was, either a co-worker, a random on the street, or his wife if he'd had one.

Tears began to fall down her cheeks. There it was. Her relief, her stress reliever, her distraction away from her pain, was walking away from her.

Just then, a man walking alone had made eye contact with her. He was tall and good-looking enough.

Impulsively, she grabbed his arm. "Please, are you busy? Do you want to stay with me?" her voice cracked.

The man nudged her off in disgust, making her feel gross and dirty.

"Fine!" she shouted after him.

She attempted to push him, though her hands had just missed his body. "Fine!" she shouted again; Louder the second time.

Two men stood on the opposite side of the street, watching her. One was tall, the other short. Katie peered into the distance at them as she sniffled, recognizing the taller man as Harold Dyson. Her jaw dropped and her face flushed. Horrified, Katie backed up, praying he hadn't recognized her, and that the darkness of the night had disguised her well enough. She wiped her tears and quickly rushed away.

An ambulance raced behind her as she continued to walk home. Soon after, another followed. Both had turned the corner at the upcoming intersection. Home was straight, but curiosity had directed her toward the blue and red lights that'd lit up the night.

Her stomach twisted as she rushed up the street to turn the corner. Was it another death caused by the killer who'd stalked Virginia? Had he struck again so close to home? Why was it taking the police so long to take him down?

When she turned the corner, there was a throng of emergency personnel surrounding a person lying on the ground, a white sheet covered their body. Fifteen feet away was his or her crashed motorcycle. Nearby was a vehicle that had a busted headlight and a dented front bumper. A woman who Katie assumed was the driver, spoke to police, her expression, horror-struck.

Katie backed away, sniffling once again. Her thoughts had returned to all the other lives cut short around town and the state of Virgina. Life was short. Very short. You never knew when life would be taken from you. It reminded Katie of all the events that'd happened surrounding the disappearances. Another death. Another incident. It was becoming too much. Slowly, she backed away, heading home once again.

Chapter 27

Katie woke up with thoughts of Jay on her mind. She'd had an idea to go to him—Not to visit, but to gather information from his property. Most normal people would call it breaking and entering; however, Katie called it protection of the neighborhood. Who wouldn't appreciate someone caring enough to gather evidence, potentially helping to put danger behind bars.

If she weren't going to return to counseling any time soon, considering Harold had seen her in a moment that wasn't her best, at least she could help with the investigation.

Katie returned to her notes she'd taken that day she'd seen Jay unloading boxes for the house. When she'd jotted the address down, she figured she'd need it one day, and it turned out she was right. All she needed to do now was plan the perfect time to go—and go unseen.

Her phone vibrated with George's number on the screen. For a moment, she considered answering it. She allowed it to ring until there was silence. It rang again. And again. And again. On the next ring, Katie answered.

"Hello?"

"Landen's awake," he said.

"That's fantastic, George. When did that happen?"

"Last night," he said.

"That's good news. I'm happy for you."

There was silence on the other end. Katie wondered for a moment if they'd gotten disconnected somehow.

"Are you alright, George?"

Again, there was silence.

Katie checked her phone screen. He was still on the line.

There was a slow sigh on the other end. It wasn't anything Katie expected after news of Landen's improving condition.

"We now know what happened to Landen."

A name immediately came to Katie's mind, but she knew better than to say it.

"It was Caleb. I knew it was Caleb."

"Wow, I'm so sorry, George."

"Me too."

Katie nearly flinched at the way he'd said it. In circumstances like this one, Katie expected to hear hurt in his voice. However, Katie heard anger and vengeance. Hatred almost, and it'd made her even more fearful.

Chapter 28

Katie talked to George for a while on the phone that afternoon. He'd told her that Caleb swore it was an accident, and there was no malicious intent. However, George didn't seem to believe it. According to Caleb, he and Landen got into a fight. Caleb pushed Landen harder than he'd meant to. Landen fell back and hit his head on a brick. Caleb ran, making an anonymous call to 911. George hadn't sounded totally convinced of Caleb's story. Katie pondered his doubt. If it wasn't an accident, then it was purposefully done, and if done on purpose, it would seem like the intention was either to seriously harm Landen or to kill him.

Katie realized that she now had something in common with George. They both had people they suspected had done something terrible, and they both needed proof of what they'd thought. And both of their suspects were family members.

George would be the last person Katie ever thought she would have something like this in common with, but here it was right before her eyes. She found comfort somehow in the least likely of people.

"Can I ask you something?" Katie said, her cheek pressing the phone against her shoulder.

"What is it?"

"Why did Mathias agree to follow me? What was in it for him?"

The silence over the phone lasted so long Katie wondered if she'd accidentally hung up.

"He got paid," George answered. "Everyone likes money."

"Okay…" It wasn't satisfactory, but Katie didn't push any further.

Later, she'd found herself again at her laptop, playing the role of detective. She'd looked up every case she could find about the disappearances.

A message popped up on her phone that laid beside her on the couch.

It was a text from Ian. How are you, Katie?

Katie hadn't been in contact with Ian since he'd revealed to her that Colin was his nephew. She didn't know how to deal with it. She cared for Ian. He'd become the one that Katie ran to and relied on in her many times of need. She sat with her hand cradling her head. She knew she couldn't demonize Ian for what he'd done—not fully anyway. She understood why he'd done what he did. He mentioned that he couldn't take his eyes off of her. Even though the words were nice, she knew the adoration wasn't truly meant for her. She'd been someone who simply reminded Ian of the love of his life. She hadn't actually been the one who was. It wasn't her. It was Amanda, so why bother in this relationship that was only going to damage her reputation further?

She replied with a simple, *I'm ok*.

Her attention was back on her laptop. She'd searched up everything on everyone in her life: George, Ian, Landen, Mathias, and Caleb. All she could find were pockets of useless information leading nowhere. Lastly, she'd searched for Annabelle. Nothing but her Facebook and Instagram had popped up on the search engine. Katie scrolled through them, smiling at what she was looking at. Dozens of pictures of Anna with her husband, friends, and their dog. Katie wiped the tears from her eyes before slamming the top down. Rising up from the couch, she paced in the living room.

She tried not to let her emotions take her back to Jay, as they always had. It was never good when that would happen. It only led her to feelings of grief, pain, and paranoia. She wondered though what he must be doing now. Katie wondered how he would feel about Ruth's passing or if he'd even known about it. She never really knew what his relationship was like with Ruth. The only memories she'd have of them interacting was back at the house when Katie and Jay were just kids. From what Katie could see, he seemed to have a normal relationship with both Ruth and Allen.

Katie's phone vibrated from the couch's armchair. She looked at the screen, reading Daphne's name.

Did you want to maybe come by tonight? Carson's working late.

Katie surprised herself at how excited she was to have something to do with someone other than George, Ian, and Jay. She'd missed

Daphne, but she knew how busy she'd been with her twins and a relatively newborn.

Of course! Katie texted back. *When?*

After fifteen minutes of waiting for a reply, she decided to call Daphne.

"Hello?" Daphne answered on the last ring.

"Hi, Daph. What time did you want me to come over tonight?"

There was a slight pause, which made Katie consider things not working out after all.

"Um, I'll let you know, Katie." This sentence alone had confirmed it.

"I'll have to see how the baby does. She's turning out to be not so—"

Katie waited for a reply, but quickly realized that it wasn't coming.

"Don't worry about it, Daph. I understand. Just let me know." Before she could reply, Katie remembered Daphne's word of maybe, as in not a sure thing.

Katie's excitement quickly dwindled. It was something to do other than obsess over the disappearances.

Katie waited for a response for longer than she'd expected to. However, she decided she wasn't going to waste time hanging out by the phone. With a free day to do whatever she'd wanted, she figured she'd try her hand at baking.

She had an odd craving for homemade brownies. After looking through the cabinet above the fridge, she'd realized the only ingredient she had for it was eggs. Katie contemplated going to the store, or just ordering a dozen from the local eatery downtown.

After pondering the decision for a half hour, she'd finally decided to go to the store. Katie got her purse and lifted the keys from the key rack beside the door.

"I'll be back Casper," she said, as he laid beside the armchair.

It was busy inside the store, with Katie swerving past several shoppers.

When she'd reached the baking aisle, she'd recognized the silhouette of a tall man and his very familiar hairstyle. He was with a woman several inches shorter than him with a beautiful Rolex watch just like the one Landen and Caleb had worn.

Mathias's eyebrows raised as he laid eyes on Katie, "Hey," he said. "Didn't expect to see you here."

"I didn't expect to see you here either," she said. The thought of him following her had crossed her mind. She couldn't help it, but after what he said about what George had put him up to, it was hard for her to forget it.

Katie's eyes landed on his shopping partner. She looked older, with crow's feet and slight wrinkles on her overly tanned skin. For a second, Katie wondered if she was Mathias's mother. Mathias could in fact pass as mixed race, considering his loose curls and light skin. However, the way the woman was holding onto his arm, signaled to Katie that these two were probably romantically involved.

Katie stared at Mathias, waiting for him to introduce the woman who'd clung to him. When he didn't, she'd volunteered herself.

"Hi, I'm Katie."

"Hello there," she said, smiling. "I'm Catriona."

Catriona, Katie thought. It was the same name of George's ex-wife he'd mentioned before. She remembered it because of how uncommon of a name it was. She looked close to the same age as George, so it was quite possible for this to be the same woman he was once married to. But if it were, what was she doing with Mathias—a boy who visibly looked half her age, and was it something George had known about?

"So, what's been going on, Katie?" Mathias asked.

"Nothing much, just thought I'd do some baking. What about you guys?"

"We're just here to get a few things," Mathias said. "Nothing crazy."

"Well, you guys have a good night," Katie said, turning away. "Maybe we'll run into each other again—hopefully by accident."

Mathias turned to Catriona. "Can you get us a root beer?"

"Sure."

"Katie, wait," Mathias said, once Catriona headed down the opposite end of the aisle.

Katie stopped in her tracks. Slowly, she turned toward him. He rushed over to her. "I'm not following you," he said.

"Glad to hear it."

"That's over with, you don't have to worry about that."

She nodded. "That woman you're with—just out of curiosity, is that George's ex-wife?"

He hesitated before answering. It was as if he were pondering whether or not to tell her the truth or to let the question go unanswered.

"Who told you?" he asked.

"Her name. I've only known one Catriona in my life, and it was the name of George's ex-wife. It's not very common."

Mathias said nothing.

"Does he know?"

"Does who know?"

Katie gave him a look that read she didn't appreciate him playing coy.

"No, and I'm glad he doesn't. He's not really one to be messed with, so I'd appreciate it if you didn't—"

"What do you mean he's not one to be messed with?"

Katie's fears and suspicions about George had all come back to her in that single moment. The night of their in-home date had entered her mind. The way George had accidentally on purpose forgot his wallet, only to seduce Katie into sleeping with him. She thought about his possessive and controlling nature at the hospital, where he may or may not have allowed Lydia sufficient time alone with her own son. She thought about how he'd hired Mathias to keep watch on her, jealous of her new-found relationship with Ian.

"He can be a little demanding and aggressive when he doesn't get his way, I'll just say that."

"I picked up on that at the hospital."

"He's not dangerous to my knowledge, but—just don't—."

"Here you go," Catriona said, approaching with the soda.

"I'll see you later, Katie," Mathias said. "Let's go, Cat."

Katie watched the two of them walk down the aisle together.

Just then, Katie's phone alerted her of a text. It was from Daphne.

Sorry, we'll have to forget tonight. Baby's sick.

Katie sent a quick text back, letting her know she understood, and that she hopes the baby gets well soon.

Katie got the item she needed for the brownies she was now going to eat alone; sighing as she turned to leave.

Katie's phone buzzed throughout the morning with texts from both George and Ian. Katie thought a lot about her relationship with Ian. He was fun, and good to her when they were together. He would listen to her problems attentively and try to come up with solutions as if he cared. It'd been so long since she'd had that from someone other than her therapists, Max and Daphne.

Another text from Ian appeared. `Can we talk?`

`I'm sorry I can't`, is what she'd texted back, one final time. It just didn't make sense. If she was going to get her career back, and if she was going to get her dream location on Windsor Street with a solid reputation again, there's no way she would tarnish it by being with Ian. Even though she wasn't working with Colin anymore, the stigma still stood. If word got out to the wrong people, questions would be asked, such as when did this relationship start and how long had it been going on. Katie simply didn't see a way that she could make it work.

She'd kept George's request to see her in the back of her mind as she made herself lunch. It was a tasty meal of chicken and rice, with broccoli florets on the side.

Casper approached his food bowl, taking a bite at the same time that Katie had placed her plate on the table.

Katie watched as the steam rose from the bowl. Another text appeared on her phone.

`Will you think about it?` George texted again.

Katie considered it. It wasn't as if she'd had anything else to do tonight. No clients. No Daphne. No Ian. And no Max. She didn't know when Max would return to the states. As per usual, she'd made her promises, but who knows if she could actually follow through.

Without Ian now, realistically, all Katie had was herself, and Casper cooped up in an overpriced apartment. She remembered Mathias's words, "He's not dangerous." Maybe she should meet with him? After all, the two of them were now faced with similar grief and frustration. Perhaps it could be something they could discuss together in deeper detail.

She picked her phone up as she waited for the food to cool, and texted back a simple, Yes.

Katie drove herself to George's place in the evening. She'd said goodbye to Casper like usual when she'd leave the house, promising him she'd be back later.

She drove several miles away from her apartment, passing through the neighborhood of the wealthy. She drove up to the black gate that enclosed his million-dollar estate.

On the intercom, she dialed him. Shortly after, the black gates slowly opened. This time, there was no corvette beside the water fountain.

No boys dressed in school uniforms standing in George's hallway. Inside it was just as clean as the last time she were here. He'd still had all his hunting gear on full display. Katie remembered how uncomfortable it'd made her. However, this time she'd been a little bit more used to it, though she avoided stepping on the bear mat.

"What kind of drink did you want?" George asked from the kitchen.

"Water please," she requested, looking around the room.

"So I'm going to be the only one drinking?"

"Looks like it," she replied.

She waited for a comment of retaliation, but all George said was a simple, "Okay."

She wandered to the tall bookcase by the wall that she hadn't looked at before. It was loaded with books on every shelf. At the very bottom to the right, was a large book that resembled a scrap book. Katie bent down to get a better look. She looked over into the kitchen at George, who was still preparing their drinks.

Lifting it up from the shelf, she carried it with her to the couch. As she flipped the pages, she quickly realized it was a photo album.

Pictures of babies, and different faces Katie didn't recognize were on every page she flipped so far.

"Okay," George said, entering the room with two wine glasses.

"Oh," he said, sitting beside her, "You found the album."

Katie noticed that unlike last time, this time around, George had left a little more space between them. Katie took her glass from

George, taking a small sip and then placing it on the coaster on the coffee table in front of them.

George began naming every person that she saw as they flipped the pages.

Katie watched the woman she'd met at grocery store with Mathias. She appeared multiple times throughout the album.

"Catriona," George said. It'd started out with old pictures of her—some by herself, some with George, and some with George and Caleb. Katie turned the page to a newer picture of Catriona, Katie guessed it couldn't have been more than a year old, since the face of the woman had matched exactly the face of the woman she'd seen with Mathias just yesterday.

She was by herself on the same couch that Katie and George were currently sitting on. She was smiling as she appeared to be opening either a birthday or a Christmas present.

Katie looked up at George, "Why did you guys get divorced?" "Irreconcilable differences," he said. However, his focus on her didn't seem to last long. He took a sip from his wine glass, and then another. And another one after that.

Katie flipped another page. It landed on a picture of Landen, Caleb, Mathias, Mathias's brother, Bryant, and Catriona. Catriona stood closely beside Mathias; her arm hung over his shoulder. Katie lingered on the picture of the two of them.

Looking at the photo, Katie wondered how long they'd been together, and when this relationship had started.

Katie felt there was more to the story than what George was letting on, but she decided it wasn't any of her business anyway.

Mathias's words had come into her mind again. Katie already knew George was more than a little pushy, but was Mathias trying to warn her of something deeper? Katie was already on edge because of Jay. She didn't want to become that person who was suspicious of everyone.

Although there was a killer on the loose, George hadn't given her any reason to suspect he was involved in anything like that. After all, pushiness didn't equal murder.

"Thank you for coming, Katie," he said. "I know I don't deserve it but thank you. Not having anyone to talk to about this just makes everything harder."

Katie nodded. "I know what that feels like."

He stared at her, waiting for her to continue.

"Right now, I don't have too many people in my life I can talk to either. My sister, who's been the only one I've kept close in my family just moved to a new country. My best friend since college has twins and a newborn, so she's got her own life."

He nodded at her, slapping her thigh, "So we understand each other."

The gesture had caught Katie by surprise, but his hand wasn't there long enough for Katie to react negatively.

George sank back into the couch. Katie made a point to stay exactly where she was.

"Did you want to watch a movie?" he asked.

Katie looked at the time on her phone screen. It was still fairly early. She hadn't had anything to do but to enter an empty lonely apartment with a sleeping cat.

"Sure," she said.

George rose up from the couch and knelt beside the entertainment system. He pulled the sliding door back, revealing dozens of DVDs all lined up together.

Katie's eyebrow lifted. She hadn't seen a DVD in anyone's home in years. "No Hulu, Netflix, or Paramount Plus?" she asked.

"I'm old fashioned," he replied, shrugging. "Are you in the mood for something dramatic, suspenseful or horrific?"

The end of his sentence nearly sent chills down Katie's spine. This was definitely not the time to watch a horror movie. The fact that George even suggested it had made her a little nervous.

"How about a comedy?" She suggested.

"That's the one genre I don't own."

"Guess I won't even bother to suggest a musical…"

George then rose from the floor with the Sound of Music film in his hands.

He approached the couch and showed her his pick. "How about it?"

Katie's eyebrow lifted, her tongue, tied. Instead of talking, she simply nodded.

About halfway through the movie, George slowly closed the gap between them on the couch. In her peripheral vision, she noticed him staring at her. There it was again—that time she'd gone home with one of her college dates to "watch a movie," only to have a guy do this very same thing, watching her until she looked back at him, and then once she did, her dates would always choose that moment to lean in for a kiss.

"You look great tonight," George said, leaning forward once again.

"Thank you," she replied. She made a point not to move a muscle.

George reached for her hair. She swiftly leaned away.

He tried a second time, and Katie did the same. "Do you mind?" she asked, her voice harsher than before.

"I do," he said, leaning in.

Katie shot up from the couch. "What's wrong with you?"

Katie stared at him. His face was clearly beginning to flush, and his eyes were glossy.

He stood up, inching closer to her. Katie stood her ground. He reached for her hair once again, and she recoiled.

"Come on," he said. "I'll be quick."

He reached for her cheek this time, and she slapped his hand away. "You're drunk."

"A little bit."

She rolled her eyes and headed for the couch. "This was a mistake." Immediately she'd felt like a moron. Why had she come here? What was the real reason why she had? Desperation? Loneliness? There was no real good reason why.

George followed her toward the front door. Katie picked up speed to top his own. She ran to the door, swiftly unlocking it. George raced over, but she was outside before he could reach her.

She rushed to her car and slammed the door, locking it immediately. George stood outside of it, staring menacingly at her. Her heart raced; her hands shook rapidly as she struggled to place her key inside the ignition. She sped down the driveway. The gate opened before she could ride straight through it.

As she drove down the narrow pathway, she began to collect her breath. Mathias's words had suddenly entered her mind. He can get demanding and aggressive when he doesn't get his way. She exhaled deeply; thankful this would be the last time she'd ever see him.

Chapter 29

At lunch, Katie stood at the stove cooking salmon, rice, and red bell peppers. Her phone dinged a text from Daphne. The screen read, I'm so sorry to cancel again. Maybe I can make it up to you next week? Katie replied, okay, but she didn't hold her breath. It was easy to be disappointed, but she tried not to hold it against her. She knew life for Daphne was much different than her own life. Daphne had a husband, twins, and a newborn. Katie was in no position to judge her very busy friend.

Even though she understood Daphne's cancelation, it'd inevitably reminded Katie of the people she could no longer be around, either due to distance, ethics, or death. The latter thought caused Ruth's face to enter her mind. She'd thought about the way her mother died. She thought about all the things she hadn't said to her mother. She still had questions. She still had lingering thoughts.

Her phone dinged another text from Daphne. `I'm so sorry, Katie. Did you want to come over at least?`

Katie thought about it, but the image of screaming babies wasn't exactly desirable.

She typed a kind decline to her offer and then proceeded to cook the rest of her food.

The question she'd had regarding her brother had popped into her mind once again. Why now, what purpose would Jay have in doing something like that? Surely, he wouldn't be doing it simply to mess with her. That time had likely come and gone. He would have more than enough opportunity to practice his manipulation and control over his own family he'd created. The thought nauseated Katie. What had he been like with his wife, his son, and his daughter? Beth had behavioral issues, but Katie wondered if that had anything to do with Jay.

How had he treated her? Was she truly safe? Katie didn't have a relationship with Beth that was close enough to know. Was it wrong? Was it wrong to distance herself as much as she had? In the current moment, she didn't know. It depressed her to know that the only person she could speak to about any of this was in a different country. She had Daphne of course, but Daphne was busy with her husband and the kids. Katie knew there was only so much time Daphne could give to her. It was understandable, but she'd missed being able to pick up the phone and call her anytime, or take night drives late at night to whatever was open. Those were the days with Daphne she'd missed. At times like this, when Max and Daphne weren't available, who did she have?

A loud knock on Katie's front door caused her to flinch. Her heart sank just a little. She remembered the last place she'd left her gun, wondering if she should grab it. It was late in the evening, and she wasn't expecting any visitors tonight.

Katie peered through the peephole of her door. She sighed before opening the door.

"Hi," Ian said. "Can we talk, Katie?"

Katie sat Ian on the couch. She stood at the stove, preparing two mugs of hot chocolate for the both of them. Rather than heating them in the microwave, she'd opted to boil the water at the stove.

Katie had wanted to berate him for stopping by unannounced, but the fact that she'd shown up without calling herself kept her from it. She wondered if that was what Ian was counting on.

"So, how've you been, Katie?" he asked from the living room. It was a simple question that'd come with a loaded answer. If Katie were to tell him everything, he may want to get up and leave, which wasn't such a bad idea, Katie thought.

"I've been okay," she simply said, washing her hands off at the sink. She shut the water off, hesitating there.

"Can I help you with something?" he asked.

"No, you stay there," she commanded.

Ian hadn't replied. The room was quiet and seemingly undisturbed.

Katie poured the chocolate mix and hot water in two mugs. She'd walked with them into the living room, handing one to Ian, and then taking a seat on the opposite side of the room.

"I appreciate this," he said, holding it up.

Katie nodded.

"Thanks for seeing me," he said. "At short notice—or no notice I mean." he smiled innocently, but it'd had no effect on Katie. "Why are you here, Ian?"

He took another sip from his mug before responding.

"I came to see you. It's okay if you don't want to see me anymore, but I just have something to say to you before we part ways."

Katie braced for impact. She never felt like Ian was anything like George. However, the way George acted at his home when drunk, surprised her, and now nothing was surprising to her anymore, nor did she trust anyone.

"What do you mean?" she asked.

"Katie," he began. "I know that it came as a shock—Colin being my nephew, and I know that my initial reasoning for wanting to get to know you sucks, but if—"

"Your initial reasoning?" Katie interrupted. "As in it's different now?"

"Of course. I like you. I'm sorry I didn't tell you, but you already know why I didn't."

"I know why, and I understand it. I'm not mad, Ian, really, I'm not."

Ian's lips curved into a smile as he stared at Katie.

"But I don't know if we should speak anymore."

His smile quickly faded. "Why not?"

"It looks terrible—you and I."

His confused look made Katie second guess the way she'd phrased her sentence.

"I just mean professionally."

He nodded. "I know, and I'm sorry about that, but didn't you say you no longer work at the office?"

"I'm not fired, and even if I was, people would wonder when we started seeing each other. If word got out, I may be accused of starting a relationship with you while I was seeing Colin as a client, which is technically true."

"But you didn't know," he said.

"You and I believe that, but who else would?"

The silence between them was very telling. Ian's eyes dropped to his lap, leaning back and looking pensive.

"I'm really sorry, Katie."

"Thank you." It was all she could think to say. It was in fact a sorry state of affairs for the both of them.

Ian looked up at her. His face still apologetic.

"Are you sure about this?"

"No." she surprised herself at how quickly she'd answered that. She had nobody left. Nobody in her life that she could run to and ask for help except for the therapist she'd been assigned by her boss. It was helpful, but it wasn't enough.

"What do you want me to do? I don't have to leave—unless you want me to."

Katie sighed, pondering her options. Finally, she said, "You can stay."

Katie prepared hot chicken noodle soup for the both of them. Even though it was late March, it was still chilly outside, mostly at night.

Ian stayed on the couch as he waited for Katie to come back. She glanced over at him every once in a while; sometimes catching his eye, other times he was busy on his phone. Katie walked back into the living room with a bowl of the soup she'd poured from the pot.

"Thanks," Ian said, taking it from her. Katie went back into the kitchen to retrieve her own, taking a spot beside Ian. She could feel his eyes on her, which immediately reminded her of George, and how he'd waited for the perfect moment before making his move. However, Ian wasn't George, and he didn't give Katie any reason to feel unsafe with him. In fact, she normally felt the opposite.

She looked over at him. "Ian?"

"Yeah?"

"Can you tell me more about Amanda?"

He hesitated. His eyes staring into the bowl of chicken noodle. Katie felt a little guilty and somewhat manipulative for asking him something he couldn't back away from—not under these circumstances. However, she didn't take it back.

Sighing, he said, "What do you want to know?"

"I want to know what she's like."

"Why?"

"Because she was your wife, and you cared for her, didn't you?" Again, he sighed. "Of course I did."

His tone made Katie reconsider prying, but she felt she'd backed off for long enough. If they were to have a relationship, Ian would need to be more open.

"I met her in college. We were friends for two years before I asked her out."

"Okay," Katie nodded along.

"It was nice, you know, having a relationship like that, where we both felt we really knew each other well before entering into any kind of commitment together. I felt I knew her better than I've ever known anyone."

"Felt?" she asked.

"Before she cheated on me," he said.

It was something Katie hadn't seen coming. She had never been cheated on to her knowledge, but she imagined the feeling was likely horrendous, and it'd probably be even worse in a marriage.

"I'm so sorry," Katie said.

"I don't fully put the blame on her," he said. "We definitely had a lot of problems. Our third year of marriage was the hardest. We tried hard to have a baby in those two years, but she couldn't conceive."

Katie closed her eyes, hoping to God he wasn't going to say what she thought he could. Something horrific—something along the lines of I cheated on her first, and contracted an STD and gave it to her, and that's why we couldn't get pregnant. However, instead, Katie heard, "She was deeply hurt and frustrated by the infertility. I fought to get her to talk about things with me thinking I could help, and initially she did, but after a while she distanced herself. I didn't know how to help her, and I'm not saying it was her fault, but I think I absorbed all the negativity, and it made me become cold as well if that makes sense."

"It does," Katie said.

"We both got depressed, and we began living as roommates instead of a married couple. At first, I thought the distance was just a result of her depression, and initially I believe it was, but then I noticed she was becoming a lot more secretive as well—keeping her phone screen down, leaving it on silent, coming home late and not telling me where she was going."

"Did you catch her?"

He shook his head. "She was sick with covid the night she'd told me she was cheating. We got in a big fight—probably the biggest I've ever had with someone. I told her she deserved to die. I stormed out of the house to get some fresh air. I was gone for several hours, and when I came back she—"

Ian's eyes became glossy. He trailed off, neglecting his sentence, but Katie didn't need him to continue. She could already tell what'd happened.

"I'm sorry, Ian."

"She didn't even appear that sick, you know. But the illness took her unexpectedly. It took a long time for me to heal. I was in and out of AA for years."

Katie leaned back into the couch. She understood now why Ian waited to reveal information like this. It was a lot for him, and he probably thought it would be a lot for Katie to. The guilt he must've felt was something Katie couldn't possibly begin to understand, but knowing this had created a deeper connection to him, one that she'd felt was necessary.

"Of all the things I could've said to her—For that to be the last thing is unforgiveable."

Katie's hand rested on Ian's shoulder. "You didn't cause her death Ian."

"Yeah, I know."

"Thank you for telling me all of that."

"Not sure I had much choice."

Katie felt slightly guilty, but asking about a partner's past wasn't unreasonable. Doesn't everybody do that at some point in a relationship?

"So, you want to tell me about your brother?"

Katie wondered if this were payback for her insistence about Ian's life. She'd tell the truth regardless. It was only fair.

"Okay," she said before taking another sip from her mug.

Ian joined her leaned against the couch. His eyes stared into hers. "What exactly would you like to know?"

"I'd like to know about your life growing up with him if you don't mind."

The memories began to flash inside Katie's head—some starting with her earliest memories of Jay's twisted actions to his last before Allen took him away.

"The last thing my brother did to me was enough to get him finally sent away."

"Where'd he go?"

"To my grandparent's house. Then a reform school. And then to the best bible college my parents could afford."

"What did he do?"

"A lot of things."

"I mean what did he do to get himself sent away?"

"My parents caught him one day—with me. There was nothing that could explain away what they saw."

Ian was quiet. His eyes had never left hers.

"One day, he had me tied up. He was going to cut my hair."

"Okay…" He said, slowly nodding.

"Right off my head with his fingers."

"Ouch," he said.

"He also had a 13-inch blade in his hand. I guess he was wondering which to use first. When my parents heard my screams, that's when they rushed through the door."

"Jeez, I'm sorry, Katie."

"That was the final straw for them. They sent him away a week later. It was hard for my mom, but she eventually agreed to it."

Ian reached for Katie's shoulder, slightly pulling her toward him.

"That was a lot," he said. "You've been dealing with a lot of things, your sister, your neighbor, and your mom. With all that I have to ask, are you alright?"

Katie had to think for a moment. She was definitely dealing with a lot of stress, but it wasn't anything she'd wanted to discuss at present. "I'm okay," she answered. "I'm as good as I can be anyway."

She began to appreciate how good it'd felt being this close to Ian. It was only now that she realized how much she missed him.

"Is there anything I can do for you?" he asked.

Katie leaned her head against his chest. "Yes. Please stay with me."

Chapter 30

Ian had taken off extra early in the morning, stopping at his home before he headed to work.

Katie slept in a little, an attempt to forget about the events of her life.

When she finally did wake, she wasted no time in getting to her computer, looking up details about the Sperry disappearances and murders. One source over the internet showed a picture of the suspected vehicle. It was the same color of the car she'd seen on the news beforehand, a silver sedan.

Where had Jay been? He'd missed his own mother's death—her final moments at the hospital. It was a time where he'd known Ruth's death was close, and still, he never showed up. Max suggested he could've gone missing. However, there hadn't been any news about disappearances of men around town. All of the victims had been women. She wondered if Max had been aware of that.

Ian had texted her earlier for an evening date. She hadn't thought much about it, as she continued to be consumed with the events surrounding Sperry.

Ian picked her up later in the evening. He'd planned a date for both of them to eat at an ice cream parlor.

It was a quiet night out where he'd taken her. It was about fifteen minutes away from where she'd lived; a small shopping center close to the highway. Since it was a school night, the shopping center wasn't littered with teenagers. Rather, it was mostly couples and singles walking the outlets.

Katie walked with Ian hand in hand as they traveled the lightly populated shopping center. It was a full moon out with no breeze. Perfect weather for a date night.

Ian pointed ahead. "It's just a little further down." his tone was light-hearted and extra sweet. It'd been this way since he'd picked her up. It was almost like something good had happened to him earlier—like a promotion, or a Harley he'd just bought, and he was still feeling the joy of it.

Katie followed behind Ian to the cashier. She ordered her favorite, chocolate chip mint dipped in a chocolate cone. Ian had a strawberry cone with sprinkles on top.

They continued down the shopping center close together. "So, thanks for seeing me," he said.

Katie stared at him as they walked. "What do you mean?"

"I mean, I was a little worried that Colin being my nephew would scare you away."

Katie nodded. "It almost did."

She was indeed running out of people to talk to in her life. She hadn't felt so alone since college.

"Again," he said. "I'm really sorry about how that entire thing happened."

Katie pondered what he'd said. Even though he apologized, it was unlikely that he'd do anything differently if he'd had it to do over. Being a therapist, Katie could see it from his point of view, but she had to wonder though, was she herself glad that he'd done it this way? It was unethical of course, but if he hadn't, she'd currently have nobody. Perhaps things had worked for the better, which is something Katie never thought she'd say in a situation like this.

"Hey," Ian said, at the man who'd just grazed his shoulder. The man had acted as if he hadn't seen nor felt Ian, keeping his focus forward, not bothering to turn his head even an inch.

"You got a problem, buddy?" Ian shouted. The man kept a steady pace down the sidewalk. His hands were deep inside his pockets. Katie took notice of the way the man was walking. It was somewhat similar to the way George had always walked. Katie hadn't gotten a good look at his face as he'd come out

Katie grabbed Ian's arm, "Just leave it alone, Ian. Please."

Ian stared after him, and for a moment, Katie feared he may chase the man down. Instead, though, he'd turned back to her.

"Nice people around here," he said, rolling his eyes.

Katie turned his shoulder, "Guess we know not to come here again."

As they headed back toward the car, Katie fought to get the image of the man who'd rudely passed them out of her head. Could it be that George had followed her? The severe complications of having Covid had been over for a while, yet this man was still wearing a mask. It wasn't exactly unheard of for some people to wear them even to this day, but Katie thought about his intentions.

If she were following someone, and she'd wanted to be in disguise, she would've chosen this time to wear a mask as well. Katie knew whatever was going on—the events of her past were far from over, and she couldn't wait to be at the end of it.

Chapter 31

"Hi, Katie," Max said, as her face popped up on the computer screen. Her apparel had easily given away the time zone in Sweden. Max had on an all-pink pajama top and bottom, with a giant pillow on her lap. It was after 7PM where Katie was, so she knew it had to be around 1AM in Stockholm.

"How are you?"

"I'm good, Max. How have you been? Or, how have you been holding up, I should ask."

Max nodded, smiling almost exactly the way she'd used to. Seeing Max this way since Ruth's death had made Katie somewhat at ease.

"I want to ask you how you've been, Katie. When did you start drinking again?"

Katie hesitated. "Do we have to talk about this now?"

"No, but what would be a better time?"

Katie searched her brain for the right answer, but she couldn't find it. "Look, it was a one-time thing. I won't be doing it again."

"Isn't that what all the addicts say?"

Katie rolled her eyes. "I was in a dark place, Max. But that's over with."

"Hope it is," she said.

"It is."

Katie had little faith in her own words, and something in Max's tone and in her eyes signaled she wasn't the only one. Though Katie hadn't had a drink for days, it wouldn't be impossible for her to slip up again after another string of bad news. Katie wondered though, what could be worse than what'd happened?

"Have you heard from Jay at all?" Katie asked.

Max sighed; her eyes lowered. "No."

To Katie's surprise, Max hadn't had a look of concern on her face like before. It was disappointment wrapped in irritation. Katie assumed Max must've spoken to Aunt Becky, who was just as upset with Jay.

"I don't get it, Katie. What happened to him? Why would he miss mom's funeral and ignore everyone?"

There was a part of Katie that was a little delighted that Jay was no longer the boy who could do no wrong in the eyes of other people. He'd now turned into the man who'd missed his mother's funeral, and the man who ignored all family members who were concerned and confused by his actions. Still, this wasn't about her and her childhood. This was about the public possibly in danger by this man.

The police hadn't taken her seriously. If she needed more evidence, she was going to get it. All the years of his torture she hadn't done anything. She'd simply stood by and watched.

She decided it was going to be different now. Now she was going to make a move. She decided to do something she'd been considering for days. She went up to her room and took down the black case from off her closet shelf. Inside was the gun that was fully loaded. Ignoring Casper's meows, she took her purse, her keys off the counter, and slammed the door behind her.

*****

There wasn't much traffic on the road this time of night. It was clear as if it were 2 in the morning, but only nearing 8 at night. Katie parked the car further away. It was dark inside Jay's house, and no car in the parking lot.

Katie examined her surroundings for any sign of nosy neighbors. When it was clear, she tried the front door, which was surprisingly open. Quickly, she'd gone in, hopefully unseen.

With her phone's flashlight, Katie looked around. The house had looked normal from what she could see. The carpet was clean and clear of any items on it. The long couch stretched to nearly the same length of the two windows above it. Katie knew she didn't have much time. If Jay wasn't here, she'd have to search the house for any sign or any clue to connect him to the murders. There was no telling though, when someone would be home.

Katie moved quickly, sifting through papers in the file cabinet, looking through books on the bookcase as if there would be a hidden clue in one of them. She hadn't had much direction; she'd just had a hunch that'd taken her here—a sense of desperation and hopelessness mixed in with deep-seated rage at Jay.

She'd torn the house up, sifting through anything she could find, but she'd come up with nothing. Her hands traveled through her hair as she sighed to herself. How could this have happened? How could there be nothing here? Collecting her breath, she looked around once more. She heard an engine slowing down as it approached the home. Katie gulped, realizing she'd had no way out if this was them. She knew it didn't matter though. If she'd see Jay again, it would end in a big blowout no matter what. She was more than ready to put an end to things herself if she had to.

Surprisingly, she'd heard the vehicle outside drive past, and she'd taken that as her cue to leave.

****

Katie drove into the parking garage of her complex, pulling into her designated parking space on the opposite side of the elevator. She took her car keys out and closed the door. She sighed to herself in disappointment at her lack of evidence, unsure of what her next move would be.

Just then, in the reflection of her side mirror, a silhouette dressed in dark clothes, a hat and mask, and something in his hand, had rushed up to her. Before she could react, the man's arm reached to her mouth, covering her in a chokehold. Her screams were shielded under the pressure of his arm. A rush of emotions had made their way into her mind, fear, anxiety, and paranoia.

She'd heard the cock of a gun, and she'd felt the object brush against her back soon after. "Get in the car," he ordered, and "DON'T make a sound."

Chapter 32

In the back of her own car, Katie sat with her fingers on her lap. She'd been completely robbed of her cell phone, money, and pepper spray. Of all the ways Katie imagined herself dying, whether in dreams, or the fear instilled in her by her brother, she didn't expect to go out like this.

She wondered about the victims that'd gone missing from in Sperry, and in the surrounding cities of Virginia. She thought about their families and their friends, waiting and hoping for their safe return, despite the fact that some of the missing had turned up dead. Katie thought about Max's reaction if she hadn't made it out of this. Surely it would devastate her.

Katie studied the back of the driver's head. He'd had a hat on. His hand rested at the wheel as he drove.

"What do you want?" she asked. "Please tell me."

He simply reached toward the passenger seat, slightly lifting up the firearm. "One more word," he'd warned.

It was enough for Katie to sit back in silence. The car stopped at an abandoned building. It was large like a warehouse. Katie had no idea where she currently was, and amongst her fear and anxiety, she couldn't recall the amount of time it'd taken to get there.

The stranger got out of the car, burst open Katie's side door and took her by the shoulder, dragging her toward the building. She was tempted to scream out for help, but after remembering the man's threat of execution she remained quiet.

Her heart pounded, and her palms were full of sweat. She hadn't stopped crying from the moment she was forced into her own car at gunpoint. He led her into the building of busted windows, graffiti and overgrown grass that surrounded it.

It had an unpleasant odor inside, mildew possibly, and an odor of some kind of death, human or animal, Katie hadn't known.

A lone chair was placed inside the warehouse. It was surrounded by rope and duct tape. This scene was eerily familiar. Katie thought back to the way Jay had treated her at their family home. The day he'd tied her up and tried to torture her with Allen's blowtorch was never too far from her mind, no matter how much she'd tried to suppress it, but why? Why would Jay want to do this to her? What motive did he have for wanting to do this to her now as an adult? She didn't understand, nor did she have any other known enemies besides possibly George. What could she do in a situation like this—kept once again like a helpless puppy, the way she had been so many times before.

He placed Katie in the chair, slowly tying her up amid her struggling. She started bawling her eyes out, desperate for help—anyone's help. She never would've guessed she'd end up in the same position again that she was with Jay over twenty years ago. However, unlike that day in the garage, she didn't have a blindfold and her mouth wasn't taped.

She watched the man standing in front of her. He was tall and slender, dressed in all black. She knew she had to be sitting in the presence of the Virginia prowler who'd haunted the streets of Sperry and the other cities of Virginia.

"Who are you?" she asked.

He chuckled. "You should already know, Katie."

Katie searched her brain amid the initial shock of the stranger knowing her name. How long had he been stalking her? How long had he known about her? Did he have her address? Had he known where she worked or who she'd been hanging around with all this time? Had he watched her every move?

"I'll give you a hint," he said. "Jay Mackenna."

The man removed his mask, and his hat, which had the same logo of the diner that she and Ian had gone to weeks ago. Her eyes peered in on his. The day they'd eaten there, the eyes of the waiter had stayed with her. She'd realized it was the same pair of eyes that were staring at her now—the same pair of eyes she'd seen the other day with Ian.

As she peered in closer at the rest of his face, her eyes began to widen.

"Craig," she said. "Craig M—"

"Mullen," he finished. "Yeah. Hi, Katie."

Craig, the boy from her childhood—Jay's best friend. She hadn't seen Craig in years. She wasn't sure at what point that he and

Jay had stopped being friends, but she assumed it was when Jay had been sent away.

"Why?" she asked.

"I've waited for you for so long, Katie. There hasn't been a day where I haven't thought of you."

Katie was speechless. She knew she needed to choose her words very wisely in a moment like this. Her body was stiff with fear. Her palms were sweating profusely.

"I wanted to get you just at the perfect moment… so I can kill you without any interruption."

Her heart sank at the word *kill*. Back in her office, clients had said many things out of fear or anger, but it was usually just words. This time though, Katie could see in his dark eyes that he'd meant exactly what he'd said.

"Why involve other people then?" she asked.

"I couldn't have my only target be you now, could I?" he'd said.

"I've wanted you all my life, Katie. And I came to realize I could never have you."

Her heart plummeted even further. Under these circumstances, such a statement normally meant that if the stalker couldn't have his obsession, then nobody else could either.

"I'm going to have you sit in constant pain, the way that I have all these years. I don't owe this world anything. You know, we're taught to be good men, treat women, right, treat kids right, and what do we get in return?"

He pointed at Katie. "You women are all the same. You want perfection and we're never good enough."

Katie thought back to all the news reports on TV. All the victims were female, some of them college students, and most were young. Craig had so much hatred inside of him. It'd built up to a level that even he was unable to control.

Katie peered in at him. She'd always known there was something a little off about Craig when she'd known him years ago. However, she was young enough not to understand the depths of it.

Craig talked as if it were Katie who'd caused him to become obsessed with her, and other women who'd rejected him— that everything bad that'd happened because of it was somehow her fault. Katie prayed inside her head that somehow, by some miracle she would make it out of this alive. She thought about her life leading up to now. From that day inside the garage with Jay, how he'd tortured her and gotten away with so many things for so many years. She thought about Max, who'd been the only family member she could count on all her life. Finally, she thought about Ruth, who ended up being the most remorseful Katie had ever seen her, along with her father, who'd apologized in his own special way.

The man flinched as arms appeared around his body. The gun quickly dropped from his hand.

"What do you think you're doing?" A familiar voice called out.

Katie's eyes immediately landed on Jay, who'd just rushed Craig. The two of them wrestled on the floor, closing in on the gun. Katie urgently struggled for freedom, hoping to be the first one to grab the weapon. It was no use though; Craig had tied her too tightly. She felt just as helpless as ever, praying this time for Jay's safety. Her anxiety soared through the roof as she watched them tussle. They both struggled for the gun, tumbling out of Katie's line of sight. A gunshot went off, and Katie shivered in her chair. She sat frozen as the harsh chill ran up her spine. She hoped, and she prayed it wasn't Jay who'd just been shot. She gulped as she slowly turned around.

Blood had flowed onto the floor, soaking them both. Katie's heart plunged deep inside her chest.

"Jay!" she shouted. "Jay!"

Slowly he'd gotten up, watching Craig as if to make sure he was no longer a threat. He then rushed toward her, untying her bound body.

They embraced warmly, immediately sending warmth to Katie's body. She cried hysterically on his shoulder.

*****

Later, the warehouse was loaded with flashing red lights and sirens.

Ian held Katie close to him. "Are you okay?" he asked. "Yeah," she said.

She watched Jay standing away from the warehouse, watching the police handle their investigation.

"I'll be back," she said to Ian.

"Okay," he replied.

She walked toward Jay, standing beside him.

"I'm sorry, Katie," he said.

"What could you possibly have to be sorry about? I owe you my life."

"Everything happened because of me. He was my friend."

Katie shook her head. "I'm the one who should be sorry, Jay. Can I ask you something?"

"Go ahead."

"Why was Annabelle's ring inside your car? I found it in the backseat."

It was a question that'd haunted her since the night she'd found it. She went over explanation after explanation inside her head. It simply didn't make sense why it should be anywhere near Jay's car unless he was the one who'd done it. However, recent events suggested it probably wasn't what Katie had thought.

Jay slowly nodded. "I gave her a ride. I never saw a ring, but if you found it in there than I assume she dropped it."

Katie flinched. "Why? Why give her a ride?"

"Because it was raining like crazy outside, Katie. I was in the area, and she was soaked when I pulled up to her. When she told me where she lived, I figured it would be a good time to stop by and visit with you, but pulling up there again I decided not to—since it was last minute."

Katie thought back to that long consistent week of rain. It did come down hard some of the time. Just then, she got a visual of Anna rushing to Jay's car and climbing inside. Annabelle's words began floating in her mind. "Nothing fits anymore," she said, the day she'd gotten on the elevator with Katie. The image of her ring loosely turning as she rotated it on her finger, emerged in Katie's mind. It was making sense now. All of it—coming together like an old puzzle finally put together.

"I didn't do it you know," he said. "Any of it. Hopefully you see that now."

"I do. I'm sorry, Jay."

"I know, and I'm sorry about Anna."

Katie nodded.

"Why'd you disappear though? Why didn't you show up for mom at the hospital?"

Jay shook his head. "Craig wouldn't allow me to. He said if I spoke to anyone—or warned you in anyway— He'd finish the job on you, and then come for my family."

"But you knew I was here," she said.

"I had to guess. I came home to find the house ransacked. I knew where Jenna and Griffin were, but Beth was missing. I knew Craig had his eye on her."

Katie's hand covered her mouth. She could only imagine what kind of evil Craig must've had in store for if he'd ever caught her.

"When we were kids, Craig always talked about torturing someone in a warehouse. We were both—sick people," he'd said. "This was the closest one I knew of. And at that point, I knew I had to call the police or end everything myself…."

He took his phone out— "And according to Jenna, Beth ran away to her friend's house."

"Well, I'm glad she's safe…. And sorry about your house."

Jay shrugged. "Wasn't your fault."

"I'm not so sure about that."

He stared at her. "What?"

"Let's just say we're even after all these years."

Jay shook his head, a smirk appeared on his face.

Katie leaned her head against his shoulder, and they'd both watched the old building together.

8 months later

The deck orchestra strummed softly. The soothing sound of the violin complimented the night, as the waves lightly crashed against the vessel.

Katie's puffed white wedding dress partially hung off the bench as she and Ian sat along the deck. It was quite the star-filled night, with a slight breeze that ran through the night air. The majority of the guests had been near the middle and east wing of the ship, leaving just a few guests, the orchestra band, and Katie and Ian on the west wing.

Ian looked over at her. "It's getting late. You want to retire?"

She smiled at him. "Yeah, you can go ahead though. I'll be there in a minute."

"You sure?"

She nodded.

He leaned to kiss her, "Goodnight, Mrs. Alexander."

She smiled as she pulled away. "Goodnight."

He rose and smiled at her.

Katie watched him, dressed in his white and black wedding attire travel the large boat until he turned the corner for their quarters.

She stood up and headed for her purse beside her. Beside it was the large rose petal vase that had now housed the ashes of her mother.

Katie walked up to the ledge, looking out at the reflection of the full moon imprinted along the dark waves. Her hair lightly lifted in sync with the gentle wind.

Ruth would've loved to be here, loved to watch her get married, and loved to be near the ocean. Katie knew that this would be the final act of honoring her mother—the best way she could officially say goodbye.

With both hands, she poured the contents of the vase over the rail, watching the little sand-like substance fall into the dark sea.

If ever there was a moment of serene calm and freedom, Katie was experiencing it now.

Along with the ashes, Katie was also letting go of her resentment— the very thing that'd held her down the longest. It had nearly killed her career, sent an innocent man to prison, and ultimately might've destroyed her life. Never again would she allow it to consume her. Never again would she allow it to take her down a dark path full of hate, loathing, and a painful emotional death. From now on, she'd choose life.

www.ingramcontent.com/pod-product-compliance
Lightning Source LLC
LaVergne TN
LVHW041655060526
838201LV00043B/438